# CARA MASSIMINA

Tim Parks's novels include *Tongues of Flame*, which won the Somerset Maugham and Betty Trask Awards, *Loving Roger*, which won the John Llewellyn Rhys Prize, *Cara Massimina* and *Mimi's Ghost*. His non-fiction work includes the bestselling *Italian Neighbours*, *An Italian Education* and *Adultery & Other Diversions*. His ninth novel *Europa* was shortlisted for the 1997 Booker Prize. His latest novel is the acclaimed, *Destiny*. Tim Parks lives in Italy.

## ALSO BY TIM PARKS

### Fiction

### Non-Fiction

Tim Parks

# CARA MASSIMINA

VINTAGE

Published by Vintage 2000

2 4 6 8 10 9 7 5 3 1

First published in Great Britain in 1990 by
Hodder and Stoughton Ltd

First published in paperback in 1995 by Minerva

Vintage
Random House, 20 Vauxhall Bridge Road,
London SW1V 2SA

Random House Australia (Pty) Limited
20 Alfred Street, Milsons Point, Sydney
New South Wales 2061, Australia

Random House New Zealand Limited
18 Poland Road, Glenfield, Auckland 10, New Zealand

Random House (Pty) Limited
Endulini, 5A Jubilee Road, Parktown 2193, South Africa

The Random House Group Limited Reg. No. 954009
www.randomhouse.co.uk

A CIP catalogue record for this book
is available from the British Library

ISBN 0 7493 9680 6

Papers used by Random House are natural, recyclable
products made from wood grown in sustainable forests.
The manufacturing processes conform to the environ-
mental regulations of the country of origin

Printed and bound in Great Britain by
Cox & Wyman Ltd, Reading, Berkshire

'The realms of thought, philosophy and the spirit break up and shatter against the unnameable, myself.'

Max Stirner, *The Unique and his Property*

# I

Morris walked across the square faster than he would have liked. The twilight had a curious liquidity about it that had to do with the freshness after an afternoon's rain and the way first streetlamps stared into the dying daylight. It wasn't a moment to hurry, Morris thought. It was a moment to loll outside a bar sipping a glass of white wine and feeling the space between things, their weight, their presence. It was a moment to watch the shadows sharpening slowly and coolly as daylight bled away and the lamplight strengthened – to watch the colours die on stuccoed walls when the bright neon stabbed out beneath. A magic moment.

But Morris hurried on, across the square and into the maze of narrow streets beyond. He was quite out of breath with hurrying. It was the fourth time across the city in as many hours. Certainly he'd arranged things badly today, he thought. Getting wet like that between Paola's and Patrizia's. His right foot was cold and damp in its shoe and his trousers too were soggy and flapping around the bottoms. Morris stopped a moment to gather his breath, then leaned on the bell. He gave it a good hard ring. At the same time his lips slowly and clearly formed the word 'Drudge'. He repeated it out loud, 'Drudge!' trying to roll the 'r', but it was difficult. He tried again, then switched to 'boring,' where by now he had the rolled 'r' off to absolute perfection. 'Bor-r-rrring.' He leaned on the bell again. Damn them!

Morris was standing outside a huge arched gate of blackened wood and now the little loudspeaker under a row of bells in the stone wall beside, finally crackled into life.

'*Chi è?*'

'Morris.'

I

A pause.

'*Chi?*'

'Morris.' He drew a breath as one who is preparing to confess. 'The English teacher.' The words, quite seriously, were dust and ashes on Morris's lips.

'Ah, I'll just see if Gregorio's in.'

Of course he was in, dammit! It was time for his lesson. Otherwise the English teacher wouldn't have come, would he? So why didn't she open right away? Suspicious race they were! Morris glanced impatiently at his watch. Ten to six. He was going to have to hurry after this one too.

A sharp buzz snapped open the lock. Morris pushed his way in and, barely glancing at the courtyard where a fountain in delightfully deep shadow splashed over naked fauns, he hurried, faster than he would have liked, up the marble stairs. Always faster than he would have liked. Which meant that when Signora Ferroni opened the door his Italian was less perfect than it might have been from trying to catch his breath. She smiled sympathetically and he felt humiliated. She was dressed in wonderful taste in a soft grey wool dress; her posture was perfectly elegant, her make-up flawless and manners likewise. Could she offer him something to drink? Tea, orange juice? No, she couldn't. Morris, feeling scruffy, refused. He had an acute sensation his hair must be in a terrible mess.

Gregorio arrived, all hair oil and the adolescent's love affair with aftershave, and led him into the sitting room where they sat opposite each other over a glass table under a frescoed ceiling. Morris reached for his books from his leather document case only to discover that that was wet too. He must get some cream or something to treat the leather. It was the only beautiful thing he had. The pages of the book were damp.

'What did you do at the weekend, Gregorio?' – the opening gambit of every Monday lesson: asked it five hundred times today already. He felt weary and trivial.

'I went to the mountain.'

'The mountain*s*. We don't use the singular unless we're referring to a specific mountain.'

2

'I went to the mountains.'
'How did you get there?'
'Who with?'
'What for?'
'Where exactly?'
'What did you have to eat?'
'What was the weather like?'
'How much did it all cost?'
'Did you enjoy yourself?'
'When did you get back?'

Gregorio had been skiing it seems. He'd gone up in his father's Alfa Romeo to Val Gardena where the family had a second or third or perhaps even fourth house and he'd spent the night there with his friend. 'Me and my fr-riend,' he grinned, delighted as Italians always were that the word didn't oblige you to declare whether male or female – as if Morris could give the most piddling of piddling damns whether Gregorio's trip had come complete with sexual experience or not! All the same, he smiled brightly back at his student. The weekend routine was worth a good ten easy minutes when all was said and done, which was 16.6 (recurring) per cent of the whole hour, or exactly two thousand five hundred of the fifteen thousand lire he was going to get paid for this lesson, because he asked the rich ones for more.

They switched to Gregorio's schoolbooks. The final school exams were near at hand and Gregorio's future hung in the balance. He had already been sent back a year once and he must get through this time. Morris was encouraging. They would make it together, he said. Where were they now? Ah yes. Out of the corner of one eye he looked at a fresco behind the cocktail bar where a goddess was twisting herself around a slender tree trunk. To his right a small bronze dryad paraded on a pedestal, arms uplifted and breasts stretched tight in a gesture of triumph. The place must be worth millions, Morris thought – of lire, billions – and this poor lad was sweating over his exams as if they could possibly matter. If he'd had half enough intelligence to pass them he'd have

3

seen how utterly insignificant they were in the shadow of all this wealth.

They read a set passage from *The Old Curiosity Shop*, where the old man and Nell, homeless and hungry, take shelter in a factory full of monstrous machines and sleep in the ashes of yesterday's coal. Gregorio's well-to-do pink tongue stumbled over the difficult words, as well it might.

The boy's mustard shirt was from Standa, Morris noticed, the Marks & Sparks of Northern Italy. Was there no limit to the economies of the rich? Morris stopped for a moment and studied his watch shamelessly. Five minutes to go. He was trying to hold back what would be a truly thunderous fart.

Finished. Morris slipped his book off the table and down into the document case. The leather really was going to require some attention. It was the only thing that gave him any appearance of being professional, scuttling round from one place to the next through puddles and cobbles as he did. He sat up now, perfectly straight and immobile, placed one hand calmly over the other on the table and smiled, eyebrows lifted interrogatively in what he knew was an attractive expression. Gregorio responded with his usual, elegant, aftershaved blankness, while on a dark canvas behind him Christ had been quite savagely crucified by some fourteenth-century painter. The only whiff of bad taste, Morris thought, but it was probably a family heirloom. Inwardly he began to count if only to see how long it would take the boy to catch on. 'Ten, eleven, twelve . . .' Every second stepped up the pressure in groaning intestines and was a breath faster he'd have to hurry back across town again in sodden shoes; but there could be no question whatsoever of leaving first, even if he had to sink to asking the boy what date it was. 'Twenty-two, twenty-three . . .' Should he shout thirty-first out loud?

'Ah, I should pay you, it's the end of the month,' Gregorio cried and dashed off to speak to his mother. A maid crossed the room with an armload of brooms and eyed Morris suspiciously. She had heard the word 'pay' perhaps. Morris had no difficulty rewarding her with the frankest of frank smiles, a '*Buona sera, Signora,*' and even a small bow of his blond head. They were on the same side after all. But the woman clattered tightlipped into the kitchen. Next thing, Morris thought, she'd be urinating in the corners to show it was her territory. Stupid old cow. They'd probably made her think she was part of the family or something.

Gregorio rushed back. Outside his lessons everything was all go obviously. In a big hurry to get out and see his 'f-friend' most probably. And in his hand was a cheque. Of all things. Sixty thousand lire and they paid you with a cheque! What did they want? For him to start paying his taxes or something? Or was he supposed to offer a reduction if they paid him in cash? BANCO NAZIONALE DEL LAVORO. At least five days before they'd clear it, naturally. Morris took the cheque, baring his teeth in a savage smile that left Gregorio not at all crestfallen. Then he was at the door, with the signora mother crying *arrivederci* over a wailing television.

'*Buona sera, Signora.*'

Gregorio said: 'By the way, we'll have to miss this Friday because I'm off to Cortina.'

Fifteen thousand lire lost in the frozen alpine snows.

'Never mind. Monday then. Enjoy yourself!' Damn you. And he was scuttling off down the stairs already to where that fountain now played away in a subtle web of spotlight beams, catching a faun's flanks here in a shower of silver, there his stony face, and one beam held the shining drops at the very apex of their parabola. Morris gave it the fart. He felt like spitting. 'Drrrrudge!' God, that 'r' was tough to roll. 'Drrrrudges bear grrrrrudges.' He turned into Via Quattro Spade, Via Mazzini, Vicolo San Nicolò, walking briskly back to the school and the last hour. What did you do at the weekend, how did you get there, who with, what for, where exactly, what did you have to eat, what was the weather like, how much did it all cost, did you enjoy yourself, when did you come back? Monday lessons almost over.

Later, Morris stood at the bus stop on Stradone San Fermo and clenched his teeth tight, as if defying wind and rain, though there was none. It wasn't a night for seeing Massimina, he thought, not with trousers wet and shoes scuffed and his beautiful document case rather the worse for wear and tear. He had sent some flowers earlier in the day, so she could hardly complain, and then he could always ring her when he got home. That should give the impression of the earnest suitor, wiped out after a day's slog and still hanging on the end of the phone to hear all the sweet gossip of his *signorina fidanzata*. He had made a good start there, Morris thought. It could be the one.

'Hi man, Morris buddy! What you up to?'

The tongue was English – or rather American. On a ramshackle bicycle, displaying no lights, a bearded young man wobbled dangerously across the street, knees splayed out wide to get his feet on the pedals. Morris was annoyed.

'Where d'you live then? Out of town?' Stan was a teacher at the school, from California.

'Montorio.'

'Montorio?' The American's accent murdered the name. And he had been in Italy twice, three times as long as himself, Morris thought. He felt pleasantly superior. Enough to keep him affable anyway.

'Where the hell's that?'

Morris said it was at the end of the bus line, seven kilometres away.

'Aren't you a bit lonesome out there on your own, man? I could find you a place in the centre if you like. That Susie's got a spare bed in her place. She's looking for somebody to move in. Cheap too. Bouncy girl. Could be fun.'

Stan was trying to be friendly and Morris should have been grateful. The American was grinning in a welcoming sort of way and obviously imagined that Morris was just shy. 'Got to stick together, us immigrants,' he laughed. 'Brits and Merks the same. Otherwise we'll get lost in this place with all these Eyeties.'

Morris kept his peace.

'Bunch of us are going down to Naples for Easter if you're interested. Wanna come?'

'How are you travelling?' Morris asked politely.

'Hitching it, in pairs, then meeting up there. But we've got one too many girls right now, so if you want to tag along . . .'

The arrival of the bus spared Morris another refusal. He jumped on, savouring the pleasant lightness of his body as he skipped over the steep steps, punched his ticket, sat down and closed his eyes.

He had chosen to live out in Montorio precisely because of its isolation from the rest of the English community. They lived for the most part in an extremely dilapidated section near the centre of town. They had a fixation on living in the centre, feeling part of old Italy, near the art museums and chic shops (otherwise why on earth had they bothered to come?), and seeing as the prices of any property in the nicer areas of the centre were quite exorbitant, they settled very happily for ramshackle and dingy bedsits in the decadent and often foul-smelling area around Ponte Pietra. Morris too would very much have liked to live in the centre, but only in the more elegant, well-to-do areas and certainly not amongst a feckless group of fellow immigrants. He had chosen his flat in Montorio because it was modern and practical and not, by Italian standards, too horrifically furnished. He had removed all the bargain madonnas and supermarket crucifixes on arrival and now the walls were thankfully bare, apart from one or two tasteful prints a rich student had given him, plus the spotlights he had wired up in every corner to make the place bright and very white.

Morris sat down on the high kitchen stool to eat a supper of parmesan and dry bread from off the counter, washed down with a glass of Valpolicella. He fiddled with an old valve radio and listened to a quiz show on the BBC World Service. Reception wasn't very clear tonight and the programme was awful. It made Morris wince with its utter inanity, but he forced himself to listen as a sort of medicine almost. Nothing better than reminding yourself you'd done the right thing leaving the place.

Then, at quarter to ten, he telephoned Massimina. Just before it was too late, in fact, because she would be off to bed

7

any minute. After the rest, the food and a change of socks and shoes, his Italian was near perfect and quite ready to confront the mother should there be any trouble.

Morris had met Massimina in one of the courses he taught at the school, a hopeless student despite her great show of diligence and then the exam that loomed for her at the Liceo. She caught a bus home from the same bus stop as Morris and noticing that she had taken a strong liking to him and that she was pleasant, well-mannered and shy, Morris had got into the habit of offering her a glass of wine in a bar during the half-hour wait they both had. Massimina had a wide, open face, freckled and friendly, and in reply to Morris's detailed questions about her home and family she replied with such a generous account of provincial riches that Morris had taken her out to the cinema on a number of occasions (when there was a film he particularly wanted to see) and every time they said goodbye he held her hands and kissed her carefully on both shy and freckled cheeks. '*Morrees!*' she said. '*Morrees, quanto sei dolce!*' She was just seventeen and a half, with a slim but generous figure, and she was failing in every subject at the Liceo Classico.

The previous Friday evening Morris had asked her to become his *fidanzata*.

It was big sister answered the phone, Antonella.

'Was it you sent the flowers?' she asked, rather coldly Morris thought. And then, who else?

'Did she like them?' he demanded, and got the tone just right, he thought. Eager, a trifle breathless. Quite indifferent as to what big sister might think.

But obviously Massimina had liked them, because now she was wrestling the phone from her sister.

'*Morri!*'

'*Cara!*'

'*Ti ringrazio tantissimo, tantissimo, sono bellissimi, mai visto fiori così belli.*'

Two lessons' worth, Morris thought. The worst of all seasons for roses. But at least they seemed to have done the trick. Morris wasn't actually sure whether he really would marry Massimina, even if her family were to let it go that far. He imagined probably not. He'd have to be crazy. Yet he was tantalized. And it wasn't pure mischievousness, it really wasn't. He wanted to test the water, to see if such a thing was feasible, to see if in the final analysis he might expect to save himself in this way. He had had a growing sensation of late that something was changing inside himself, that new paths of action were opening to him, paths that in the past he would simply never have dreamed of. Even that silly business with the document case, for example. It was as if a fundamental inhibition had finally been removed.

'*Scusami cara*?' He had lost track of what Massimina was saying.

Her mother wanted to meet him, have a word about it all.

'Fine. When?'

'She says as soon as possible, Morrees. Like tomorrow night. She'd like you to come over to dinner. She's a bit concerned, not having met you and so on.'

He was working late tomorrow, Morris said. Clearly that was the right impression to give. Hard-working man.

'The next night then, or Friday?'

Morris thought quickly. He was going to have to charm the pants off the old battle-axe, obviously. And he could do it. He really could. He was feeling very confident in that department these days. The only thing was, to go when *he* felt up to it. Not when they wanted.

'The thing is Mamma says I'm not to go to any more lessons until she's approved of you!' Massimina wailed, and was clearly upset. Morris was really beginning to like the girl. She wasn't at all like those tweed-skirted, toffee-nosed types one had felt obliged to court in one's student days, always ready to air some opinionated opinion on any and every subject, the spirit of contradiction prompt and bristling under their powdered Oxbridge skins should you try to do the same. He'd be over there Wednesday, he promised, voice as soft as it could go. Or absolute maximum, Thursday.

# 2

Morris's large blue Moroccan leather diary was dated 1977, but the days of the week were the same as for 1983. He had found the thing in his little flat along with various other papers left by the late last tenant. After marking off lessons done and earnings taken, Morris sat in the bath and considered tomorrow. The same rush around town. The school twice, then Alberto, then the school again, Matilde, the school again. In the morning he must do something about the zip on his best trousers, get some cream for the document case, get some food, cheese, bread, some more dish-washing liquid, something for his dandruff (him, Morris, with dandruff!) and some more tickets for the bus of course. He soaped shaved armpits, tracing time-saving itineraries across an imaginary map of the city.

No, it was awful. He was living from hand to mouth, from one day to the next, one month to another, week in week out. From the point of view of career, social advances, financial gain, the last two and a half years had been completely wasted. More than that, they had left him physically exhausted and mentally addled by all these stupid lessons, besieged by boredom and mediocrity. Did he have one bright student? Even one? Was there any of them recognized Morris's uncommon talents (the way he could make up exercises on the spot, invent the wildest stories for listening comprehension)? Did any of them have any idea of his calibre? No, the only thing he had truly gained these last two years was the ability to speak a foreign language near perfectly and the curious freedom that ability now appeared to give him in the way he thought. As if he had shifted off rails. His mind seemed to roam free now over any and every possibility. He must make a big effort always to think in Italian as well as speak it, Morris thought. It could be a way out of himself and out of the trap they had all and always wanted him to fall into.

Twisting the wax out of his ear with a Q tip, Morris considered himself in the mirror. Yes, perhaps it was precisely the change of language that had slowly been altering his way of thinking. (Had he been thinking in Italian when he stole the document case?) His blue eyes glared at themselves in a mirror that was misting. 'Dr-r-rrrudge!' he said, but with a smile about the corner of his lips now, a slight baring of long teeth. It seemed a new smile to Morris. He really couldn't remember having seen that particular smile there before. So much inside oneself one didn't know about. '*Cara Massimina*,' he mouthed, '*cara, cara, Massimina*,' and he felt rather pleased with himself.

'Dear Dad, you remember you always used to go on at me about having my eyes on the ground? You used to put a fist in my back, cup your hand under my chin and force me upright. You said studying would turn me into a worm.'

Morris paused, clicking off the dictaphone and using it to scratch an itch behind his ear. What was he trying to get at?

'You said I looked like a spina bifida case the way I was always bent over reading. I said you were hardly bloody Adonis yourself. You didn't know who Adonis was but you belted me for swearing all the same. As if you never did.'

This was tedious: infant-trauma-equals-adult-misbehaviour stuff. Never been convinced of that. And yet at the same time he did feel vaguely excited. Explaining yourself was always exciting. Especially when there was some new evidence to hand.

That new smile, this new idea.

'And then when I was about fifteen and did start taking care of myself and using aftershave (like Gregorio!) and combing and trying to walk with my chest out and bum held in, you said I was a pansy. (Why was that particular word so wounding?) So that I couldn't win either way.'

In the end, of course it was quite simply a question of identity. Morris the good boy, the greaser, mother's helper, the bumsucker, the social climber, the masterly filler-in-of-forms, struggling from terraced Acton and dumb unionized dad to Cambridge lawns – champers and prawns – or Morris the rejected, the despised, the hard-done-by, miss is as good as a mile, irretrievably alienated (at least the ILEA had given you the words), determined to take revenge.

'Revenge, Dad. Because . . .'

One was both of course, both Morrises, and yet the two personalities were not easy to combine.

'. . . because you were right about having my eyes on the ground. At least metaphorically. (I think I stand up a great deal straighter than you, actually.) I'd swallowed the English society-is-a-meritocracy line. I was studying to get out, to get up. To get out of our crappy mediocre house, our ugly street. Away from your beer-drinking, farting, darts friends. And instead if I'd looked around I'd've seen I could study till doomsday and never lift my head an inch out of the shit.'

Morris stared. The sheets he lay in were so gritty they were almost sandpaper, and yet the idea of washing them seemed quite insurmountably tiring and tiresome. What he really needed in the end of course was a maid. Or a wife? He smiled wryly and wondered if it was that new smile he had come out with in the bathroom. Or even a mother.

'You remember when Mother died you said I should go right out and work and not fart about studying pansy things like . . .'

No, that was wrong. That was the wrong tone altogether. And he'd let himself be driven off course. He was supposed to be developing this looking-down idea. He wasn't concentrating. Morris wound the tape back a little and rolled over. He felt warm and comfortable on his stomach in green cotton pyjamas.

'I was ashamed of you. I . . .'

Oh God.

'Mother understood. Mother . . .'

No, keep off Mother. Anyway, she hadn't understood. So

12

damned religious. Mother, Morris appreciated this now, had only sided with him over studying because she somehow felt it was virtuous (probably because it seemed to involve mortification of the flesh) and hence associated with religion, which was the weapon she opposed to Dad's drinking. When you got down to it, both of them had tussled over his future the same way they'd argue what colour to paint the walls in the loo. Or whether to have sex or not.

'Anyway the point is there's been a change of heart. I'm going to look up, look sharp. Italy's a funny place and it's taught me a lot of things. But most of all it's brought me round to your form of socialism, though not in the way you understand it. The rich deserve everything we can hit them with and I'm going to start hitting just as soon as I can.'

No, that was awfully shrill. That wasn't right at all. It didn't say why he had stolen the document case, or started this strange courtship with Massimina. After all, he really rather admired the taste of the Italian upper classes. It was joining them, not beating them was the problem, living artistically as they lived, with style, with flair. Whereas Dad hated the rich because he didn't want to be like them. He hadn't explained himself at all.

Start again then.

'You do realize that I admire you Dad. I admire you and hate you. And here's another interesting contradiction, if you will. My desire to humiliate is curiously mixed up with a desire to be *in the right*. I see that quite . . .'

But the whole thing had lost all sense of direction now. He'd noticed the same problem whenever he'd tried to write a letter to the newspapers. You began with a very clear idea – the change of heart, the looking up – and then halfway through you realized it wasn't clear at all. It was a mess in fact.

The dog started barking at two. Morris woke to a howl, long and bloodcurdling as a werewolf's. Then came repeated barks only a yard or two from his window. His jaws, as always when he woke, were clamped together tight, his tongue sore down one side and swollen. He lay listening to the dog, brain pounding with the most profound black anger, anger that seemed to bulge out from between his tired eyes. It wasn't enough to have your mother die on you then, the only person who'd cared for you, who'd encouraged you. It wasn't enough to have been born poor, to have a peasant of a beer-swilling, stinking, pork-scraping father, to have fought upstream every moment of your life, to have been kicked out of university and rejected for more jobs than appeared in the *Guardian* in a month – no, to add to it all you had to have a dog next door shatter your sleep in the middle of every night, so that you could lie there rigid and horribly awake, going over and over everything again, the sense of frustration, of failure, of being taken for a ride, of having made the wrong decisions, been ignored, of having nothing, but nothing to look forward to, ever, nothing to show for all that effort.

The dog's tireless barking rang between courtyard walls and seemed to hack at his tired brain like a pick sinking into mud. Lying on his back, Morris began to cry, miserable tears of self pity. His cheeks ran. He was damned, merely. Damned. Nothing less. What gave it away was that nobody else seemed to worry about the animal. They were immune. The barking didn't wake *them*. But he was cursed with some terrible disease that brought these troubles to him. And he didn't deserve it. He really didn't deserve it.

Next morning, in Piazza Erbe, Morris bought a postcard and wrote the following polite and pleasant message to his father.

'Dear Dad, hope all is well your end. You'll be working hard in the allotment to get things ready for spring I suppose. Everything fine here. Never rains. Splendid sunshine. Work going extremely well. Maybe if I find the time I'll book a flight for a week in summer. All the best, Dad. MORRIS.'

That sounded all very enviable. (Why was it that life seemed a constant conversation with Dad sometimes?) He scribbled the address: 68 Sunbeam Road, North Acton, London NW10, Gran Bretagna, bought a stamp in the tobacconist's and posted the thing at the bottom of the square. Then off in search of a new shirt and trousers.

Dash or simplicity was the question. Modern or classic? What they wanted of course was basic business dress. A serious lad who could offer a girl something stable (even if they already had enough money to look after the both of them handsomely till kingdom come). It would be nice, Morris thought, to go in something different and shock them into appreciation, even admiration, of a different kind of person altogether, not the man they had wanted but something they would see at once was even better. That was what a real artist would do. But he was feeling rather doubtful of his ability to pull it off just at the moment. Probably it would be better to keep the dress simple and then leave any inspiration to the moment itself, the conversation, the gestures.

In the end he settled for a very faint and tightly checked greeny shirt to go with his dark tweed jacket (an Englishy touch, along with the college tie, so dark against his blond skin), and then brushed wool Italian trousers that would be presentable anywhere. He was overspending of course and it did make him wonder briefly quite how the gas bill would be paid. But then the winter was over. Who cared if they cut him off? Anyway, Morris had a curious feeling that very soon he wouldn't have to be worrying about the odd thousand lire here and there, or whether he managed to find himself twenty lessons a week or not. He had reached the end of his tether was the point, surely, he had played the game their way too long, without success, too hard, too earnestly, too honestly. Either he strangled himself now, or the tether broke.

Shelling out a hundred thousand lire, Morris felt as one who is spending recklessly to be rid of a currency that will soon no longer be of use to him, and he was rather pleased with this metaphor and smiled generously at a dark young shop assistant.

Next to Standa to hunt out a cream for the document case. He liked taking care of beautiful things and chose his product carefully, reading all the instructions on all the tubes and tins there were. Normal things he was rather careless about (his scuffed shoes, for example) but with beautiful things it was different (and that was the mystery in the end, to have opened one's eyes in North Acton and yearned for class and style before he even knew they existed). And Morris thought that when one day he had finally got a good number of beautiful possessions together, he would spend a long time looking after them and get a great deal of pleasure from it. (He could train Massimina if it came to that. She seemed trainable enough.)

The main thing about the document case, though, Morris thought, rubbing in the cream with his fingertips at the school before lessons, was the aplomb with which he had taken it; precisely the kind of aplomb with which he would have liked to live his entire life, precisely the aplomb that was so miserably absent when you spent most days scuttling about in the street from one lesson to the next, grubbing together a few lire.

Morris had been on the train from Milan where he'd gone to renew his passport and there was only one other person in his compartment. Late at night this was. He had been feeling particularly buoyant after a day off work in a different town and when the other fellow insisted on striking up a conversation he had felt loath to admit he was a mere language teacher. What was a language teacher in the end? A nobody. A mere failed somebody else. Who would ever be a language teacher by choice? Morris said he was American (why not?), a member of the diplomatic service based at the American Consulate in Venice; he had been in Italy only six months so far but . . . His Italian was exceptional for such a short period the other man interrupted politely, and Morris had smiled and nodded pleasantly.

His fellow traveller introduced himself as a representative for Gucci's, and it was at this point that he had lifted the soft leather document case onto his fat knees and tapped the thing with such broad and chuckling satisfaction that Morris was rankled and almost told the man directly that he would

16

have no truck at all with a flashy bunch of tricksters producing super-useless products that depended entirely on the name and sold at exorbitant prices to stupid fawning Americans who had to have everything preselected for them by this farce of legendary trademarks (so easily forged) that in reality meant nothing at all (while millions starved! – himself potentially amongst them, come to think of it). But the document case was extremely elegant, Morris couldn't help noticing, so he kept himself to himself and spoke politely about the leathergoods market and the admiration of his countrymen for Italian designers.

The conversation turned to politics and the man from Gucci's said how much the Italians were grateful to the Americans for having helped to keep the Communists out of government and Morris warmed to the subject and came out with an extraordinarily powerful invective against the red menace, even though he'd recently been seriously considering going to live in the Eastern bloc. (LONDON LAD SEEKS BETTER LIFE IN MOSCOW! banner headlines in the *Morning Star*.) He would work for Radio Moscow jamming the BBC since they'd always refused him a job. Why not? Who *needed* Brain of Britain, Radio Newspuke?

After about half an hour of this friendly conversation, the man got up to go to the lavatory and by pure chance his absence coincided with a very brief halt at the small station of Desenzano. Morris didn't think about it at all. Or if he did, he thought in Italian and so barely recognized it was himself doing the thinking. He placed one hand on the doorhandle and waited calmly till the train made its first slow lurch into motion again. Then, with quite perfect aplomb, he lifted the document case from the seat opposite and leapt out onto the platform. He had never felt less like a drudge in his entire life.

The train he had stepped off was the last one that evening; he was obliged to pass the night in a pensione near the station. But Morris didn't mind. He felt jubilant, exhilarated, surprised at himself. He should have started doing this kind of thing years ago.

Sitting on the narrow bed he went through the contents of the case, which were less attractive, frankly, than the thing itself – a sheaf of brochures with photographs of Gucci products, a copy of *Penthouse* (dirty bastard, with his polite conservative small talk), a bag of peppermints, various business letters and memos identifying the representative as a certain Amintore Cartuccio, based in Trieste, and finally, a big brown leather diary full of scribblings of appointments and their results.

Morris sucked the peppermints one after another and studied the diary entries for upwards of an hour, finding a variety of figures written by the names of what must be shops he supposed, and then occasionally the name 'Luigina', followed by an exclamation mark. This name, he discovered, always coincided with that of a certain store in Bologna and appeared at intervals of around ten to twenty days. Two visits to Milan were also accompanied by the name 'Monica', in the margin of the page, and this time the definite hour of an appointment.

It had occurred to Morris once or twice since that night in the pensione that there might be some mileage to be had out of Cartuccio for anyone with a modicum of courage. He couldn't actually remember seeing a ring on the man's fingers, but he was just the type to be married. It was curious how all the piggish, salacious, conventional types would quite certainly be married, whereas a gentleman like himself was forced in that direction only by extreme poverty.

' 'ello Meester Morees!'

His first student had arrived, a small nervous fellow with the inevitable, grey-black, sad Italian moustache. Morris started. Caught in the act of rubbing cream into the stitched seams of thirsty leather, he felt almost as if he'd been found out in some kind of lewd activity, caught with his hand in his pants.

'I see you 'ave the Gucci bag,' Armando said, taking his seat in the classroom.

'That's right.'

'Ees very nice the Gucci bag.'

Morris said he had always admired the quality of Italian leathergoods and gritted his teeth ready for the lesson.

'Have a good weekend, Armando?'

'Yes, I 'ave.'

# 3

Morris was telling an apocryphal story about Stan. There were the mother, the grandmother, two older sisters (how was it he had understood there was only one?), a certain curiously-named Bobo, and Massimina herself who watched him with full dark eyes. The maid had served hors d'oeuvres of chopped spinach and sour cream in little balls (delightfully known as 'priest stranglers'), a pasta course of lasagne and ham, a meat course of simple, lightly done and deliciously toothsome steak, and now a dessert called *Tiramisu*, which seemed to be some kind of soft smooth coffee cheesecake, extremely swallowable and topped with cocoa. Morris had made appreciative but not overly enthusiastic comments on the food, giving the impression, he hoped, that he was perfectly used to meals of this kind. Despite a raging hunger he had not only managed not to wolf things down, but even to leave a morsel on each plate and to refuse (ever so politely) every offer of seconds. His clothes perhaps, and especially the college tie, had proved a shade more formal than those of his hosts, but that was rather as it should be, Morris felt, on a first and humble appearance. And his Italian was excelling itself. He was in form.

'But the point is,' he wound up, 'that Stan is really *very well off*. Yes!' His bright eyes gleamed at their surprise. The fabricated story was at its twist and they seemed to be enjoying it. Morris paused for effect and smiled. (It was always he who did the entertaining. He had noticed that. The boring people fed off anybody with a scrap of imagination.) 'Yes, his family owns *a whole string of motels in Los Angeles!* And he had no need to live in the abandoned house at all. No. In fact, Stan could easily have taken up a nice flat the very day they'd married, if *only they'd been allowed to marry*. In the centre even. And if he'd just had the good sense to sit down with Monica's parents and explain his real situation then they'd never have worried at all most probably. Because for all his hippy ideas and clothes and beads and beard and things, Stan is really awfully nice. You know these Americans. But as it was, of course, what could they do? They had the impression the boy was from the gutter and that their daughter was going to end up there too. So they sent poor Monica off to Paris to a convent school, even though she didn't know a word of French, and poor Stan was left destitute in his abandoned house with his vegetarian cookbooks and Oxfam clothes and all his money that he never wants to spend.'

Morris, narrating, shot regular glances at Massimina which the others could hardly fail to see. The story, in one sense, given the circumstances, was extremely ingenuous and pointed. But that was precisely Morris's intention. It would indicate at once his fears, his appreciation of their fears – their legitimate fears he seemed to be saying – and his explicit intimation that he was on their side and that there was no problem in his case anyway. No beads, beard or Gandhi posters with Morris. For a moment he almost wondered whether he shouldn't finish up the story with a real moral wallop, have the poor fictitious Monica hang herself in the loos at the Gare du Nord, or turn lesbian and make porno films or something. But perhaps it wasn't the moment for a risky self indulgence.

Massimina smiled. 'More *Tiramisu*?' She was already busying herself with the great cut-glass bowl. This time Morris accepted – 'just a spoonful' – watching her attentively. Massimina had a curious mixture of long black hair, light freckles on a camellia textured skin and clear big generous dark brown eyes. Her nose and facial structure had a fine sharpness about them and when she smiled she was definitely attractive, though in a kindly rather than sexy way.

Considering the obvious wealth of her family, Morris found it odd that he should be the girl's first suitor, but he put it down to her youth and painful shyness. One fact he had learnt from their long chats in the bar after lessons was that ever since her father died, when she was two, Massimina had slept with her mother. The thought of the two females going to bed together, the one old and heavy and stale, the other fresh, young and virgin, stirred a curious sensation in Morris that wasn't quite excitement, or quite repulsion, but as it were an intensification of interest pure and simple.

He prided himself on his interest in life.

Bobo, short for Roberto, who it turned out was Antonella's *fidanzato*, had some more *Tiramisu* too. He was scrawny and jawless and ate rather too fast with his head right down near his plate. Morris felt definitely superior, especially when he kindly remembered to offer his arm to the infirm grandmother as they moved from the dining room to the sitting room for the coffee and cognac. He was a gentleman, damn it, despite his background, and of how many so-called gentlemen could you truly say that? The only thing he absolutely must remember was not to drink too much. Absolutely not. He'd already gone through three or four glasses of Soave from the family's own vineyards. Just a nip of cognac now and that must be the end of it.

In many respects the sitting room was very much like the dining room – heavily furnished and dark with an over-whelming sense of straight lines and woodenness about it. This was certainly not the nouveau riche. The floor was marble, black-and-white chequerboard squares, the fur-niture painfully upright in coffin quality mahogany, while ivies of the more sombre kind trailed dark leaves across a tiger rug (genuine down to the bullet hole). Yet surprisingly, the old-fashioned curiosity of the room put Morris at his ease, rather than the opposite. It was the theatricality of the place. How could you feel responsible for anything said in a room like this? And especially if it was said in Italian. He sat down on a viciously straight-backed chair, careful not to jerk his head too much lest dandruff should sift down onto his jacket.

Apart from the decrepit grandmother, all the women were

now out of the room for a moment, fussing after biscuits and petit fours. It was the moment, it seemed, for the scrawny Bobo's interrogation.

'You're a teacher, I hear?'

It amused Morris no end to hear people say, 'I hear', of something they knew perfectly well. After all, they must be aware he had met the girl through the school, mustn't they? But he would have to be careful with Bobo. A couple of remarks over dinner had indicated that the lad was nothing less than the son of the largest poultry magnate in the Veneto. A coup for the signora mamma who was doubtless happy to the point of wetting her pants. And hence Bobo's opinion would count for everything. Morris smoothed his face blank with humility

'That's right, I do some teaching.' He hesitated. From the corner of his eye he caught a glance of Massimina's mother, standing at the doorway, her face grained with the hard lines of fifteen years' most businesslike widowhood.

'But that's an extra really that I do more for my own pleasure than anything else, and then as a favour to the director of the school. My main job here is as an import-export agent. I'm associated with the London and Bristol trade boards and when companies in those towns are looking for customers or suppliers in this area, I do the contacting for them.'

Morris then very casually mentioned the names of three Veronese companies he was working closely with at the moment, two clothing producers and one wine exporter, names you saw on posters and local television commercials. There was a fair chance, of course, Verona being the tiny, tight-knit place it was, that either the signora or Bobo would know people in these companies. But precisely the aplomb with which Morris took that risk should prove the clinching factor.

Having said that, Morris waited. He mustn't, at all costs appear to be defending himself. There was a space of almost a minute. The signora's mouth had a definite, sunken, false-teeth look about it.

'And why did you come to Italy?'

'Fell in love with the place like everybody else. Holidays, you know. You do have such a marvellous country. Then, when my father in the Trade Board said he could get me this job, I jumped at the chance. I'll be here permanently I imagine.' Morris smiled, his own teeth being, as he knew, perfectly white. The fact that it was his father's patronage that had got him the mythical job would be just what they wanted to hear. Strong family. Plenty of leverage. And then one could always have the man die if the whole thing got dicey.

Over coffee, Antonella wanted to talk about Massimina's studies. Antonella and the other older sister, Paola, both sat cross-legged and straight-backed on their straight-backed chairs with an atrocious air of nunnery about them, and for the first time Morris felt a twinge of genuine sympathy for the younger girl's plight as the family dunce. He said he felt Massimina's main problem was nervousness when it came to the exam, since in his evening class she worked hard and well. He accepted a piece of marzipan in the shape of the tower of Pisa. Massimina smiled a meek thank you. Then at the mere mention of photographs from somebody or other, Morris insisted on wading through all the family albums to the polite boredom of everybody else bar Massimina and the grandmother (charmed *her* pants right off!). Here was an afternoon on Monte Baldo, here another when Antonella was born. Here was Massimina at five. *Oh che bella! Che carina!* And what a fine man Il Signore had been, my word! Very handsome.

Morris didn't even have to grit his teeth. He felt marvellous, was the truth. The smell of polished wood mingling with expensive female perfume was like a drug taking him up and up; the taste of quality cognac, Vecchia Romagna (how could he refuse a second glass?), and then the wonderful, the quite exquisite straitlaced opulence of it all . . . perfect! At the front door he kissed Massimina most decorously on both freckle-dusted cheeks. *'Coraggio!'* he whispered.

'I left my car down in the square,' he explained to the

others – and then all the way home on the bus he was trying to remember whether he had ever told Massimina he didn't have a car. (Why on earth did he go home by bus every evening if he had a car?)

The letter arrived only two days later, quite a feat by Italian postal standards. And it was typed.

*Egregio Signor Duckworth* – how Morris hated to see his ugly surname! And where on earth had they got it from? Had he ever mentioned it to Massimina? Had he? No. They *had* checked up, then. How terrifically suspicious they all were! And on what possible grounds?

> *Egregio Signor Duckworth*, I am writing to let you know that Massimina will not be attending any more lessons at the school. You will appreciate that this is a decision we have taken together as a family and we trust you will not try to contact her. Massimina herself agrees with us that you are not the right person for her.
> > *Distinti saluti,*
> > LUISA TREVISAN

There was nothing in the world for Morris then. Nothing. He couldn't even take in a handful of wealthy peasants with their pocketful of real estate and plonky vineyards. And what had he done wrong? He, Morris? His manners had been impeccable, hadn't they? He hadn't eaten too much, even though he was near starving. His hand had been firm and dry when he offered it to the mother and Bobo. He had even given the old crone of a whining grandmother his arm, for God's sake, to get her into the sitting room! Not a crumb had he dropped, not a drop of wine spilt. What on earth could they have against him? His Italian had been faultless, bar the ghost of an accent. Okay, so they'd discovered he was exaggerating a little about the import-export thing. But who wouldn't? They had brought that upon themselves with all their bourgeois need for solid incomes. And it was the kind of job he was bound to get hold of in the end. Someone of his capacity. Morris was furious. Who the hell did they think was going to marry their dumb freckled daughter when all was said and done? Who in his tiny right mind! And to have to put up with those two nuns as sisters-in law!

He went into the bathroom to look at himself. Red eyes, tousled hair. Morris! 'Promising' they had always written on his school essays, on his reports, his university papers. So much promise come to this! Very deliberately, slowly, he stripped himself naked to look at himself, his real skin-and-bone, fingers-and-toes, prick-and-scrotum Morris self in the mirror. Promising! He was quite bubbling over with self-pity. An anguish of it. Never felt failure so acutely before. Beaten and beaten. He saw his tears in the mirror. He looked at them up close, how they gathered along red eyelids. Mocked and trounced. So undeservedly! He picked up his Philips adjustable-head cartridge razor and hacked a tiny chunk from his arm. A bead of blood welled out slow and bright, turned into a trickle, and Morris laid himself out naked on the cold tiled bathroom floor and closed his eyes on the darkness of nothing to do and no one to be and nothing at all ever to look forward to.

# 4

When Father hit her she had come to his bed and slept there. She pulled him into her breasts, kissed his hair. It was difficult to believe a memory could be so vivid still. A person of such quality like that. Even if she was dumb. Of how many people could you really say that they were people of great quality? And with that special female quality. Generosity, giving, sacrifice. The quality had to do with the dumbness in the end. That was most curious, and also true of Massimina perhaps. The quality of a sacrificial victim: dumb, as a sheep to the slaughter. Because she had never understood Morris at all. She had never realized that even as she got into his bed and wrapped him in her warm arms and pulled him into her breasts, all love, Morris was already experiencing the shame of the remarks Dad would toss at him later, already wishing she were gone.

If he thought of Mother's largeness in his bed, her warmth and smell, her slight dampness and breath in the morning after those nights – not frequent, but frequent enough – that Dad had hit her, Morris felt surges of emotion, confusion, deprivation. When she died it had all been rather easier in the end.

Her photograph was on the bedside table. She had his own straight thin nose and blond hair, but otherwise she was rounder, more fleshy and her flesh had a defeated look, a lack of tone that the eyes simply confirmed, big and weak, with a slight flutter, something half-alive trapped between the fine net of wrinkles she'd had at only thirty-eight. And they weren't smile wrinkles either. It was difficult to know what to think of people like his mother.

Perhaps he had been in love with her was the truth.

Though Morris held no truck at all with psychoanalytic clichés that aimed to reduce your personality to the most animal determinism. If he had loved her, it hadn't been Oedipus style. No, he had loved her for her unthinking thoughtfulness, for that stupid, blind generosity (to bastard Dad!), that incredible trusting acceptance of (satisfaction with) her own lot, that mad, religious belief in life, that had her always knitting refugee blankets and saving milk bottle tops.

'I do, dear Dad, appreciate your reaction though. I suppose it could all be rather suffocating, coming back from the pub to find . . .'

But the dictaphone had run out of tape. Another expense.

Yes, it had definitely been easier when she was dead. Less confusion. In fact it was a period he remembered as one of the happiest. He flaunted his grief. With Dad, at school, with himself. Flaunted and nursed it. There was a certain distinction in having one's mother die so young. They even stopped hissing 'greaser' when he shot up his hand to answer every question (not that he had really minded. It had been a confirmation really of his superiority, their jealousy). A great period. Dad had tried to be so nice and Morris had shaken his head and refused to speak and burst into tears. Serve him right as rain. He kept all his mother's old cosmetics in a plastic bag hidden in the curtain pelmet. All her old colours and smells. Because it was difficult to keep grief fresh (and ready for use). When Dad caught him putting on the lipstick, stretching his mouth the way she had, he called him a raving pansy, but Morris didn't explain they were Mother's. That was *his* business. And if he knew in his own heart that he was *not* a raving pansy then that was all that mattered.

After six months or so, Dad found a new girlfriend, a skinny, giggly woman whose peals of laughter could be heard halfway down to Western Ave. Incredible that he'd expected Morris to be nice about it. Incredible he hadn't seen this was just another psychological stick Morris could get back at him with. Dad was a novice, you almost began to pity him.

Morris refused to sit at table with her, to watch TV. He heaved his books up to his room and studied.

One gravitated, perhaps, towards what one could do best, the position of most power.

Of course Dad, in his incredible pig ignorance, somehow related higher education to homosexuality, so that when Morris was the first student at Acton High ever to get to Cambridge, it was all confirmation to him. They more or less said good riddance to each other. And what riled Morris most of all when they threw him out two and a half years later, was that he had nowhere to go but back to Acton, and Dad's told-you-sos.

He had had, for the only time in his life, and for no more than ten minutes, ten milligrams of cocaine in his trouser pocket twisted into a piece of tin foil. He thought he would wait till he was sober before deciding whether to take it or not. If he hadn't been drunk at one of their pathetic parties he would never have accepted the stuff. Never in a million years.

The master's point was that he was making an example. Morris was the kind of person they made examples of, not being connected to absolutely anybody who was in any way remotely anybody. As a result the whole thing passed quite obscenely unnoticed and no example was really made. The kind of irony Morris could do without. Even the students' union, which Morris had repeatedly snubbed (he was interested in his studies, the first he was going to get, not in playing adolescent politics and sending money to Chile) seemed determined to let the matter drop without conflict.

'I miscalculated on two fronts, Dad.' Who cared if the thing was working or not. 'If I'd made a big show of being working class from the beginning, instead of hiding it and spending all the grant on dressing well, then the union would have stepped in. If, on the other hand I'd dedicated myself to making useful friends, then somebody might have brought some influence to bear. But I got my head down from the start.'

One of the things Morris most admired about himself, and

that any eventual biographer would have to dwell on with some warmth, was how he had kept his morale up after what seemed must be a fatal blow, the destruction of everything he had worked towards. He was chucked out just two weeks before the finals and with firm offers for postgraduate places already under his belt. Which fell through at once, naturally enough. And yet in no sense had he lost his nerve. Serenity came partly from knowing you were in the right of course. And then he had been reading late Lawrence. There might be something to be gained from a reconciliation with Dad. He would get a job, work his way up. He still had his mind and a world to conquer. Youth and enthusiasm were on his side and university wasn't all it was cracked up to be anyway. They might even have done him a favour (a postgraduate student hardly lived like a king). Winning is a state of mind, Morris told himself, and the May light was like honey all over the grit of Sunbeam Road as he dragged his suitcases back to Number 68.

Why hadn't they offered him a job? Why hadn't they offered Morris a position? It was inconceivable. Thrown out, yes, but he had got a first in his Part 1. Then he never told them about the expulsion. His letters spoke eloquently of dissatisfaction with academia and eagerness to ply the trade he was applying for. And those letters were okay obviously, because they invariably won him an interview. Then his first interview usually won him a second; yet face to face at last with the man who actually held the gift in his hand, something always went wrong for Morris. But why? He presented himself well, he thought; he was polite but never obsequious, ambitious without even a suspicion of arrogance, respectful, faintly witty. What on earth was going wrong? Morris would watch himself in the big wardrobe mirror, searching for a fault. Nothing. Dark suit and tie, hair brushed to a blond treat across the intelligent forehead. Perfect.

Still watching the reflection, he would explain himself to himself, his cv, modestly, warmly, recording it all on his dictating machine. Why did he want the job? Well, he felt he could offer certain qualities that . . . He looked himself in the eye and found strength of character perfectly controlled and restrained within the acceptable social conventions – what else did they want? His eyes were a shade too close together maybe, his nose a suspicion sharp, all right, but he could hardly help that, could he? And then the 'real life', anti-glamour look was in these days; the men on the BBC seemed afflicted by boils, had nuisance hair, sticky out ears, and nobody seemed to mind. His accent still had a trace of Park Royal about it, did it? He would change it then. And he did. To no result. Or was it that his accent didn't have enough of Park Royal about it? He sounded affected when he should have been earthy? Roots were in. Revert then. Morris tried everything, to no avail. He started with the BBC, the ITV (he sensed he was a media man at heart), the press, the publishers, and then worked his way down; big industry, medium industry, the civil service (nobody could say he hadn't swallowed his pride), small industry, service industries. It was a full scale assault (a bonanza for the post office), but the last interview always did for him. The blue eyes, the frank open face, the blond hair; there was something threatening somewhere about Morris that the Captains of Industry were wise to. 'Following our interview of the 14th, we regret . . .' Always the same scrap of paper, electronically personalized on their processors. Then Gestetner offered him a minor position in their administrative department in Southgate (a mere London Transport marathon from Park Royal) from where, after three weeks of pushing papers between accounts, publicity and production, Morris retired, utterly dissatisfied.

'Scrounger,' was his father's sour comment on finding his son back on the dole. 'No sticking power,' he said, between fried eggs. 'No gumption.' And try as he might, Morris simply couldn't reconcile himself to his father's reactionary, working-class virility. (Lawrence had rediscovered Dad from a distance of course.) The ground-floor council flat they lived in seemed full to bursting with the man, his beermugs and boiled-egg sandwiches, string vests stale with sweat, abandoned cups of cocoa and a booming voice locked into constant argument with the television, *Nationwide* and *World of Sport* – Ron Greenwood had chosen the wrong team again. No, it was impossible for Morris to escape his father, the fearful smells and noises, and impossible in that claustrophobic crushing space to hope for any kind of romantic reconciliation.

So on a fine night a year after his expulsion, some weeks after the Gestetner episode and following a desultory second interview with the Milk Marketing Board (what was life for?), Morris left his Sunbeam Road home, and some four hours later his country, on a 'Magic Bus' that he hoped might live up to its name. Morris was to hear some months after this that the Milk Marketing Board had awarded him a key position in their publicity department. But by that time his boats were carbonized mentally, morally, and what really counted, practically – he had no money to get home.

'When did your family come to Verona?'

Friday afternoon, last lesson. The not-so-merry month of May. Two years on.

'My family ees in Verona these many hundreds of the centuries.'

Oh God.

'Ask me.'

Blank.

'Ask me why I came to Verona.'

'Why did you came to Verona?'

'Come.'

'*Ah si* . . . did you come.'

'It was the furthest place I could afford a ticket to.'

Incomprehension.

'Money. Finished. Here. I must stop. Find job.'

Puzzlement. Fleeting smile of the young Gregorio amongst family frescoes. To his left was the little bronze dryad on her pedestal that Morris had winked at so often throughout the interminable boredom of his lessons with the boy – and never a wink back. A nice statue though, breasts

32

pressed almost flat with the exuberant stretch of the body upwards, holding a branch of some kind. Worth money.

'You are the 'eepy then?' Gregorio's face was a smiling Latin blank, polished hair oiled back from the roots, dark eyes uselessly alive. 'You are the Jack Kerouac?'

'God forbid!'

'*Cosa*? I would like to be the 'eepy too.'

By which he meant he would like to move into a state of permanent holiday, Morris thought. 'Maybe I'll take you with me some time,' he said. '*Ti porto con me.*'

Gregorio was surprisingly quite excited. 'Would be very nice. If my parents would be agreed.' He paused and switched to Italian, grinning white teeth. 'They would think it was educational.'

Morris considered those bright, dark eyes for a moment from his own, ice-clear and Anglo-Saxon blue.

'Okay, time's up.' The lesson was just finishing when the telephone rang. Gregorio, all energy as ever now his trials were ended, rushed to grab the thing.

'Be there in a minute!' He had to dash over to his grandparents in the next block, from where the family was setting off to Cortina for the weekend. So nobody, Morris thought, with a lucidity quite fatally cool, would be back in the house again till Monday. And already he had decided. He was going to steal something.

'I'll show myself out,' he shouted to Gregorio, who was hurrying up to his room now for his skiing outfit.

'*Bene, arrivederci a martedì.*'

'*Arrivederci.*'

With one calm look about the room and particularly at the windows, Morris lifted the little bronze statue from its pedestal and jammed the thing to the very bottom of his document case, nearly splitting the leather seams. The bulge was obscenely obvious. Should he unlatch the window to give an explanation of the crime? Morris started in that direction, but Gregorio's quick feet were already padding down the stairs. Morris turned sharply to the door, then changed his mind and stopped still. Was there time to put the thing back before the boy appeared? Was there? No.

'Look, do you need any help down the stairs with your bags?'

Gregorio had appeared at the bottom of spiral steps, laden with gear. The absence of the statuette from its little pedestal seemed horribly, glaringly obvious. And likewise the huge bulge in his document case. What a fool! Morris deliberately looked at the pedestal, inviting the worst. But Gregorio was already gliding down the snowy slopes above Cortina with his 'friend', twisting and turning through gulleys, slithering round beginners. And perhaps he had never really noticed the statuette anyway. Morris felt prickled all over with sweat and excitement. His buttocks were tight together in his trousers.

'Here, let me take the poles at least.'

'*Bene, grazie.*'

They were out of the apartment on the stone stairs that led down to the courtyard. Morris watched Gregorio turn the key over two, three times in the lock, then use another tiny key which must be to activate the alarm. A small green light glowed out beside the door. Then they went down to where the fountain played over the faun's flanks in the twilight and out into Via Emilei. Gregorio's father had the Mercedes packed up and ready at the corner of Via Fama.

'*Buona sera, Signore, Signora.*'

'*Buona sera, Morees! Come sta? Tutto bene, il lavoro?*'

'*Grazie, grazie,*' Gregorio was saying as Morris laid the poles alongside others on the roof-rack.

'You must come with us one time,' the signora said and smiled indulgently at their boy's teacher. Her face, under a thatch of peroxide blonde, was absurdly young, all powders and creams most probably, Morris thought, and glancing down at his case he caught a faint, tell-tale gleam of bronze from the bottom. Anybody could see it.

'I don't ski, I'm afraid.'

'Gregorio will teach you.'

'*Sì, sì,*' the boy agreed. He was taller than Morris and smiled down with long teeth.

34

'Gregorio likes you very much,' the father said, as if this was some kind of terrific compliment. 'We'd like you to come.'

'I'll look forward to that very much,' Morris said.

They would never invite him in a million years.

# 5

Late the following evening, Morris walked quickly down Via Portone Borsari, Via Fama, Via Emilei, and found the great oaken doors of the palazzo which Gregorio's family owned and in part of which they lived. It was near midnight. He hit a bell at random. *Famiglia Zane.*

After a few moments the intercom crackled. *'Chi è?'* The distortions of the thing would cover any voice characteristics.

*'Sono Gregorio, Signora.* I can't find my outside doorkey. I hope I didn't wake you.'

*'Va bene,'* the woman was clearly annoyed, but after just a second the gate buzzed open and Morris passed through. Gregorio was, after all, son of the padrone.

He could go upstairs to the apartment door, but there was nothing to be gained there with that alarm. Instead he went through the porch into the tiny courtyard where the fauns postured in the middle of a fountain that had now been turned off. Morris sat on the edge of the great stone bowl. Midnight. The various clocks of the city gonged and chimed. The night was pale and the dark air of the courtyard had a spongy, damp taste. He considered the internal walls around him, smothered with vines and wistaria up all four storeys, the plants parting only for the windows, two of which were yellow with light. Nothing for it but to wait.

He sat on the stone bowl, shifting from one buttock to the other against the cold. Half an hour, an hour; but he wasn't bored. It had occurred to Morris that in all his long and tedious education and then his meagre round of lessons, not to mention the paperchase his year of unemployment had been, this was the very first time he had ever dealt shrewdly with the world of things and people for definite gain – bar the document case of course, and that had been too easy. This was definitely more exciting.

Perhaps it was mostly a question of passing one's time in the end. Without feeling an utter fool. He had thought of that before. And if they wouldn't let you arrive at money honestly and honourably, nor marry it, perhaps it wouldn't be so terribly out of order, or even difficult, to steal it. Perhaps it was just a matter of keeping your eyes peeled, an extension of the sort of Morris-against-the-world feeling he had always sensed at school.

And then it wasn't even a question of money really, but of style. Was he to go on living for years and years, counting each teaching minute as so many lire, wrapping himself in blankets wintertime, doomed to public transport, envy – while these people lived, due to accidents of birth, with the grace of emperors? What advice, what alternative counsel did the world offer him? How was time to be passed, life to be spent? The popular wisdom (find a job, chin up, work hard, there are always the weekends) offered only oblivion.

If they gave you nothing to do, at least you could give them something to think about.

At one fifteen the last light went off and the courtyard settled in a deeper dark. Morris gave it fifteen more minutes. It might have been wise to wait longer but he was getting cold now and eager to have done. Enough. Standing up, his bottom stiff and numb, his lips dry, bowels weak, he felt the same kind of nervous flush he had felt as a young student before an exam. Excitement and fear. The next few minutes deciding everything. And Morris had always thrived in that kind of competitive situation.

If only life really were decided by exams!

He went and stood under a vine whose trunk climbed to the second floor near the sitting room window of the Ferronis. He trampled the little patch of open earth where the thing sprouted and then shinned up a few feet breaking off leaves and branches. A fine mess. He dropped down and considered the windows. The hole would need to be big enough for an arm to go through to give the impression someone had reached in and opened the thing from inside.

He took the largest of the stones from his pocket and aimed carefully. In the narrow courtyard his throw would have to be steep, near vertical. He heaved up the stone and missed. The thing struck the wall a yard or so to the right and clattered down through a sea of vine leaves. The noise was appalling, a fearfully loud rustling with sharp echoing cracks as the stone bounced on branches and finally struck the flagstones of the courtyard like a gunshot. Morris dashed through the arch to the outer door and had it half open before he paused to listen. Despite the coolness he suddenly found himself bathed in sweat. Why on earth had he got involved in this crazy business for the sake of that stupid little statue? God! But there must be some sign of a break-in or he was finished. It wouldn't take them ten minutes to work out who had done it.

After a few moments he crept back into the courtyard to discover that no lights were on. Nobody had woken it seemed. Amazing. He found his stone behind the fountain, took up exactly the same position as before and this time threw with a slight bias to the left. Dead on. The window must have been made of the cheapest glass because it flew into fragments which fell in a shower through the vines. But before they could hit the ground, Morris was already out on the street. He thrust his hands in his pockets, pursed his lips to whistle and, given that the last bus was long gone, set out briskly on the long walk home. What he whistled was, 'When the Saints'.

Morris had the statue boldly placed on his coffee table beside the photo of his mother and glanced up at it from time to time above the pages of his book. He would have to wait till Monday's or Tuesday's papers to hear how much it was worth. But it was not urgent. In fact, he wasn't sure he really cared, or whether he would make any attempt to sell the little lady whatever she would fetch. It was nice just to have her there, a smooth, bronze, upward lift of form; knees, thighs, breasts, arms and tilted face, all swinging from right to left and exuberantly upwards. He would keep the thing, damn it, unless he was desperate. Perhaps he would even buy a pedestal.

'The difference, Dad,' he remarked into a dictaphone humming with new batteries, 'if you must know, between stealing and exploitation, is this: that with exploitation the victim knows he is getting fucked, like you at the factory, and has to accept it, to put bread in his mouth as you say, and so is humiliated. But stealing is a more generous transaction. The victim isn't obliged to assent to his own ruin and therefore remains proud and free. Hence stealing would appear to be the more honest and morally superior of the two.'

# 6

It was the first of June they turned off the gas. This was quite reasonable, seeing as Morris hadn't as yet paid any of the bills for the expensive winter months. He had been expecting it even. Nevertheless the event plunged him into a grand depression, the kind of gloom that sent him scuttling out after other people's company, his students and neighbours mostly, but even the English community on occasions with their bangers-and-mash and Valpolicella parties. He dressed carefully, not wanting to wear out anything valuable, yet at the same time determined to distinguish himself from the jeans and T-shirt brigade. Once arrived, he skulked in the corners of their shabby living rooms in Dietro Duomo, trying to pick up from their boozy cackle and chat whether anybody had any idea how to make money through the summer months.

The schools closed the second week of June and most of the private students would probably give up around the same time, thus condemning the expatriate teaching community to three months of penury. During this period most of the teachers gave up their rooms and flats to save themselves the rent and disappeared on hitch-hiking holidays to the cheapest possible destinations, or cheaper still, back home to regroup again the following autumn when the schools re-opened and the same squalid rooms would be as readily available as most squalid and undesirable things generally are.

The prospect of this summer, looming as an interminable scorching hot hazy blank, nothing to do and no money to spend, had Morris floundering in the very depths of self-pity. He was a waif and a stray was the truth. An orphan, in the true spiritual sense of the word. He was a nobody, without dignity or recognition. Without repose. He thought how the noble Italian upper classes would pass the summer season, strutting through the shaded squares, parading along the sun-drenched lakeshore with their godlike bodies and stylish clothes.

Poverty was endurable in England, Morris explained to Pamela Pinnington, a slim, limpish girl from East Croydon, because it had been institutionalized; the whole country wore a façade of poverty and the rich were guilty of their money and kept it well hidden while the poor were proud of their tribulations and flaunted them like banners or battle scars.

'But in Italy only fools are poor,' Morris said. 'And everybody can see how marvellous life is with cash.'

Pamela asked, did he really think so? She thought the most wonderful thing about Italy was that if you had a lot of friends and shared your flat, you really didn't need too much money at all. Morris watched her as she spoke, nervous middle-class fingers twisting round a beer mug full of wine, and immediately regretted the rashness of having said what he had, exposing himself like that. The girl had huge, brown, blinking eyes and wore a dirty T-shirt with no bra so that you had to feel sorry for her breasts which were no more than nipples.

'Perhaps you're right,' he said politely, trying to extricate himself. He wasn't in any way lascivious about women, but he did like them to be beautiful.

'You could have a go at getting a job as a travel guide,' Marion Roberts interrupted. Marion was a tall bleached blonde who wore the same kind of electric lollipop make-up so common in places like Camden Market or the Portobello Road. One of the many who hung around the awful Stan. 'Give them some bull about having been to university and knowing the city backwards and they're bound to give you some work.'

But the idea of dragging groups of pensioners from Great Yarmouth around the streets and squares of ancient Verona to have them snapshot each other with hankies knotted over their heads under Juliet's balcony, complaining there was nowhere public to spend a penny and giggling over the name Piazza Bra, was more than Morris could even begin to imagine. Not his cup of tea, he said.

Stan came to join them. He wore jeans and a goldish Indian smock and his beard was speckled with crumbs. Simonetta, another girlfriend, Italian, hung mouselike behind him. Marion's inked eyelashes flickered.

'Poor Morris has a problem with the summer,' she said. 'He's stony broke.'

Morris had actually said nothing of the kind, but didn't protest. He was long since used to being made fun of. If fun you could call it.

'No shit man!' Stan scratched in his beard under a broad Jewish smile. He seemed as pleased to see Morris, Morris thought, as a priest who has found a new sheep in his flock. Stan, the community leader.

Morris shouldn't have taken such an expensive apartment, he said. He was paying the price now for not having shared a place earlier and saved on the rent. Still, if he wanted to come and live with them for the last couple of weeks and then maybe join them on their microbus trip out to Turkey, he was most welcome. There was an island off Izmir where you could guarantee to live for less than a dollar a day. Stan linked his arm into Morris's as he said this and Morris felt suddenly so completely disorientated by the desultory, inferior conversation that he said, yes, he might do that, and then was furious with himself, of course, for not having immediately burnt a boat that was so patently unseaworthy.

But what grated most of all – as he had told Massimina's family at that fateful party when he had invented a fiancée for the American – what grated most of all was that Stan actually was rich! His mother really was sitting on a whole string of motels back there in California. And what did the boy do? He played hippy dippy poor man in Italy, where to live well certainly didn't cost the earth, squatting in a pigsty with five others ('us immigrants have to stick together') secure in the knowledge that he could step out of his muck any moment he chose and take the first plane home to Sunset Strip.

At least I'm not a hypocrite, Morris thought. At least I can say *that* of myself, and he left without a word of goodbye.

At home, he stood up from his bread and parmesan to pull out a drawer from the cabinet behind him. Amongst the stacks of dictaphone tapes there was a bundle of papers which he took out and spread on the kitchen counter.

AGILE THIEF DOESN'T KNOW WHAT HE'S AFTER, the back page headline of the *Arena* had announced; with typically facile journalistic amusement the article went on to describe how some poor idiot had gone to the risk of climbing six metres up a wistaria and smashing a window to take nothing more than a cheap bronze reproduction barely worth the metal it was made from.

Morris went through the other papers. There was the letter from Signora Trevisan, letters from the gas company, two laboriously penned postcards from his father ('You're only putting off the evil day, lad.' Why on earth did they bother to stay in touch, insist on reminding each other of their respective existences?), various rejections for jobs he'd written off for in Milan, a long sob note from Massimina, to which he hadn't as yet found time to reply, and finally, all the Gucci brochures and the diary of Signor Cartuccio with the exclamation marks by the names of Luigina and Monica.

Munching the cheese, Morris reread everything with great care. The tedium of another exhausted empty evening was before him. When he was at university, he had noticed how everybody, himself more or less included, had a sense of prestige and of belonging quite by right to a great mutual admiration society which bore you up and gave you a constant relation to others and to the world. And the same must be true, Morris thought, if you were involved in some kind of religion, or part of a family, or married even; you shared hopes and fears, hate and trust, and developed communal callouses against the stings and treadmills of the world. Common illusions was the correct description.

But on your own, and in a foreign country . . . on your own you had to find self-esteem all by yourself; you were turning to the mirror for company, clutching at straws – a terrible, virtuoso affair. In short, the real thing. It was incredible how an evening, a weekend, a whole summer, could simply open before you like a chasm, uncrossable, unfillable, paralysing. One was even tempted to start writing books or painting pictures or something, like half the rest of the immigrant community (Pamela Pinnington of all people – 'I'm a bit of an artist actually'). Or to play the libertine and gather your trophies that way. (Dear bi-sexual Stan with all his tribe around him, like some lascivious latter-day mormon.)

Yet Morris was determined to steer well clear of such desperate remedies as these. No, he was damned if he was going to play the sucker who flogged himself over canvas or manuscript from dark dawn till dusk only to have his creations condescendingly brushed aside by the nincompoops who doubtless commanded in that zone (could you imagine anyone ever publishing Stan's 'New World Immigrant Zaps the Old'?). Anyway, he had too much respect for great art to dabble himself. And the idea of playing Don Juan had never appealed, the details of such a life would be so untidy; it was the wholeness of his own body, his own image, he was interested in, not the possession of others.

'Every man is an island,' he informed his dictaphone. 'Entire unto himself. Click. Or God help him.'

Yet he had to do something! Anything, absolutely. However reckless. Or this life would simply trickle and trickle away, with all the talent and taste and energy he had gone completely to waste. He turned back to the drawer, fiddled through the heaps of tapes and used train tickets and pulled out his writing pad. There were only four or five sheets left. So he practised first on the back of the gas bills.

(What was life for, exactly? Where, in particular, if anywhere, was Morris Duckworth going?)

*EGREGIO SIGNOR CARTUCCIO;* he went for the most fiercely childish block capitals, not simply because he would have to

44

disguise his handwriting, but because he knew there was nothing more threatening than childishness. REMEMBER ME? THE AMERICAN DIPLOMAT. HA HA. I STILL HAVE YOUR DOCUMENT CASE AND DIARY, AND NOW I HAVE FINISHED MY RESEARCH. IF YOU DON'T WANT YOUR SIGNORA WIFE TO KNOW ABOUT YOUR DISGUSTING ADVENTURES WITH SIGNORINAS LUIGINA AND MONICA, THEN WILL YOU PLEASE BE SO KIND AS TO LEAVE THE, I THINK, MODEST SUM OF FIVE MILLION LIRE . . .

Where? Obviously there was no question of him mailing the cash to this address. On the other hand, Cartuccio lived in Trieste and Morris was damned if he was travelling nearly two hundred miles on the off chance that the chap would be fool enough to pay (if he ever sent the letter at all). But then it wasn't really such an awful lot of money. Cartuccio probably earned that every month. Maybe every week. (Heartbreaking to think how many people earned in a week what would do Morris for a year.) What to do?

He picked up the diary and flicked through the pages for the month to come. Cartuccio was in Rome this week it seemed, returning via Florence, Bologna and Vicenza on the tenth, eleventh and twelfth of June. Vicenza was just twenty miles away from Verona so Morris might stretch to that, he thought. The problem being that he didn't know the place at all. So where could he arrange for him to leave the money? This was an interesting question and weighing it up Morris at last began to enjoy himself. It would be quite a tour de force if he pulled it off. A challenge equal to his imagination. If the man paid he would give half away to charity, just to show he wasn't the common criminal. Or at least a million anyway. Some orphans' charity.

He went to his bedroom, pulled down an old suitcase from off the wardrobe and dug out a Michelin guide from the bric-à-brac inside.

VICENZA. Principal Sites (visit, 1 to 1½ hours): Piazza dei Signori – like St Mark's Square in Venice, this is an open meeting place for all . . . No, nothing there. Bissara Tower – this occupies one entire side of the . . . No, no accurate description. The Basilica then? Too crowded by the sound of it. Minor Sites. Yes, here was what he was after. The Church of the Holy Crown – This magnificent edifice was constructed in the mid-to-late thirteenth century in honour of the Holy Crown of Thorns donated by St Louis, King of France. Two signed paintings are to be admired within: a *Baptism of Christ* by Giovanni Bellini (5th altar on the left), and an *Admiration of the Magi* by Paolo Veronese . . .

Morris tried to picture the church. A string of altars up the left-hand side with candles burning here and there in the gloom, probably a little machine at the fifth altar where you could slip in fifty lire to illuminate Bellini's *Baptism* and hear a description of the thing's history in two hundred foreign languages. There would be a little group there most of the time, but hardly a stampede.

FIVE MILLION LIRE – No, make it six, may as well get enough to survive the summer at least. In style. Especially if he was supposed to give one away. SIX MILLION LIRE IN THE CHURCH OF THE HOLY CROWN, VICENZA, ON JUNE 12TH. THE MONEY MUST BE IN BILLS OF ONE HUNDRED THOUSAND IN A REGULAR ENVELOPE. GO TO THE FOURTH ALTAR ON THE LEFT. SIT ON THE NEAREST CHAIR WITH HEAD BOWED AND TAPE THE ENVELOPE UNDER THE CHAIR WITH SIMPLE SELLO-TAPE. NO TRICKS OR MISTAKES OR YOUR MARRIAGE IS FINISHED.

Morris could see the scene perfectly and was delighted. It was pretty well foolproof, damn it. Cartuccio would put the stuff there on the twelfth and he himself would pop in the following day to pick it up. If Cartuccio didn't oblige, okay, then at least he got a look at the paintings by Bellini and the Veronese. Which had to be better than the old waste-bin-at-the-bus-terminus trick.

Morris went over the letter, rewriting it on the back of another gas bill and changing a few details. It was important to sound more threatening and a bit crazy, he thought. If you weren't crazy, nobody would believe you'd ever really do anything. Begin something like, *EGREGIO SIGNOR CARTUCCIO*, YOU STINK, YOU KNOW THAT, STINK, YOU AND

ALL YOUR FILTHY RICH LEATHERGOODS BOYS WITH YOUR COPIES OF *PENTHOUSE* AND A SLUT IN EVERY TOWN. REMEMBER ME?

He checked up a few words in the dictionary and a couple of points in his grammar book to make sure he had the Italian just so and then copied out the final thing in an uneven, disturbed looking hand, making the low quality Biro smear sticky blotches all over the place.

When he had finished and popped the thing into an envelope, he felt so hugely entertained (he'd never mail it anyway) that he started another one directly, and this time straight onto letter paper.

*Gentile Signora Trevisan,* he used his own handwriting now, at its most sloping and lyrical, occasionally wiping the Biro on his handkerchief. Beside his left hand he kept Massimina's letter with its long sob sentences like, 'Oh Morris, if only we could arrange to meet somewhere, if only I had your phone number, I miss you so – ' and then the cries of desperation – 'Mamma's saying I must do nothing but study because I'm so behind at school and I have no time for silly crushes on older men, but Morris, truly, I do love you and . . .'

*Gentile Signora Trevisan,* Many thanks for your communication of last month. I do appreciate the care you are determined to take of your beautiful youngest daughter. I also realize that you must be aware of what I now confess to my shame, that I lied to you all about my work and prospects, though I insist I did so simply for fear that had you known my real and modest situation you would have severed any relationship between myself and Massimina immediately. After receiving your letter I felt I had lost everything and I decided to try and accept it. But now I have received a letter from your daughter telling me her feelings for me are as strong as ever, and with this to give me courage I find I simply can't and won't let go. I love Massimina, Signora Trevisan, and wish more than anything else to

47

be beside her. What I now beg you to do is to let me see her sometimes, albeit in the presence of others, and to give me two or three years to prove myself as a prospective husband. I swear, on whatever scrap of honour remains to me, that I will never take advantage of any affection Massimina may have in my regard and that I will do my utmost to make up for my disgraceful behaviour as a guest in your house.

Most sincerely, MORRIS DUCKWORTH

It was awfully overblown, Morris thought. But that was the Italian style (don't think a single word in English was the secret). And at least it saved him having to come up with any less conventional expressions of emotion. The following morning then outside the post office in Verona, Morris tossed a coin to decide whether to send the letters. Heads yes, tails no. Both times the coin came down tails. He tossed it again and still tails. The hell with it. Morris mailed the letters anyway. They could do no harm.

'But it does seem amazing to me they managed to drag themselves up to the second floor on just that bare wistaria.'

Morris was speaking to Gregorio between lessons. It was a chance meeting in a café that spread its tables out onto the stylish esplanade of Piazza Bra; and Gregorio said yes, the police thought it must have been a teenager, or even a young child, because whoever it was hadn't broken a single branch near the top. And then it would explain his taking something so basically valueless.

'Good job they didn't spot the little silver Neptune though, the one on the mantelpiece, you know. My father would have gone crazy. It's worth a fortune.'

A gesture of the hand, as if brushing away a fly from his face, hid Morris's wince. He was teaching Chapter Four of *Simply English* this week, which was all about where people keep things ('in the kitchen, second cupboard on the right, top shelf, behind the sugar'), and just for fun, to add some spice to the thing, he made a point of asking people if they

48

had any sculptures in the house and where they kept them. 'In the lounge. A Renaissance piece with Jupiter as a bull carrying off Europa.' 'And what's it made of?' (Chapter Three, materials, legitimate revision.) 'Of silver.' Incredible how ingenuous people could be. Maria Grazia said her grandfather had picked the thing up in a junk shop and later discovered it was worth a lot of money. Morris would be going into arrears on his rent, he calculated, around the end of June.

He looked out over his wine across the square at the gently milling promenade of shoppers. It was precisely this aspect of Italy that kept him here really; the *passeggiata*, the stylishly flaunted wealth, a sense of repose he enjoyed in simply watching beauty all around him – a liquid clear sunlight across the square, sparkling the fountains, baking the ancient unblinking façades – and these people who had inherited so much, the stones, the sunshine, the style – all laughing and floating through these golden pedestrian streets.

But how to become a part of it? Morris, who had never been a part of anything, who doubted if such things were possible? (Every man is an island . . .) Yet the desire was achingly, shamefully strong. Precisely the strength of desire, Morris reflected, if experience was anything to go by, confirmed the unattainability of the object desired.

Gregorio, meanwhile, was discussing his summertime plans. He was going to stay at the family villa in Sardinia and recover from all the studying he'd been doing before facing university. If he'd passed his exams that is.

They sat sipping wine under a torch of a sun.

'And you?'

'Oh, no plans as yet. Depends on work of course.'

'Not going on one of your long travels to the ends of the earth?' Gregorio smiled softly, rather effeminately, Morris thought. And it occurred to him that Gregorio did have rather a curious way of looking at one. Too intense. As if you were an object of interest. Which was perhaps why he liked the boy in a way. One felt flattered.

49

'I was thinking of going to Turkey with some others. Like to come?' Invite to be invited. There was an idea.

'Love to,' Gregorio said. 'If only my damn parents would let me. They'd never give me enough money for the trip.' Again the smile.

'There are problems though. (Carefully does it.) I haven't decided a hundred per cent myself. These people are going in a dormobile and I'm afraid the company isn't so hot.'

A long, glass-draining pause, and then, there it was:

'Would you like to come with us, then? There's plenty of room. For a few weeks at least. My parents won't get there till August, but I'm setting off any day now. Saturday probably. We could have quite a time.'

Morris held his breath. It was like having a creature walk into a trap before you'd barely set it. How many invitations had he had in his life? You could count them on the fingers of one hand.

'If I could make it, I'd love to see Sardinia. It depends on work though, you know. I've had a couple of offers for interpreting at conferences.'

'Suit yourself, but the swimming's excellent there. Plus there's always plenty of company, not to mention a boat or two to play with.'

What could be better? And having managed not to jump at it right from the very start, Morris was just going to accept quite definitely, and rather prematurely really, because the lad could easily go and cancel on him the next day and then he would look a complete fool – just about to accept, when all at once there was a voice calling out his name across the square. Morris's name.

'*Morrees! Eccoti qua! Che meraviglioso!* Oh Morri, I have to speak to you.' The girl was in tears, you couldn't say whether of joy or pain. 'I saw your letter, Morrees!'

Morris looked at her. Massimina was in a complete mess. Red in the freckled face, make-up all over the place, hair tousled, body apparently quite shapeless in a running outfit of all things. And out of breath to boot – nostrils flaring and eyes puffy. Rather horrible.

Just when he might have settled things with Gregorio too! Morris didn't stand up.

'Morrees, thank God I found you, thank God, if you knew, if you only knew what . . .' She stopped, unable to go on and burst into tears. Gregorio stood, embarrassed, but curious too, eyes flickering from the girl to Morris. His long delicate fingers moved inside his shirt for his wallet.

'No, look, I'll pick up the bill,' Morris told him quickly. 'And I'll give you a call as soon as possible about Sardinia, okay?'

Gregorio turned to where Massimina stood there panting, and was obviously waiting to be introduced, but Morris didn't oblige. Introduce friends and they end up going off on their own together. To talk about you behind your back.

'Are you sure it's okay?' Gregorio asked.

'Yes, I'll get it,' and he winked at the boy with just the right kind of ambiguity.

'I'll leave you to it then,' Gregorio grinned, nodding at the weeping girl, and he had obviously decided to find the situation amusing. His slim figure swayed off across the square in white bermudas and neon-blue T-shirt.

Massimina sat down and had found a handkerchief. Her tracksuit was brilliant red with white flashes down the arms. Her black hair, fallen forward, stretched down as far as the table. Sympathy was in order. (This was the girl he'd asked to marry him.) Morris put out a hand and took the girl's wrist gently.

'Tell me about it. Come on. Cheer up now, everybody is looking.' When the waiter passed he ordered two martinis, which would just about break him.

He looked over Massimina's body, but there was no sign of a bag or purse.

'Come on now, tell me.'

So bit by bit, sniffling her martini and pushing the back of now one wrist, now the other, into her red eyes, she told. Everything had gone wrong at home, just everything and again everything. Yes? Morris tapped his feet on the marble flagstones under the table. The martini was making him feel extremely comfortable and rather distant, as if he were at the other end of the square.

Grandma was ill, she said, that was the first thing, dying most probably with her angina, and all the others were being so horrid about it saying it was probably better if she went now, if she was going to be so demanding and helpless all the time. Then she, Massimina, had failed all her end-of-term exams, everything, completely, which meant she would have to study all summer to retake them in September, and it just wasn't fair, it wasn't, nor even sensible, because there was no point in her studying, because she just wasn't that sort.

'No,' Morris said.

Anyway, then she had discovered his letter, which Mamma must have been hiding from her for days, and so now she *knew* he loved her and she was more sure than anything in the world that she loved him and her mother was just being horrible saying the things she did about him. Paola had sent her running to get Grandma's pills in the middle of the night from Mamma's handbag and she'd found the letter by accident. So after lunch she'd put on her tracksuit and said she was just going for a run and then she'd run all the way into town to find him, because she wasn't going home any more.

Morris watched the coloured dresses shifting in the steadily slanting light across the square. If the mother didn't want Massimina to see the letter, why hadn't she simply destroyed it? A far more sensible line.

'So, what are you going to do?'

'I'm not going back, that's all. Not to spend all summer studying for exams, and with Mamma not allowing me to see anybody. I wasn't made to do exams.'

In about five minutes she would change her mind, Morris thought. After all, she had never even slept in a different bed from her mother. He waited, watching as she dabbed the tears away from her round, faintly freckled face. The prettiness of the camellia coloured skin was coming back now. Extraordinarily smooth skin when you compared it, for example, with Gregorio's. Or any boy's over fifteen. And that was something Morris always looked for in girls and that never failed to fascinate him when he found it. Simply as an extraordinary fact, that skin could be so smooth, life seem so fresh.

'What were you made for then?' he asked.

Fair question. Not at all cynical.

She looked into his eyes and her bottom lip puckered out into a childish dimpled smile.

'Maybe for you, Morrees.'

After Morris's last lesson, Massimina was waiting at the bus stop as she had promised. Hoist with his own petard, was the way he saw it. There was no point in courting the girl outside her family's approval. He had no taste for it at all. And particularly he had no desire to start some kind of awful affair that could only end in disaster. He had written that letter to get *himself into* her family, not to get *her out* of it. The difference was neither academic nor subtle.

'I should really take you straight home.' That should win some approval. 'Come on, let's find a taxi.'

'No, Morri,' and quite impetuously she threw her arms around him. 'I'm not going back.'

At which precise moment, Stan wobbled past. Stopping his bike under a lamp across the street, his face was a wide bearded grin.

'Hey man, you made up your mind about Turkey yet? We're off in a week now.'

Massimina pulled away.

'You can always bring your friend,' Stan laughed. 'Drop in and tell us as soon as you can.' A bus swept between them and Stan disappeared.

# 7

It was seeing her together with the money, so much money, that brought the idea into his head. He had been explaining, quite reasonably, in the plain light of another day, that simply from the financial point of view she couldn't possibly stay, when she unzipped the red tracksuit top just three or four inches and, reaching inside, produced after a few seconds of fiddling a small wad of notes that must have been hidden in her bra.

'I took out all my life savings yesterday. I've got loads of money, enough for a couple of months anyway. And after that they won't be able to do anything about it anyway, will they? I mean, in cases like that they have to let you marry because of thinking you've been to bed together.'

Morris's mouth, which had been open wide to speak, snapped shut.

'And anyway, I'm eighteen in August.'

Well, they definitely had not been to bed together. In fact the evening had passed rather well. Massimina had made up a cold salad, laid and cleared the table and then taken a bath, re-appearing afterwards in the tracksuit, but without, Morris noticed, a shade unnerved, her bra. Her breasts were larger and heavier than he had imagined, and indeed than anybody would have imagined, given her slim body. He stayed sitting at the kitchen table where she was safely opposite and for conversation, to fill the time, he simply asked her questions, as he had always done at the bar after lessons waiting for the bus, and she chattered happily in reply: Bobo did this and that, he had got off his military service by getting a doctor friend of his father's to give him a certificate which said he had an ulcer, Mamma had had an accident which made her deaf in one ear, Antonella was studying law, Paola had a crush on a married man and wanted to go away for a year to get over it but Mamma . . .

It really wasn't too difficult at all, Morris thought. As long as the absence of that bra wasn't supposed to be a signal for something or other. At eleven, he said quite abruptly that he had to be going to Vicenza next morning. In fact, he'd have to be making a very early start. Very.

Better get to sleep now then, she said. She had found his brush and was brushing out her long black hair, which under the spotlamps had strange reddish lights in it. Should she, she asked, sleep on the sofa, or would he? He would, Morris said, rather too quickly, too gallantly.

Where would you find a nice girl like that in England? he asked his stolen statue, undressing. All he could remember from university parties were vamps and sluts who ignored you when you couldn't dance and then rediscovered you later when you were the only one free or sober and tried to drag you back to their rooms as if you were so much hot meat. Obviously there was something to be said for the Catholic provinces after all. He had chosen well.

Though not so well with the sofa perhaps. For eight hours he had half slept, huddled into a question mark, waking occasionally to the dog's barking, his teeth clenched, tongue sore.

Now, with the first morning light streaming in like a great boiling white girder against the red material of that sofa, Morris rotated his head to chase out the cricks from his neck.

'How much is there?' he asked involuntarily, knowing he shouldn't. But the idea was already there. And ideas, like weapons, can't be uninvented. (Speaking of weapons, Morris had a nasty habit, an illness he sometimes thought, of seeing them everywhere. He could hardly butter his toast of a morning without respectfully fingering the handle of the knife, inescapably aware of its terrible potential.)

'Two million. That's all I had in my account. But if we live cheaply we can last a while I think, until one of us gets a job or something.' She stopped. 'Don't you have to go to Vicenza today though?'

'Look Mimi' – it was the first time he had used the diminutive form of her name, 'it's only going to take them about one hour to call all your friends and work out you must be with me, right? Then about another hour to contact my school and get my address and they'll be over here determined to take you away.'

She was silent.

'So if you want to stay with me, we'll have to go on a trip, otherwise they'll force you home. They could even arrive any minute.'

'Yes,' she said dubiously. 'The only thing is, though, I should stay in Verona in case Grandma gets any worse. They had to take her to the hospital yesterday.'

He swallowed the coffee she had made for him and looked at her, making sure that that new little smile didn't play about the edge of his lips.

'It's one or the other,' he said tenderly. 'Home or the trip. But we can't stay here. Grandma or no Grandma.'

If she says home, he thought, then fine, well and good. But if she goes for the trip . . . Morris suddenly felt his whole body swimming and tingling with blood, his trousers tight round the crotch.

'You can always,' he said, 'phone as soon as we're away and then come back if she gets really bad.'

'Yes,' and she smiled brightly. 'Yes.' She leaned down from where she was standing by the table with the sculpture and photograph of his mother, and ruffled his blond hair with her fingers. 'Let's go on a trip then, Morri. Let's! That would be marvellous,' and she bent down to kiss his mouth.

'Right.' Morris was already standing up. Right right right right!

'But just let me phone home first. So they'll know I'm all right. It's a bit mean really, making them worry any more.'

No, if they knew she was with him from the start then there would be no point in it at all. Morris wasn't sure yet whether he had quite made up his mind, but he was determined to keep such a very exciting idea within the realms of possibility. He put his arms on her shoulders and moved them inwards – gestures you saw on television – to find he was caressing a neck softer than any simile could tell. But he didn't let that confuse him. (It was, after all, the waste that was a wonder to him with human beauty. So much loveliness for nothing.)

'Let me phone,' he said. 'I can ask about Grandma. If they talk to you they'll be totally intimidating. You know what your mother's like. She'll have you back and studying all summer in no time.' He suddenly felt very affectionate.

She hesitated. 'Okay.'

They went into the hallway and stood over the telephone.

'*Trenta-sei, sessanta-sei, novanta-due.*'

'*Giusto.*' Morris licked his lips. This wasn't the decision itself. He could simply enjoy it for what it was, a clever practical joke. The point of no return was miles away. In Vicenza? '*Trenta-sei, sessanta-sei, novanta-due.*' He dialled the numbers very swiftly until, on the nine, he lifted his finger away almost an inch before the dialling stop. Massimina was watching his face with a worried smile and noticed nothing. There was a curious mixture of flirtiness and fear about her, timidity and courage. Very female. Not unlike Mother when she dressed up for darts club lunches but was worried Dad would get drunk. That way they had of enjoying and suffering together. Scrubbers and martyrs both. Morris was suddenly feeling quite sure he could handle this.

Then he was surprised to hear that a phone had begun to ring somewhere. He had expected simply the no-connect signal. Damn. Beads of sweat broke out on his forehead.

'*Pronto?*' A stranger's voice, thank God.

'*Pronto, Signora Trevisan?*'

'Sorry, who? There's no Trevisan here.'

Morris waited for the other to hang up, but she didn't. Massimina looked at him, raising a thick eyebrow. He'd have to make her pluck that if they were going to be in each other's company for much longer. He covered the mouthpiece.

'It was Paola. She's just gone to get your mother – *pronto, Signora Trevisan?*'

'I'm afraid there's no Trevisan living here, you've got a wrong number.'

Why in God's name didn't she hang up then? Damn.

'*Sono Morris Duckworth.*'

'This number is three-six, six-six, seven-two. What number were you after?'

'It's about Massimina, Signora Trevisan.' Ninety-nine cases out of a hundred people were rude and hung up when there was a wrong number – and this woman had to try and be helpful!

'Hello, can you hear me? Hello.'

'I just wanted to tell you that Massimina is here, Signora.'

And finally the line went dead. Morris relaxed. He smiled at Massimina who was biting the cuff of her tracksuit.

'No, Signora, I had no part whatsoever in encouraging your daughter, and I certainly haven't made any attempt to take advantage of her. Rather the opposite. I've been telling her she should go home. But she insists she wants to stay here. Not only because she's in love with me, Signora, but because she finds the way you run her life totally unacceptable and dictatorial.' This was perfect. Morris almost wished for a moment that Signora Trevisan really was at the other end. But it was too late now. He left a long pause for an angry reply.

'No, I don't intend to discuss anything of the kind with you, Signora. Nor does your daughter. I merely phoned to inform you that you needn't worry, and also because Massimina would like to know how her grandmother is.'

He paused again, but this time Massimina grabbed his arm to take the phone off him. The receiver came away from his ear for a moment so that he was sure she must have heard the whine of the empty line. 'No!' he pressed the thing back to his ear and shook his head firmly, frowning.

'Thank you, Signora, I'm very glad to hear it. And now I'll . . . no, Signora, I told you I haven't, we haven't . . .'

He hung up.

'No point in trying to speak to her. She was shouting the most awful things.' He smiled sadly. 'Better move quick now, or she'll be over here.'

'And Grandma?'

'She's fine. They're bringing her back home this afternoon and they reckon she'll be on her feet in a week or so.'

In the train Morris watched Massimina while she watched out of the window. Once you got to know it, her face certainly had its character; oval and freckled with wide, liquid deep brown eyes and an expression that generally settled into a little practical frown, showing the light down of hairs on her puckered upper lip. But it was a practicality born of sweeping the stairs and dusting the furniture, not a discerning quality, certainly not a mark of intelligence. It was not that she could represent in any sense for Morris either a mind he wished to court or a beauty he would be for ever pleased to contemplate; yet if she bothered him as little as she had so far, stayed quiet and sensible and more or less content, then it would be enough.

Watching out of the window at the countryside flung by in bits and pieces, Morris was now feeling perfectly calm. He wouldn't make the fateful decision for a couple of days anyway, until he'd seen how things were panning out. So for the moment he could just relax and enjoy. In comparison, the Vicenza thing was beginning to seem rather a minor, silly, far-fetched affair (say it was all a joke if there was any trouble – nobody surely could take it seriously – get off with a warning). Who knows though, he might have another five million lire before the afternoon was out. Or had he asked for six? One should keep copies of that kind of thing.

'Morrees!'

'*Si, cara.*'

'What a strange look you had on your face.'

'Really? I was just thinking.'

'What about? Tell me.'

There were two others in the compartment, a nun and an ageing peasant and the nun smiled indulgently. Massimina reached across the space between the seats and took his hand.

'What shall we do for lunch?'

'Perhaps we should celebrate, in a restaurant. That's what I was thinking in fact.'

The frown puckered. 'I think we should be careful with the money, Morri. If we want it to last.'

'But at least the first day we should celebrate.' He had been looking forward to a wholesome, slap-up meal. He hadn't eaten well in ages.

Massimina insisted. They should buy bread and cheese and make a picnic. They could sit on the steps at Mercato Vecchio and feed the pigeons. That would be wonderful. The nun smiled again. Morris felt suddenly hot and angry. He wasn't going to be dragged around Italy playing lovey-dovey hippy-dippy on the steps of public monuments, feeding scruffy winged rodents. There was nothing he hated more than people who cluttered up beautiful places with their backpacks and sandwich papers. If you didn't have money, you shouldn't travel. He stared at Massimina, boiling now (Morris Duckworth playing soppy boyfriend for a nun's regretful smiles!), but held back. The worst thing would be to draw attention to themselves.

'Whatever you say, *cara*,' he said, and the old peasant glanced up and grunted.

The day stretched before them, a great hazy blank with everything to be invented and not a shred of routine to hang on to. This did not seem to worry Massimina, busying herself with bread, cheese and cooked, the cheapest, ham. She was in love, she had escaped from home, everything was new and she had the energy to carry herself into a thousand empty days. She had wound her hair into tresses and knotted them over her head to keep herself cool and now she sat straight-backed on the steps of the monument with a fine ivory neck exposed to the blazing sun.

Morris, on the other hand, already felt bored and some-what annoyed. It would be two or three hours yet before the Church of the Holy Crown opened after the siesta and meanwhile there was nothing at all to do. He brushed the crumbs off his lap. They had left his suitcase in left luggage at the station because Massimina had refused to get a taxi into town. She wanted to search out the cheapest pensione on foot and then walk back to the station, pick up the bag and carry it there. Morris wilted at the thought. The sun was boiling, the air unpleasantly still. Better a million blown in a week of air-conditioned comfort than this eking out into a future that held no special attraction for him.

'We'll have to get you some clothes too,' he said, but she said no, as long as there was a sink to wash what she had now, she'd be fine. Wash it at night and it'd be dry in the morning in this weather (amazing how the pampered were just dying to live lives of privation). She leaned over and hugged his leg, resting her head on his knee.

'It's really marvellous to have got away like this.'

'Let's move into the shade,' he said. 'I'm baking.'

'We could walk up to Monte Berico on the hill and get the view.'

But this time Morris insisted he needed a beer and Massimina gave way with a giggle, saying how English he was.

In the bar Massimina talked about Catholicism, so as to let him know, Morris soon realized, where she stood on sex. She was devout. She helped with collections of old clothes for needy children. Perhaps after a month or so, when they felt truly sure of themselves and she had reached her eighteenth birthday, they would find a priest to marry them and they could go to bed together and Morris could find himself a job in another town, teaching; then they could make a family and after a while her mother would give way, as soon as the first baby arrived that is, because she adored babies, and then everything would be all right. Morris could imagine his mother saying exactly the same thing to his father; with this difference: that Dad, no doubt, would have been pushing his hands in her clothes as she said it.

Still, it did give him a breathing space. He was thankful.

'My mother was a Catholic,' he said, and after a couple of beers added, 'Maybe we should go to a church and pray – I

61

mean, I'm not a Christian myself, but I don't mind you praying about things – about us, if you like.' She would immediately start a crusade to convert him. That was the kind of romance that would really turn her on.

The church was gloomy with just a faint echoing shuffle of sparse tourists. Dotted here and there, twenty or so people were praying in air spiralling with dust and incense. Massimina crossed herself and genuflected. The gestures were attractive. Morris led her towards the left side of the nave.

'There's a picture we ought to see,' he whispered.

And she said, 'I didn't know you were interested in art.'

'Very,' he said.

*And then there was somebody sitting in precisely the seat that counted!* He couldn't believe it. An old woman in black, muttering and crossing herself. Shit! He turned to the Bellini, Massimina squeezing his hand rather irritatingly with devoted enthusiasm. Her fingers were sweaty. The painting wasn't anything in particular. Christ emerging from the Jordan, arms raised to heaven from where a bright light was shining and John the B with all the rest of the crowd standing in the background and staring like a bunch of idiots. The woman stayed put in her chair.

'Let's pray then.' Massimina stood on tiptoe to whisper in his ear.

He took her to the chairs behind the old woman's, scanning the tourists to see if there was anybody suspicious hanging around. No one. Massimina sat and bent forward. Himself likewise. But the other chair was too far in front to reach under. Why on earth hadn't a detail like this occurred to him? Massimina's eyes were tightly closed while her lips formed silent words. Five minutes, ten. Shit and shit, this was thoroughly stupid! For nearly fifteen minutes she prayed, as if God would ever want to listen to all that stuff about her studies and her croaking Grandma and leaving home and whether she should surrender her virtue to Morris, etc. etc. Until finally she turned to him with a calm smile.

'Let's go then.'

'I'd rather like to stay for a moment or two,' Morris said sombrely. 'I love the atmosphere here. So moving.'

'I'm afraid I have to go to the bathroom.' She was embarrassed.

'You go. I'll follow in a few minutes.'

*That* surprised her. A moved Morris. (Or perhaps it didn't surprise her at all. Because the whole mystery was, what did she think of him?)

'Right.' She stood and tiptoed away, genuflecting and all the rest again when she reached the aisle. Perhaps she imagined her prayers had been answered, Morris thought, with him staying. He turned round quickly and saw she was already out of the church. The woman in the critical chair was still there, but there was nothing for it now. He simply counted to ten, then shamelessly tumbled forward on his knees, ran a hand quickly along the underside of her chair – and tugged the envelope away! *It was there!* The woman twisted round.

'*Scusi*, I slipped, so sorry.'

'*Niente, Signore, niente paura.*'

He had the envelope right there in his hands! This was incredible. Crime paid. If the money was all there he could slip out through another door and dump Massimina for good before it all got too oppressive. His fingers tore open the envelope. But it seemed a shade slim. He prepared himself. And out came just a slip of paper with only two crumpled bills for a thousand lire each.

*Caro Signor Blackmailer*, seeing as I was passing through, I thought I would leave you this little note. Luigina and Monica, you will be relieved to hear, are my daughters. My dear wife died some years ago. No money for you then. However, I would be very happy to have my diary back; there are various phone numbers and addresses there that I don't have other copies of. Could you please, therefore, mail the diary to my address as soon as possible. If I don't receive it within a week, I will inform the police of this whole affair and give them your letter plus a description of yourself.

*Cordialmente,* AMINTORE CARTUCCIO

PS In case you're short, I enclose 2000 lire for postage. You can keep the document case.

# 8

Mórris washed carefully, wiping behind his ears with a flannel, and considered himself at length in the cracked mirror. A cracked Morris. Handsome, but flawed. He puckered his lips grimly. The little bathroom of the pensione was all lagged hot waterpipes, trapping the dust in corners, and a whitewash the colour of chimneysmoke. The bidet was stained and gritty. A million other people had seen their cracked faces in this mirror. Not to mention other mirrors. Millions and millions, puckering their cracked lips. And the figures told against you. The sheer immensity of the figures. The number of noughts behind every significant statistic. That was nausea, Jean-Paul. Where was the prestige of being a Morris among millions? Unemployed, unobserved. Nowhere. Morris observed himself unobserved. He smiled his smile at himself and pulled his tongue. But the same considerations counted against the others too, didn't they? Oh yes, the figures counted against every last one of everybody. Against Massimina also. Perhaps especially against Massimina. Ten million like her. Ten billion. The numbers damned you, and they freed you.

'I'll have to go back to Verona for a day. There are a few things I forgot to do if we're going away for a while.'

They were in a single, dingy room with a double bed, but Morris had promised to sleep on the eiderdown on the floor.

'That's okay. I can wash my things while you're away. Explore the town a bit.'

Morris poured for himself liberally from a bottle of wine, which provoked the inevitable small frown on her girlish face.

'You mustn't, Morri!'

'It helps me not to think.' (Something Dad could never claim.)

'About what?'

'About all the things I should and could have done and will never do now.'

'Oh Morri! Don't say that!' She came round and sat next to him on the bed and had her arms around him. The tracksuit under her armpit was damp.

'I could have had a terrific job or done something really important and instead, look at me! Nothing more than a crappy English teacher.'

It felt odd saying it to Massimina. As if while saying the thing that was always and most urgently in his head, he nevertheless wasn't being sincere.

'But being a teacher is a respectable job. I could never do it.'

Well, that was true.

Morris shrugged his shoulders, downed the glass of wine and immediately poured another. She laid a gentle hand on his wrist to stop him and he rather enjoyed the little drama of resisting it. It was like a moment in one of those films Paul Newman had done from Tennessee Williams's playscripts.

'I could have done better for myself,' he pronounced with sudden and extraordinary self-pity.

'Then why don't you, Morri?' she pleaded. 'Why don't you?'

It was too late now, he said. And meant it.

No it wasn't. 'Look, Morri, honestly, as soon as Mamma sees it's all decided between us, I'm sure she can arrange a terrific job for you with Bobo's family.'

'Your family will never accept me after this.'

'Oh yes they will,' she insisted. 'Morri, I promise they will. Really. I'll do everything. Look, when you go back to Verona tomorrow, why don't you go and see them and tell them it was me who ran away and everything because of the thing with the school and that you're trying to persuade me to come back.'

Morris was rather moved and pressed her freckled face

into his shoulder a moment, pretending to cheer up. He drained the wine which was a rather insipid Soave. If only one could make the girl spend, for Christ's sake, the situation would be ideal.

'I know,' she said. 'I can write a letter to take from me to them saying exactly what the situation is. I mean that we're not even going to bed or anything and that we just want to take a holiday in each other's company and she should trust us. You can take it and give it to her.'

'That's an idea.' He wiped his mouth. 'Look, in fact, while you write the letter, why don't I rinse out the tracksuit. It could do with a wash.

'There's no need.'

'But I should do something for you, *cara*. You're doing everything. Shopping, preparing the food, finding the pensione. Let me do something for you. I'm not one of those Italian men who has to be served hand and foot.'

'*Morri. Quanto sei caro!*' She turned away to pull down the tracksuit bottoms and unzip the top, showing baggy blue cotton panties and a tight to bursting white bra. Morris glanced with no more than discreet interest. Her face flushed. She sat down on the room's only chair at a tiny wooden table, found pen and paper in Morris's (Cartuccio's) document case and puckered her lips into the usual frown.

In the bathroom Morris plunged her red suit into a tub of cold water and having rubbed a little soap into it for effect, left it there to soak for the night. With nothing to wear in the morning she'd be stuck in the pensione most of the day waiting for the thing to dry, and he hoped to be back by four, or five at the latest.

'Morri?' her face loomed over the edge of the bed as he was drifting off to sleep. 'Morri, are you awake?'

He was now. Flat on his back the oval face hung pale and worried above him.

'Morri.' She was whispering for some reason, like a child who doesn't want her parents to hear she's awake. 'You don't regret coming away with me, do you? I mean, that's not what you were thinking about when you wanted to stay in the church for a bit. You seemed so distant when you came out. As if you didn't care about me at all.'

'Of course I don't regret it. Maybe it's about the smartest thing I've ever done.'

'You know, Morri, you have a lovely voice, the way you speak, your accent. I think that's what first made me fall in love with you. In your lessons.'

Morris said nothing.

'After you come back tomorrow, we'll really go on a trip, somewhere exciting?'

'We'll have to see. I have some friends who are going down to Turkey for the summer. That would be nice maybe.'

'Yes, let's do that, Morri. Let's.' She bent down suddenly and kissed him on the lips. He didn't move.

'*Buona notte.*'

'*Sogni d'oro.* Golden dreams.'

There was Gregorio too in Sardinia, he thought. That would be another place to hide up if things got hot.

'You do realize, Dad, you do realize that I'm kidnapping her. Which is more than you ever did with a woman for all your bragging. The perfect synthesis of class warfare and womanizing. Aren't you surprised you didn't think of it?'

Morris was up at first light and dressed in the bathroom. He put on a clean white shirt and trousers that he had folded at the bottom of his suitcase and a thin leather tie left slightly loose. He put on cufflinks too and got his hair carefully into shape with a wet comb. This was six a.m. Then he left a little note: 'Back at four, MORRIS,' and eased the door open, listening to her deep even breathing all the way.

In the railway station he bought four likely looking detective novels and a return ticket to Verona. It was going to be a hectic day. And the joy of it was he still hadn't done anything anybody could reasonably expect to put him away for. Minimum risk till the very last moment, that was the watchword.

First he read her letter that she had sealed up and made him promise not to read, 'or you'll never get your head through a door again.' Her handwriting, he noticed, was as full and plump as her breasts, touchingly innocent, and each of the strokes below the line had curious, flirtatious little tails.

*Cara Mamma*, I know it's an awful thing I've done but I had to. I'm old enough now to decide what kind of life I want to live and I love Morris very much. Very very much. I don't care what you say about him, I feel he is a good man even if he is a bit lazy maybe. He's been very restrained and kind and gentle with me and hasn't tried to force me to do anything with him at all. Maybe he does lie sometimes like you said. But I think he does it because he feels inferior or because he is afraid other people will think he is. So it's something I feel sorry for and will try to help him with, not something to be nervous about, as if he was trying to get money from us or something (he hasn't asked me for a single lira). Anyway, we're setting off on a trip for a little while now to decide if we're really fit for each other. Lots of love to everybody, and I'm so glad Grandma is getting better.

*Un caro abbraccio a tutte*, MASSIMINA

So he was lazy, was he? And he lied because he felt inferior – him, Morris, inferior! And this was what they called love. A month to see if they were fit for each other! That is, if he was fit for her. As if he was somebody to be weighed up like a sack of potatoes and given five or six out of ten on the matrimonial ratings. Which settled it. He was going through with it. They needed a damn good shaking up, the whole lot of them.

As soon as he was off at Verona Nord, swinging his detective novels in a plastic bag, Morris bought the *Arena*, the local Verona newspaper, then caught the Number 8 out to Montorio, arriving at his flat shortly after nine o'clock.

During his bus trip he had already found what he was after in the paper.

LA BELLA MASSIMINA STILL MISSING, an inside headline announced, ELOPED OR KIDNAPPED?

There were a few details of Massimina's sudden disappearance on Friday night with nothing but a bright red tracksuit. Until the police had managed to contact Signor Morris Duckworth, however, *il fidanzato* rejected by the family, there were still hopes that it was merely a question of passionate elopement, although as each hour passed the possibility of something more terrible became ever more likely. (Indeed it did.)

Inspector Marangoni, in charge of the case, said they couldn't rule out kidnapping, murder, or even suicide. In an interview with the press, the director of the Nelson School of English, Horace Rolandson, had described Morris as a subdued and conscientious teacher, certainly not the rash or overtly passionate type, and he was sure Morris would be back the next week to pick up his pay cheque for the courses he'd just finished (though he probably hoped the contrary). The fact that Morris hadn't as yet been paid for his last two weeks' work was considered a strong element against elopement (what a cynical world!).

The mystery, the *Arena* concluded, remains unsolved, while the anxiety of the family grows; Signora Trevisan remains firmly convinced that in the unlikely event that Massimina has run away, she would certainly make at least some attempt to contact the family and spare them this agonizing uncertainty.

'Massimina is a generous, traditional girl,' Signora Trevisan told us, 'not a drug addict or a spoilt modern child. She certainly would not have left her home while her grandmother was dangerously ill in hospital.'

You could see there wasn't much going on in the provinces, Morris thought. The *Telegraph* wouldn't have given it two lines.

To one side of this article there was an extremely flattering portrait photograph of Massimina which would be of no help to anyone in identifying the girl. Family vanity had won hands down over practicality there. The only remaining problem being that Stan and Gregorio had actually seen him with Massimina Friday evening. But Gregorio would already be on his way to Sardinia and it was extremely unlikely that Stan ever read or even was capable of reading Italian newspapers. Still it was dicey. Maybe he should admit having been with her for an hour or so. Go and tell the police right away. Morris wrestled a while with the problem but couldn't resolve it. Play it by ear then.

Once in the flat the first thing was the diary. He wrapped it in brown paper and inserted the following letter, scribbled in the same fiercely childish script:

TOUCHÉ CARTUCCIO! MANY THANKS FOR YOURS OF THE 25TH. NOT WISHING TO INCONVENIENCE EVEN A DISGUSTING FELLOW HUMAN BEING LIKE YOURSELF (REMEMBER *PENTHOUSE*), I ENCLOSE YOUR LEATHERY DIARY. BE SURE THOUGH, MY PIGSKIN FRIEND, THAT I HAVE PHOTOCOPIED ALL RELEVANT PAGES AND THAT MY ENQUIRIES WILL NOT END HERE. IF YOU HAVE ANY CAUSE TO BE ASHAMED, YOU SHALL HEAR FROM ME AGAIN. *UN ABBRACCIO MORTALE, IL TUO AMICO, IL DIPLOMATICO.*

Morris considered this letter for some time. He didn't feel happy about some of the phrases. It was all rather heavy-handed, children's TV stuff, but he didn't have time to think of anything else. It would have to do, that was all. He must hang on till he was back in Vicenza before posting it though. Shouldn't send the man two letters from Verona.

Next the detective novels. Morris dropped onto the couch in the sitting room and spread out the four books in front of him. Then almost at once he stood up again and was off into the bedroom looking for scissors. And Sellotape too. He must have some Sellotape somewhere. And gloves, dammit! Because the Sellotape would show fingerprints. He was proud of himself a moment then for having thought of that. No fool he, oh no.

He stopped, passing through to the bathroom again, and watched himself in the mirror there – tall and blond, smiling, elegant in his white shirt and trousers. Quite charming. A garden-party type. He had enjoyed the garden parties at Cambridge. Quite the only part of the social life he had liked. For a few seconds, Morris had a wonderful sense of the attractive physical presence of himself. The flesh was firm in his trousers, the neck rose clear and clean over a clean Italian collar. What more did they want, for God's sake? And who could blame him now if they'd brought him to this? He hurried back into the living room and sat down with his novels.

They were stupid of course. Crimes of passion, crimes of politics, murders for love(!) and money, murders to settle old enmities, old debts; clever little eccentric men solving everything with their polite interrogation methods and winning ways with women. Crap and crap. The same humanistic garbage over and over, the world a nasty place where the good guys take a beating but somehow win through on the last page and who cares whether it's Maigret, Miss Marples or Bond. Garbage. You wondered whether any of them had ever read a newspaper in the end, or tried to get a job. And failed, that is. Again and again. Failed to find a place for themselves. No, failure was certainly what they didn't seem to know about. Or rather, it would feature for a while and then happily go away – tension and release. If it continued then it was deserved. And if it led to drastic decisions then it was perverse.

Not novels of the '80s, Morris, critic manqué, reflected. Nowadays the motive could be taken for granted. Humanity.

But the days when he could permit himself the luxuries of philosophy were numbered. He had a hell of a lot to do if he was going to get back to Vicenza this evening. He dampened an index finger and leafed through a silly Simenon. Sulky passions and murky Parisian bars, but nothing he was really after. No. Agatha Christie then: long dresses and love letters, people lighting pipes and scratching behind pink ears, traces of arsenic in an apple crumble. Zero. But the third book was more promising, even if more stupid, and on page thirty-five Morris found just what he was after.

Sheik Shaktiar, Your beloved son is in the hands of Bedouin Freedom Fighters who will not hesitate to dispatch him to the most doleful destiny if you do not comply with our every demand. Before the third sun sets, therefore, you will place a thousand dinars in gold, wrapped in camelskin, on the Tomb of Abdullah The Barbarous at Ouajakd Oasis. Should you try any kind of subterfuge, your son's doom will be sealed and he will be dining with his blackguard ancestors in hell before the first moon wanes.
The Avengers of Islam

Morris was rather delighted with this splendid ransom note. As a first stab, it fitted the bill perfectly. To a camel's hair, no less. Nothing more terrifying than farce, than not knowing whether it was serious or not. He slipped on a pair of rubber gloves from the kitchen and proceeded to cut it out.

Then it was just a question of finding 'daughter' to Sellotape over 'son' (there'd been a daughter on the first page of the Agatha Christie, hadn't there? The heiress. Yes.), then 'her', instead of 'him', even easier. Where the original said Bedouin Freedom Fighters, he cut out a few question marks and taped them over the top of the line, and where the ransom was described, he found a line in the Simenon where Maigret says, 'We can tackle that problem when we come to it,' and taped the sentence diagonally across the whole section. The envelope he would buy in town, touching it only with rubber gloves, and the address he could lettroset on a spare counter in the post office. Who knew what modern science mightn't be up to these days, but certainly this way they couldn't put anything on him at all. They'd have no idea he wasn't Italian; probably they'd imagine one of the regular

73

indigenous kidnapping bands. God knew there were enough of them.

One small problem though. Morris bit the inside of his lips, very excited now. (At last, this seemed to be the life he was cut out for. It really did!). He must give some indication he really had her. Some detail, not too definite, but something that certainly pointed that way, that made what might seem a practical joke gnawingly possible. He leapt up, went over to his single shelf of books and looked up 'mole' in his English-Italian dictionary; and then 'armpit'.

He was already snipping the words out when the folly of this occurred to him. If they could recognize the edition somehow, if they found out he was using an Italian-English dictionary? No. He went to the bedroom, climbed on a chair and rummaged through the ex-tenant's belongings in an upper cupboard. After a few moments he pulled down the regular Italian dictionary he remembered seeing there; then it was the work of two or three minutes to cut out the nouns he needed and mix them with a verb and a couple of prepositions from the novels.

*Lei ha un neo sotto l'ascella sinistra* – She has a mole under her left armpit. Perfect!

Morris slipped the completed letter inside his newspaper and began to tidy up the flat. The detective books would have to go out with the rubbish; all his clothes and possessions he packed into a second suitcase and three cardboard boxes which he carted upstairs to the communal attic. The only thing he left in the flat was Gregorio's worthless bronze, gesturing on top of the living room bookshelf. It was foolish to leave it there, obviously, near madness in fact. Except that Morris had a vague feeling as he began this enterprise that the gods would side with the rash and the imaginative. Not those who weren't ready to gamble. (Let Dad call him a pansy now!) Morris, Morris told himself, was tossing his bread upon the waters (whatever that meant), offering himself as a hostage to fate.

An hour later he got off the bus at the terminus in Quinzano, climbed up two steep hairpin bends above the little square and rang the bell outside the huge, cast-iron gate that barred the long driveway to casa Trevisan. He faced the little tele-camera above the bell-push squarely and honestly.

'*Sono io, Morris.* I read the papers and came directly.'

The lock sprang and the gates swung automatically apart. Morris strode up the raked, white-stone drive between flowering magnolias. It was blisteringly hot and so he could be forgiven, he thought, the drops of sweat that were rolling down his temples.

In less than two minutes Signora Trevisan was telephoning Inspector Marangoni. The inspector, it seemed, wanted Morris to go immediately to the *Questura* in the town centre, but Signora Trevisan insisted that he come out to them. She hadn't had a moment to speak to the boy herself yet. After three or four minutes' argument the inspector said he would come.

'No, I went to Milan yesterday,' Morris explained, 'to the opera, and missed the last train home. Then I had to spend the night in the station because I hadn't enough money on me for the hotel and it was only when I saw the *Arena* this morning that I discovered what had happened.' Say he'd stayed in a hotel and they'd check up immediately. He'd found a review of yesterday's *Madame Butterfly* at La Scala, so he was quite ready there.

Signora Trevisan watched him attentively from a face grey with worry.

'Go and make us coffee,' she said quickly to Paola. Her eyes were bulging and red. 'Oh God, I was so hoping she'd run away with you or something stupid like that.'

'I'm afraid not,' Morris said politely and tried a faint smile. But she turned away. Explanation over, she had no time for him of course. He was only 'something stupid', a harmless hypothesis that sadly had to be jettisoned.

'You're saying you haven't seen her at all then?' Bobo asked curtly.

This was more difficult. Morris turned and found the scrawny lad's face a mask of severity. He was getting off on playing family protector, naturally, in the absence of other menfolk.

75

'That's correct,' Morris said, taking the plunge. 'Not since I came to dinner here, in fact.' If only the damn girl hadn't left the house in that stupid tracksuit he wouldn't have to worry about this at all. Only a halfwit ran away in a red tracksuit. He felt quite angry with her.

Bobo was exchanging glances with the mother when the telephone rang and Morris was so tense now he started in nervous surprise, a twitch of all his right arm and shoulder. If Massimina . . .

It was Antonella to ask somebody to come and take her place at the hospital. She couldn't stand it any more.

'How is the old lady?' Morris asked Bobo in a low, respectful voice.

'In coma,' he said with relished grimness. 'Dying.'

'I'm sorry,' Morris said (if he'd had a hat he'd have been holding it in his hand – he could see it now). 'All these things coming together one on top of the other,' he commiserated as Signora Trevisan put down the phone. 'I don't know what to say.'

The woman looked about to burst into tears and dispatched Paola at once to take over from Antonella. All at once, seeing those damp eyes, Morris felt genuinely sympathetic. Still, if only they'd let him court the girl in a regular conservative fashion, none of this would ever have happened.

Inspector Marangoni was bulky and somewhat aggressive. Having been obliged to drive out of Quinzano under a blazing sun, he was obviously determined not to show any excessive deference to the Trevisan family, however miserable their plight might be. He sat down hard in the inevitable straight-backed chair and addressed himself exclusively to Morris. Beside him sat his assistant, small and slim; a dry, expressionless, olive face with quick eyes. Morris was pleased to notice they were both sweating quite as much as he was.

'*Parla italiano, Signore, capisce tutto?*' The others watched.

'He really speaks very well,' Signora Trevisan began.

'Please allow me to carry out the questioning alone,

Signora. To satisfy regulations I must have the answers from the young man's own lips.'

Morris smiled, deferential and indulgent together. 'I speak fairly well. If there's anything I don't understand, I will say.'

'You have some kind of document, identity card?'

Morris felt inside his leather case and produced his passport. 'Her Britannic Majesty . . . requests . . .' Most decent of her.

'*Permesso di soggiorno* in Verona?'

'I'm afraid I don't have it with me at the moment.'

'It's not important.' The inspector paused, staring directly into Morris's eyes. 'So, you had some kind of relationship with the missing girl?'

'I wanted to have. Her mother forbade us to see each other.'

Signora Trevisan opened her mouth to object, but the inspector hurried on.

'You never had any intention of running away with the girl?'

'Not at all. In any case, Massimina is still seventeen, so any kind of elopement would be considered a crime.' He smiled.

'Technically speaking, yes.' The inspector leaned over and whispered a word to his assistant, who was scribbling notes.

'Did you ever talk about the idea?'

'She did, but I was against it. I was of the opinion that her mother would come round.' He looked up blandly at Signora Trevisan in a gesture of reconciliation, but her face was hard. So much the worse for her then. 'I thought it was best to give it time.'

'And when was the last time you saw Massimina?'

'A month ago now. More. When I came to dinner here.'

'You haven't seen her since then?'

'No, nor spoken.' He felt a muscle tremble in the corner of his eye.

The inspector exchanged another word with his assistant. 'Signora, I would like to have a word with Signor

77

Duckworth on his own. Signor Duckworth, would you mind stepping out into the garden for a moment. We can talk there.'

'Not at all.' But standing up, Morris felt his bowels almost dissolve away inside him. They knew he had seen her Friday evening, then. Stan had said something. Or Gregorio. How could they forget a red tracksuit? How could he ever have imagined they would forget it? He must keep cool. He could say he was afraid they would think him involved, perhaps. Damn it, why had he posted that stupid letter before coming here? If it wasn't for that, if he could intercept it maybe somehow, there still wasn't anything they could really nail him for. Only a few lies. But when the letter arrived . . . and then if that Signor Cartuccio went and saw something in a newspaper . . .

'Signor Duckworth.' They sat, incongruously, at a small marble-topped table under a lattice of wistaria that gave a green fishbowl feel to the air, hushed and cool. 'I must warn you that Signora Trevisan has informed us that you lied to the family on a number of counts when you spoke to them about your private life and that she considered you a person not to be trusted – at all. Bobo, Signore Posenato, that is, supports this testimony.'

Morris could barely conceal a sigh of relief. He pushed a hand into blond hair for a moment, covering his expression, and tried to settle his features into a look of mildly irritated resignation.

'That's perfectly correct. I lied to them about my job and my prospects and my father's position.'

'And may I ask why?' But there was already a faint grin on the heavy man's face. Morris could see it under the glistening sweat.

'They're rich. I thought they'd be very negative if I told them how precarious my circumstances really are. So I blew things up a bit. I thought by the time the relationship really became serious, if it did, I'd be bound to have a better position.'

The inspector grunted, the assistant dropped his head to hide a smile as he scribbled.

78

'I had no idea they'd be so suspicious as to go and check up on everything. I mean, you don't . . .'

'No, quite. Signor Duckworth, I have just one or two other questions to ask you while I have you on your own, and then you're free to go.'

Plain sailing. 'Go ahead.'

'There is no possibility that Massimina is pregnant, is there?'

Morris was surprised, genuinely, and showed it with a start. 'Not at all. Absolutely out of the question.'

'Excuse me, Signor Duckworth, but my job sometimes obliges me to ask unpleasant questions.'

Marangoni found a handkerchief and rubbed it thoughtfully over a big damp waxy face. He was suffering. He was thinking of his nice air-conditioned office. And his teeth were bad, poor man. If Morris had had teeth like that, he would have gone to the dentist tout de suite and paid whatever it took.

'So you weren't having sex?'

'No, no. To tell the truth, she's more Catholic than the Pope. She wouldn't hear of it. Her idea was to get married right away. Hence our engagement.'

'Quite, good. Second, then, do you have any reason at all to suppose that Massimina may have taken her own life?'

Morris shook his head quickly. 'No, not that. She isn't that kind of girl.'

'Think about it, Signore, did she have any reason to be upset recently?'

Morris made a show of thinking. 'Well, I know she was very depressed about failing her school exams, and also about her grandmother being ill. I mean, really down. I got the impression her grandmother was her only real friend in the family and the others just felt she was a bit of a dunce and bossed her around all the time.'

At which point Morris suddenly realized that if he was supposed not to have spoken to the girl for as long as a month, he couldn't have known whether she had failed her exams or not, nor her reaction to the grandmother's illness. But he kept on bravely.

'Then I suppose she was rather upset about not being able to see me. Certainly she wrote a couple of desperate letters. All the same, I still don't think she . . .'

'Could you show us those letters, Signore? Every scrap of evidence helps.'

'Er, I've only got the one still I think,' – and written before the exams, dammit – 'I'll try and bring it to the *Questura* this afternoon.' Where the hell had he put the thing? And why had he spoken of more than one letter so casually like that? Tell the truth, for God's sake, where you could. Otherwise you made them suspicious for nothing.

'We'd be very grateful, Signore. Just one final question. In your opinion, where do you think Massimina is now?'

Morris shrugged his shoulders, pursed his lips and ran a hand through his hair in a comprehensive gesture of doubt.

'I've no idea. I know what I'm afraid of, obviously, but I really wouldn't know.'

'And what are you afraid of?'

'Well,' Morris hesitated, 'some kind of awful sex murder, don't you think?'

There was a long silence.

'You don't think she may have been kidnapped?'

'Well, yes,' Morris said after a moment's thought. 'I suppose she could.' And he added puzzled, 'Are they really *that* rich?'

'I believe so,' Marangoni said quietly.

The inspector asked Morris where he would be able to contact him if necessary over the coming days and Morris explained that this could be something of a problem. He'd finished teaching now and had arranged to go on a trip with friends who were driving to Turkey. The inspector considered this for a while and then said he saw no legitimate reason for asking Morris to stay, but he would be grateful if he could keep in touch by phone every few days or so, so that they could call him back to Verona in case of any unexpected developments. A routine arrangement, the inspector explained. Any problem with money and he should feel free to call reverse charge.

Fine, Morris agreed, he would do that. But then he said that maybe he wouldn't go away after all now, he wasn't sure, with this awful affair going on. Even if he hadn't seen the girl for a month and had given up hope more or less, he still felt very attached. He was in a dilemma really whether to go or not. Either way, he would be over at the *Questura* this afternoon to let them have Massimina's letter to himself and he would let them know his movements then. At which Marangoni and his assistant seemed quite satisfied and went back into the house to have a word with Signora Trevisan.

Strange, Morris was thinking, that nobody seemed to know about Massimina's having taken that money out of the bank. You'd have thought that was the first thing they'd have checked up on. Unless she'd been lying to him of course.

Morris refused the Trevisans' invitation to lunch, then accepted when half-heartedly pressed (one was obviously never going to eat well with Massimina). They sat down to a table of two roast chickens, courtesy of Bobo & Co. no doubt, and ate in almost complete silence, what conversation there was being restricted to the most formal possible (which at least allowed one to savour the food).

Only when Morris was leaving did Signora Trevisan say she would like to excuse herself if she had offended him in any way, and Morris said, no, it was really he who owed an apology and he said if there was anything he could do for them over the coming days he would be happy to do it. He thought for a moment now they might at least have the decency to ask him to stop over regularly and share their news and suffering, seeing as he was supposed to be in love with the girl. But they said stiffly, no, there was nothing he could do to help, and so Morris hurried off on his remaining errands.

All afternoon he was in a state of what might best be described as battle-action calm; a frenzied, maniac calm, aware of the tiniest detail, the world of forms, bodies and movement impressing itself every moment on his mind with photographic sensitivity and precision, his head racing with thoughts. Yet at the same time everything he did was done calmly and carefully, walking a tightrope as it were, with life and death in mind. In short, Morris was enjoying himself.

Getting off the bus at Ponte della Vittoria, he walked the back streets through to Dietro Duomo, waiting twice behind corners to check they hadn't for some reason sent someone to follow him. The air was dense with heat and unpleasant smells drifting up from gratings and garbage. The cobbles were hot and the winding alleys behind Via Emilei had a fetid tang to them. But in a few days he would be by the sea with any luck. He could get himself a tan, loll on the beach and sort out everything carefully and in peace. Because it was a long road ahead of him now. At two fifteen Morris climbed the broken stairs of Via Accoliti Number 7.

'Getting the ferry from Brindisi around the thirtieth,' Stan told him, sipping wine through iceblocks. He was cross-legged in his underwear. 'Be great if you could join us. We'll be in Rome the week before that at the Emmaus commune. I'll give you the address if you want to pick us up there.'

Morris had some teaching that was going on for a little while, privately, he said. But he might just be able to make it if he pushed things. It would be fun.

'Oh Morris,' Marion Roberts said. She was painting something on the wall. 'I read something in the paper about you. Weren't you involved with that girl that's disappeared? What's it all about?'

She was smiling broadly through her traffic-light make-up, delighted naturally to have found out something about his private life. Why was it that everybody wanted to know about your private life? As if Morris, for example, could care less whether Stan went to bed with Marion or with the Pinnington girl, or the pathetic Simonetta – or even all three. Or none. He absolutely couldn't give a damn. He had no interest in Stan's exploits. Whereas other people thought they'd nailed you against the wall somehow the moment they'd discovered you had a girlfriend. And Morris remembered the amusement of some schoolfriends who had once found his mother's photograph in his wallet and danced round and round refusing to give it back.

'No, the papers really rather blew it up. I went out with her for a bit a while back, but I haven't seen her for ages. Somehow they seem to have got it into their heads we might have run away together.'

Stan sat up. 'Not the girl you were at the bus stop with the other night?'

'No, that's another,' Morris said, trying to listen to the tone of his voice (was it convincing?). As long as nobody mentioned the tracksuit.

'Quite a lover-boy!' Marion tittered, dashing an abstract red line into the mess she was making of the wall. Damn her. Morris was angry and felt himself, absurdly, flushing. She was the kind he just couldn't stomach. What in Christ's name did she have to paint the wall for?

'Massimina had already disappeared Friday night,' he added and watched Stan.

'Massimina hey? High society stuff. Massi-mini-mina! Rich?'

'Fairly.'

'Wow, that's weird, man. I bet she's been kidnapped or something.'

'I shouldn't be surprised,' Morris said stiffly.

'Funny the way you use "shouldn't" there,' Marion unknowingly came to his rescue, 'I always teach my students, "wouldn't". I mean . . .'

'Bringing this other chick on the trip then?' Stan asked, with a wink and a scratch in his beard. 'The more the merrier, like I said.'

Morris hesitated. He still had no clear idea what he would do with himself. Never mind with Massimina. Obviously he'd have to keep her occupied somehow.

'It depends if she can get away,' he said. 'Parent trouble.'

Stan grinned sympathetically. 'All the same, these wops. Family, family and more family. You can never get away

83

from it. Probably dying to be kidnapped the most of them if you ask me.'

'Right,' Morris said.

A half hour later he had woken up the director of the English school from a heavy siesta and persuaded the man to sign him his cheque for the last month and pay fifty thousand of what was owed in cash. Morris explained that he had already seen the police and Horace Rolandson, red in the face and obviously still recovering from a heavy bout of Sunday lunchtime drinking, said he was relieved, could do without a scandal. Rolandson was one of a dwindling rearguard of old-school emigrants who still lived in a colonial compound mentality; he had never learnt to speak Italian without a marked Yorkshire accent and lived or died by the reputation of his dingy school and the 50s' theory of language teaching he had brought over with him so many years ago. He shook Morris's hand rather meatily.

'See you again next term, lad eh,' and smiled him out of the flat, breathing gin into the dusty air.

At a quarter past three Morris was at the bus stop again, suffering from a mixture of heat-exhaustion and euphoria. He was back at his flat at nearly quarter to four, dug out Massimina's letter to himself from the case in the attic, then back to the bus again. He left the letter at the central *Questura* in Verona with a note for Inspector Marangoni promising to be in touch in the next few days or so. Then off finally to catch the five-thirty train. Two hours later than he intended, but there you were. She would wait.

# 9

Ingenuity was the thing. That was what it was all about and that was what would make it forgivable in the end. The sheer brilliance. It wouldn't hurt them to part with a little of this world's goods. Even the inspector had said that, more or less. It might damn well do them some good in fact. And if it gave the signora some twinges of remorse over how she had brought up and handled her children (not to mention how she had handled Morris), then all well and good.

He would give a tenth of the money to charity anyway. That should look good if it ever came to selling his story to the *Mirror*. Kidnapper tithes booty. No, the fact was he was a generous person, if only he had something to be generous with.

Morris started his ransom note in the hairdresser's. The thing was to get it dead right. In every department. The right sum of money, large enough to be useful, and believable, small enough to be payable fairly quickly, not to make the family throw up their arms in despair and go directly to the police. Because he would have to get it to them without the police knowing, naturally. And the police would quite definitely be screening the Trevisans' mail. It was a problem. Then the right method of delivering the money too. Some way that would make any intervention impossible. The right tone; frightening and reassuring together, authoritative. A work of art was what was required (what's always required, Dad, if you're to get your head above the crowd).

Morris looked up at Massimina and the girl smiled down at him from the hairdresser's chair where a middle-aged woman snipped deftly about her head. At Morris's insistence, Massimina was having her hair cut and permed and

85

hennaed. She'd look much more attractive that way, he said, more chic and less childish, and cooler too for summer. Also it was like a change of personality, cutting your hair, she'd feel a new, independent person, free from her mother – who had doubtless resisted any hair-cutting idea, Morris imagined. And rightly so. The girl's hair was her pride and glory. He could barely believe he'd managed to persuade her to cut it. And if there was anything he felt guilty about it was that. An aesthetic crime.

She watched him scribbling away with his silver Biro.

'Writing to Papà again?' she smiled, dimpling freckled cheeks. Morris made a show of writing his father a postcard from each town they went through and Massimina obviously felt that this was one of his safer character traits and hence to be encouraged. She also wrote a postcard to her family, but it was Morris who always went off to post both of them together.

'I was thinking actually of inviting him over at the end of summer, when it's cooler, in September time, and he'll be able to stand the heat.'

'Meraviglioso, Morrees. I'd love to meet him.'

'We should be back in my Verona flat by then and we can have him sleep in the sitting room.'

'Ottimo!' And she blushed under the flashing scissors. If Father slept in the sitting room, they would be in the same bed together in the bedroom, was what she was no doubt thinking. Married. Procreating even. Her eighteenth birthday was on August 10th. Presumably she expected to be a mother before her nineteenth. She opened her mouth to say something else, but the hairdresser bent her head gently downward and she had to look away.

DEAR SUFFERERS, Morris hazarded. He wrote the rough copy in English in case the girl saw. It was supposed to be to his father after all. She'd never try to understand the thing with her aptitude for languages. DEAR SUFFERERS, WHAT PRICE YOUR LITTLE LOST ONE THEN? FRANKLY I THINK A CLEAR *MILIARDO* WOULD HARDLY BE TOO MUCH, SUCH A DELIGHTFUL, DELICIOUS YOUNG CREATURE SHE IS – I'M

86

WATCHING HER PRETTY FACE RIGHT AT THIS MOMENT. SUCH PRECIOUS LONG HAIR! (He would slip a lock of the stuff into the envelope – that was an idea – and he bent down quickly to scoop some up off the floor. Coming up again he caught her eye a moment in the mirror and was obliged to lift the dark hair to his lips and kiss it. She smiled. Love was sweet, wasn't it?)

A CLEAR BILLION, AND CHEAP AT THE PRICE. MY COMPANIONS HERE, HOWEVER, HAVE PERSUADED ME TO OFFER YOU MONEY-MINDED PEOPLE A SMALL DISCOUNT. (This'd teach the bastards to go messing around checking up on Morris after he'd been so damned polite and formal, even offering poor tottering Grandma his arm, for God's sake!) YES, WE ARE WILLING TO SETTLE FOR EXACTLY EIGHT HUNDRED MILLION LIRE – 800,000,000 – ON THE CONDITION THAT YOU DELIVER QUICKLY AND HONESTLY. NO TRICKS. ANY ATTEMPT TO BRING IN THE POLICE OR SPRING A TRAP WILL ONLY MAKE US EXTREMELY NERVOUS WITH QUITE PROBABLY TERMINAL CONSEQUENCES FOR SOMEBODY WE BOTH KNOW WELL. (DRAGGING THE RIVERS? GROVELLING IN GARBAGE PILES? PLASTIC BAGS WITH LEGS AND ARMS UNDER MOTORWAY BRIDGES? WHAT DO YOU THINK?) EIGHT HUNDRED MILLION SHOULDN'T BE IMPOSSIBLE BETWEEN FAMILY AND FRIENDS. ALL THOSE WELL-CONNECTED FRIENDS. (It was only four hundred thousand quid in the end. Perhaps it wasn't enough). IN DENOMINATIONS OF NO MORE THAN 50,000 LIRE NOTES, ALL WELL USED OF COURSE.

Morris sat back a moment watching Massimina's face in the mirror and tried to divide eight hundred million by fifty thousand. God, what a stupid currency! Knock off the noughts. The same as eight hundred thousand by fifty. Or eighty thousand by five. Sixteen thousand. Morris tried to imagine sixteen thousand banknotes. Certainly a big pack and no mistake. Where the hell to put it? Just one blow like this though. Just one, oh God, and with careful investment you were settled for life, a life of art and leisure. Maybe he would even write a book if he pulled this one off. The confidence it would give you! You could walk on water after this. That'd show Dad who had his head screwed on right, when Morris Duckworth came back and bought old man D. a modern maisonette in Ealing. And a book published to boot. *A Citadel to Storm*, he would call it. Then, seeing as he wouldn't need money, he could get involved in good works: children's homes and things where people would respect you and . . .

'Morri!' She was transferring with a towel over her head to under the drier. 'Why on earth are you writing in such big print?' Her face with all the hair hidden away under the towel had an impish, round, pixie look, the eyes brighter and darker, nose sharper, cheeks chubbier.

Morris felt a sudden flush of blood to his face. 'My father –er – has bad eyesight. He can't read regular handwriting for more than a couple of lines or so,' he added quickly, remembering the minute script of his postcards.

'Are you telling him about me?'

'*Naturalmente.*'

'Tell me what you say. Go on. Translate.'

But the sound of the hairdrier now drowned out their conversation and Morris was able to get back to work.

. . . OF NO MORE THAN 50,000 LIRE NOTES, ALL WELL USED OF COURSE. THE MONEY, WRAPPED IN BROWN PAPER, MUST BE PLACED . . . No, that was awful. Brown paper was awful. Trite. Genius was going to have to shine here. Something that couldn't possibly be checked up on was the point. Something moving perhaps?

Morris gazed across the shady space of the hairdresser's to where Massimina's long hair lay shorn on the tiled floor. Beautiful filaments of black and gold massacred in the half light. Where? Where? Where? It was the ransom arrangements that always blew a kidnap. He'd seen those films where the person delivering has to go to a phone box and gets called by the kidnapper standing on a nearby flyover who tells him to go to another phone box, etc. But Morris wasn't up to that on his own. Not with Massimina around. Sucking his pencil he looked up and found the girl still smiling, head locked in the helmet of the hairdrier, blowing kisses. He half smiled back. A reassuring, you're-going-to-look-terrific smile. And then he had it!

THE MONEY MUST BE WRAPPED IN PAPER AND THEN PLACED IN A REGULAR BROWN HOLDALL UNDER A PILE OF NEATLY PACKED CLOTHES. THE HOLDALL WILL BE SIMPLY ZIPPED CLOSED AND THAT IS ALL. NO LOCKS, BOMBS OR TRICKS. MASSIMINA WILL BE THE FIRST TO OPEN IT. YOU WILL PLACE THE HOLDALL ON THE LUGGAGE RACK OF THE MOST FORWARD FIRST-CLASS COMPARTMENT OF THE MILAN-PALERMO ESPRESSO LEAVING MILAN AT – ON – (Have to check up the times there and decide on a date. Which would depend on when he mailed the letter of course.) YOU MUST NOT REMAIN EITHER IN THE COMPARTMENT, OR ON THE TRAIN. OTHERWISE OUR LITTLE PRECIOUS ONE HERE WILL NEVER BE RELEASED.

One felt rather cruel writing it; but then how else were you supposed to write a ransom letter?

AND NO SECOND CHANCES, GET IT? YOU WON'T SEE ANY MORE LETTERS FROM ME. (No. Not me. Us.) FROM US. ONLY YOUR DAUGHTER. ALIVE OR DEAD. AS YOU CHOOSE.

Morris thought for a moment he might persuade Massimina to sign the bottom of a letter to his father and then paste the signature over the final ransom note when he'd got it all ready in Italian. To show he had her alive. But it was too tricky. They'd want to know why he hadn't got her to sign the final copy itself. So he decided to sign it himself. *I VENDICATORI DELLA POVERTÀ*. That had a nice sound. Enigmatic, with a hint of terrorism. A truly red herring. And then something else came to him.

TO PROVE THAT I HAVE HER ALIVE WITH ME I HAVE ASKED MASSIMINA TO REVEAL A PIECE OF INFORMATION THAT ONLY SHE COULD KNOW. SHE TELLS ME HER SIGNORA MOTHER MUST GET UP EVERY NIGHT AT LEAST FIVE TIMES TO GO AND PISS BECAUSE OF A BLADDER CONDITION SHE HAS HAD FOR YEARS. NOBODY BUT HER DOCTOR AND FAMILY KNOW OF THIS.

That should reduce any desire to show the thing to the press.

'Forty-five thousand lire,' the hairdresser announced with

89

a smile that appeared to admire her own handiwork. And in fact Morris had been as wrong about Massimina's hair as he had previously been about Gregorio's bronze. She looked splendid with a short hennaed blow-wave, a long curl falling sexily to just above one eye. The face was rounder, yes, but it was more alive too, and her ears were little pearls. Who would ever have guessed? In short, an improvement he hadn't expected. He'd been fearing the worst, something gauche and ostentatious that he'd be embarrassed to be seen in company with. Dead right about the eyebrows though. Plucked to a thin rising arch now, they took the childishness out of her, adding a faint touch of sophistication. But what really mattered, good taste or bad, was that she was damn near unrecognizable.

'Such an awful lot of money, Morri,' she pouted. They stepped out of the hairdresser's into an oven of a sun with Rimini's long beach blazing white in front of them.

'But you look marvellous!' (-ly different) Morris cried, and in his sudden euphoria he bent down and gave the creature a resounding smack of a kiss right beside her mouth. And enjoyed it.

'Morri!' She hugged herself beside him, running slim fingers up and down his chest. 'You know that's the first time you've done that.'

'No!'

'Sometimes I wonder if you really do love me, you're so reserved.' The little pout again – but she didn't really wonder anything of the kind. She thought she had him for good and ever. (That humble-pie letter he'd written to Mamma.) And the pout was partly for a bright shop window, to see how it came off under this different thatch of hair. Vanity was getting the upper hand. But it made her nicer, somehow, rather than the opposite.

'It's because I don't want you to feel I'm trying to push you into anything you might regret.' Morris had his answer prompt. 'And then I'm English you know. You know what the English are like.' (God knows how he'd have convinced the girl if he was French or something.)

'*Come si comico, Morri,*' she was saying. '*Come sei comico! Ti amo sai,*' and arm in arm they picked their way down stone steps onto the burning sand and through the kaleidoscopic sunshades of the beach. The only thing Morris was worried about was that with so many women topless she might decide to do the same. Massimina had shown suprising signs of adventurousness of late (running away, for heaven's sake, cutting her hair) and to have her topless with the breasts she had was precisely the kind of attention he could do without.

They had bought her a new set of clothes the morning after his return to Vicenza. She had resisted strongly and they had had their first big argument. Morris would have liked to give way, so great was his distaste for any kind of open conflict, but the red tracksuit was just too obvious. In the end he offered to use his own money to buy the clothes (that would show her who was generous now. Go and tell that to your suspicious mamma) and Massimina had flushed and broken down in tears.

'It's too hot for a tracksuit for one thing. And then I love you Mimi, I want you to look beautiful.' Vanity was the key. 'Not always in that shapeless sweaty thing that covers up every inch of you. How can you look feminine in a tracksuit? And then I don't want you to be stuck indoors half a day every other day while you wash and dry the thing.' (Which was actually the only advantage. Giving him a chance to pop out and do things, safe in the knowledge that she couldn't make a phone call or post a letter or read something in the newspaper.)

Massimina was beaten, though she insisted on UPIM, the department store, rather than the more chic expensive shops round about; and seeing as he was going to pay, Morris gracefully conceded this point. But when they finally reached the cash desk with a handful of shirts and blouses, she wouldn't hear of Morris paying and forked out for the whole lot herself, a cool two hundred thousand lire. She reached up and kissed his neck while the cashier's fingers did a polished jig over the till.

That was such a nice thing he'd said, she whispered, about wanting to see her look pretty; and he was right. But why on earth should *he* spend his hard-earned money on her when everything she had she'd simply been given? He could hardly have put it better himself. But Morris felt quite honestly a shade guilty then and insisted on buying her two pairs of shoes (still at UPIM). He rather enjoyed choosing them. Red would go with the pearl grey skirt. No, not high heels, they were long out of fashion; flat with an open top. And then sandals for the beach. Aesthetics was his realm after all, and dressing a dressable woman was fun. He even held out for a large straw hat with a wide brim that conveniently shaded her face. After which he had to agree to a frugal lunch of supermarket mozzarella, bread and cheap Merlot.

That first day, quite frankly, the first twenty-four hours after the Verona trip and the burning of the boats, Morris had been afraid he might have bitten off rather more than he could chew and he caught himself looking over his shoulder every few minutes and shivering whenever a police car came past. Despite having got her out of the tracksuit well before lunchtime, he was so nervous for a while in the afternoon he'd got cold sweats and a touch of diarrhoea and had to pop into the lavatories of every café they passed without ordering anything, which he hated – especially because it left her free and dangerous outside on her own.

One time when he came out and found her talking to someone on the pavement he thought he really was done for and she had met a friend, an acquaintance, by chance, which would blow absolutely everything. But it was only some American army chap asking directions to the Basilica and Massimina was trying to answer him in the awful halting English she'd learnt from Morris. As soon as he'd sized up the situation, Morris made short work of the fellow.

'Right, left and right again, buddy, then carry on straight,' he said, having not the faintest knowledge of the city, and he swung Massimina firmly away. His stomach felt light and empty and his bowels as uncertain as an English spring.

'You're just jealous,' she told him happily. She was enjoying herself more than ever apparently, despite all the bad news he'd given her the previous night; his negative reception at the Trevisans, her mother's tough reaction, etc. She wanted an ice-cream now, *stracciatella, amaretto* and *bacio* ('*Bacio, Morri*'). She wanted him to put an arm round her shoulders, she wanted to go to the cinema, to have a manicure.

'Oh Morri, if only everything didn't cost so much!' And the happier she became, the harder and more irritating it was to have to explain that he had the runs and that that was why he kept popping into all these cafés, so as to empty himself over their filthy insanitary holes in the ground. It was her fault (he had an itch now too) for the godawful diet she was miserlily insisting on; but she laughed and said he should learn to see the funny side of things. She even twirled round in a dainty little pirouette which fanned out the pleated green skirt they'd bought and had men turning round to see the tops of her legs. Morris put his arm round her tight. Not an unpleasant feeling, her hip moving against his. But the publicity of the pirouette was to be avoided.

The nervousness and faint nausea had passed by the evening, however. It was as if Morris had finally got his sea legs or something. And when he slipped out after supper, promising to post her next letter to her mother (no doubt saying how sorry she was Mamma had taken the first so badly, throwing Morris out of the house like that), he felt marvellously confident as he tore the thing to shreds on the corner of Giardino Salvi and Corso Andrea.

The gardens did look so elegant in the twilight! So classical, so Italian, with their scent of cypresses and water splashing on statues. Marvellously, marvellously confident he felt. He must tell her to send a postcard to her grandmother in particular, or a get well card; that would be nice. The old dear was probably dead by now, which at least saved her any worry about Massimina (how humane Morris could be!), but a card would hearten Mimi. And to use up the time it most probably would have taken to find a postbox in a disorganized town like Vicenza he found a tobacconist, leafed through the get well cards and picked up a cartoon of somebody bandaged to the eyeballs which was presumably supposed to be funny.

A lot of things were playing his way. That was what he had realized. If she insisted on staying in the cheapest pensioni, for example, then it was all the easier never to produce one's passport. All you had to do was say you'd lost it, or had it stolen – and certainly no one was going to ask him for *her* passport. The woman was never questioned about anything. Latin etiquette. And whether they believed your story or not they always took you in the end because they needed the money. Plus of course, cheap pensioni never had televisions or radios, like a good hotel might, so there was no danger whatsoever of her seeing an item about herself. Newspapers in general she obviously had no taste for, and then even the big Italian dailies were fundamentally local, based on a single city with national news on the front page, local news inside. This made it extremely unlikely that a Vicenza paper, or even one of the quasi nationals like *Corriere della sera* or *La Stampa*, would carry news on a minor kidnap like this, or at least not for more than a day or two. The country was teeming with more ambitious kidnappers for God's sake, mafia and terrorists and all sorts of dramatic events which made his little adventure more like some kind of Sunday afternoon outing (actually, it did have that sort of enforced gaiety feel to it). Not to mention a forthcoming general election. (Inspector Marangoni probably didn't give a damn really. It was pieces of paper to be pushed about between one coffee and another for him.) So that barring some million-to-one meeting with an old acquaintance, Morris could consider himself safe. Just keep an eye on her, make sure she made no phone calls home, wrote no letters that he didn't know about, and all would be well. Then the real beauty of it was, he hadn't actually hurt anyone. On the contrary, he was giving her the time of her life. And without even having 'defiled' her or anything. No Caliban he.

Morris skipped back up the dark stairs of the pensione, whistling. The thing was, his mind was occupied, occ-u-pied. One hundred per cent. Boredom and drudgery were over. No more nothing-to-do and dogs waking him up to raw nerves in the dead of night. No. (He would have killed that dog now anyway, he was sure of it – the sponge in the meat juice for him if ever Morris went back there. He was through with suffering in silence.)

'Someone's happy!' Massimina said. She was trying on the pearl grey skirt, red T-shirt, red shoes.

He stopped whistling. 'And why do you think that is?' (Don't smile *that* smile, it's not pleasant.)

'Because you're with me, most probably,' she said.

There was an element of truth in that.

'You do look terrific,' he told her.

'Thank you Morri,' she said, and then with a new note in her voice, 'Thank you so much.'

'For what? Saying you look terrific?'

'No, no I mean for all this, the clothes.'

'You paid for them, *cara*, not me.'

'But I would never have done it without you. You know what I mean? I wouldn't have dared. I've never bought clothes without Mamma before.' And she did another one of her little pirouettes, lifting her hands together over her head, twirling till the panties showed. He did hope things weren't going to get difficult.

'Morrees?'

'Yes?'

'You know something? I've never slept so well as these last few days.'

'No? That's nice.'

'I feel so relaxed.'

Out of sheer envy, he found after a moment or two he hadn't replied to this. And wasn't going to.

'Really. You don't know how horrid it is having to sleep with my mother.'

'I can imagine.'

Then she had just launched into a description of all the things that made it unpleasant passing the night with Signora Trevisan, her trips to the bathroom, snoring (farting? Morris wondered), when it suddenly occurred to him to ask, 'But don't you ever have bad dreams?'

Hardly were the words out than he was conscious of a surreptitious confessional instinct – he had really been looking for a way to talk about his own oneiric afflictions. And simultaneous with that realization came the awareness that no, he must not, must never disclose the utter utter horror of last night's visions for example. The violence. Such a sudden deterioration too. He couldn't remember anything quite so bad. Though probably it was just the sleeping arrangements. He was getting rather fed up with eiderdowns on the floor to tell the truth.

She put her fingers in his hair, alerting his whole body with the electric shock her simple unselfconscious affection was.

'Only sometimes. Last night you laughed in your sleep though?'

Laughed? Was it possible?

As long as he didn't *talk*.

'Morrees,' she said again apropos of nothing and everything. Feigning relaxation, he closed his eyes.

They were stretched out on the beach at Rimini, Morris under a sunshade, Massimina a foot or two away in the full sun. Morris felt rather embarrassed by his dead white English skin. He hadn't done any serious sunbathing for years, and so had bought those bermuda bathing shorts that stretch nearly to your knees to protect himself. Massimina was wearing a single-piece green-and-white costume that Morris had insisted was the thing for her (she could hardly take her top off that way, could she?) and she had a yellow rubber bathing cap to protect the new hairdo.

The beach was shimmering with the heat and the encampments of sunshades and deckchairs thronged with beauty and the beast, laughing and chattering, a figure ocasionally detaching itself to plunge into the tepid still water of the Adriatic. A strong smell of coconut oil drifted aimlessly without a breeze; overhead a biplane towed an advertisement for Crodino and from the shadow of the sunshades the eyes of old men darted after the girls. Who would ever ever dream of looking for a kidnap victim here? Amongst the pleasure-seekers and the free?

'And then how can you ever have a good lie-in,' Massimina began again, 'with somebody who insists that sleeping after seven is a sin? I mean, I know I'm a Catholic myself, but where's the harm in staying in bed just a little on Sunday morning?'

'By the way, I'm sorry you missed Mass last Sunday,' Morris said. 'I'd never have left the tracksuit to soak if I'd only thought.'

She laughed. (Oh, she really was pretty damn content, wasn't she? Oh yes!) 'I'm sure God doesn't mind. I'm sure he's not just like some miserable old schoolteacher only interested in rules and things. He knows what I feel in my heart and that's enough.'

So she was a Protestant in the end, not a holy Roman at all. Next she'd be saying it was all right for them to go to bed together as long as they felt right in their little hearts.

After a while's silence she asked about his family and for no reason at all Morris went and told her how his mother had died; in a car accident when he was fourteen. He had learnt to recite this event with great sang-froid, no perceptible tightening of the muscles nor reddening of the eyes, and he knew it made a great impression.

'One day Mother was on her way home from the Co-op with the week's shopping in her little push-trolley, when a car driven by some idiot with a heart condition went out of control, rode up on the pavement and crushed her against the wall of Barclays Bank.' (But then weren't we all crushed against the wall of some bank or other?)

Morris lifted himself on his elbow and licked dry lips. Have to buy some Lip Balm in this heat. By the sea as well. The salt really did it to you.

'So then there was just me and my dad.'

After a few moments' pause, not knowing what to say, she said, 'Funny you losing your mother and me my father.'

And she said: 'I'd very much like to meet your dad. I do hope he comes over. He must be very brave, going on after a disaster like that.'

What was he supposed to do? Morris thought. Kill

himself? Dad? In the end he got up in the morning, went out to work at seven thirty, lunch at the canteen, came home, snatched tea and off to darts at the pub till closing time, the same as always. What could it possibly matter to him whether Mother was there or not? If anything it was an obstacle out of the way.

The only one who truly missed Mother was Morris.

'He despised me,' Morris announced unwisely.

'*Cosa, Morri?*' (Why)

'Dad. He was always saying I wasn't a real man because I didn't go out to work at sixteen.' Why not let the girl hear? 'And then because I spent so much time reading. He had this obsession about real men and work and women. He's always saying how socialist he is and then wants everybody to go and break their backs from dawn till dusk for some capitalist coronary candidate (the one who killed Mother for example), as if . . .'

But when you said it like that it didn't mean anything at all. He didn't seem to be getting anywhere near explaining it. And not with the tapes either. The thing eluded you. As if the problem was somewhere else altogether.

She didn't know what to say of course, though you could hardly blame her for that. You could hardly expect your kidnap victim to provide you with comfort and intelligent conversation after all, could you? To settle all your little personality niggles. No one else ever had for heaven's sake, so why expect it now. But Morris suddenly found he was near to tears.

When he didn't speak for some moments, she said, 'A bit like me and Mamma really, her wanting me to study all the time when it's obviously useless. Only with you it was the opposite.' And then she said, 'Morri, don't be upset,' and she slid a slim naked arm round his shoulders so that their warm skins came together in the heat and she kissed him with tongue and lips on the corner of his mouth. Morris tasted salt.

'Oh Morri,' she whispered, 'I am so glad I don't have to do any more exams!'

The problem with having to watch her all the time was that it left him with very few free moments to himself. And there was so much to do! So when she said she felt too hot and needed another swim, Morris declined to join her – he didn't like to go in the water too often, he said, delicate skin – and he sent her off on her own, promising to watch.

Then as soon as she was splashing away into the mêlée of the others at the water's edge, he took the nail scissors out of her beach bag and set to work on a copy of *Panorama*, searching out the right words, snipping them out and dropping them into a fold between two pages. Not such an easy task. He couldn't find 'wrapped', dammit. Nor 'hold-all', nor 'zipped', nor 'luggage rack'. He'd have to buy some different kinds of mags. Or glue together single letters maybe? But that would take for ever. Patience was the watchword though. Absolutely. He mustn't write a single syllable in his own hand. Not just because of the handwriting, but this verbal hodge-podge would cover up any oddities in his Italian as well. Borrow a typewriter somewhere in the reception of some hotel to write the address perhaps. Tell them it was something for work and he didn't have to handwrite it. Bobo's address, not the Trevisans', to cut out the danger of police intervention. He would have to get hold of a Verona telephone directory for that (or perhaps suggest to Massimina that they write the lad a goodwill postcard) and then he'd have to go to the station, or at least phone, for the times of the Milan-Palermo Espresso. No, go to the station was better where he could actually see the times written. No hurry though. He absolutely mustn't hurry or rush or frenzy. Time wasn't against him in any particular way. They had enough money for much more than a month at the rate they were spending. This afternoon he would pick up the Verona *Arena* from one of the central newsagents (or the station perhaps, two birds with one stone). They should have received his first communication yesterday and have it in the papers today.

KIDNAP OR PRACTICAL JOKE? FEAR MOUNTS FOR FATE OF MASSIMINA. Crap like that. But he had to know where they were up to. In fact it was rather in his favour if they were under the impression it was a regular kidnap. They'd bring in the special kidnap squads the papers were always crowing about and start checking up on all the millions of underground groups who were into this kind of thing, or people who might be enemies of the Trevisans and whose businesses were in financial difficulty and so on and so forth, never realizing they were up against a true master this time, an individual amongst individuals. They'd be searching every abandoned house around Verona (he'd done the right thing posting the letter there, in the city), because you didn't look for kidnap victims in hotels, however cheap, did you? And he hadn't really 'kidnapped' her anyway. Deny the letter – which they could never pin on him – and what did they have against him? A single lie to police and parents. Nothing. Disappear and they'd never bother following him for that.

'*Morri, ti presento Sandra. Ma che cosa stai facendo con . . . ?*'

'What?' He was suddenly shivering despite the tremendous heat. He savaged the scissors into the page he'd been so carefully cutting. 'Just trying to remember how we used to make patterns when we were kids, but I can't get the hang of it.'

'Morrees, Sandra; Sandra, Morrees.'

Morris was on his feet now, sweat dribbling down his back, between his buttocks. Who the hell was this woman? Tall, sandy-haired with horse teeth sticking out a mile and a prominent aristocratic nose. His hand extended automatically and he hoped the smile he felt creasing his face was the charming one. God, you let the girl out of your sight for two minutes and she was already making friends with half the beach. Unless it was somebody she knew from . . .

'*Piacere,*' he got out. Her hand was wet from the sea, his own sticky with sweat. He tried to be aloof and shy looking; that generally turned people off. '*Scusi se sembro un po*' . . .'

Massimina burst out laughing. 'She's English, Morri. That's why I asked her to come over and meet you. She's English!'

'How do you do,' Morris said, brusquely now. 'I'm afraid I hadn't understood.'

The woman had asked Massimina the way to the showers apparently. (Why did everybody have to ask the stupid girl things? Nobody ever asked Morris anything.) So Massimina had taken her across the beach and they'd shared the same hundred lire piece standing under the same shower with Massimina telling her everything about Morris and how English he was, staying hidden and white under the sunshade like a mole, while everybody else basked. And then she'd invited her over to meet him – because a holiday was for meeting people and having fun, wasn't it? And Morris would be happy to be able to talk English with a real English person.

'From Barnet – or Hadley actually – near London you know.'

The gold belt, Morris thought. Half the Conservative Cabinet taking their dogs for walks, or having their servants do it for them when it rained.

'I was brought up in South Ken myself.' Believe that . . .

Sandra had a blue bikini over no breasts at all and rather too much bum. Her suntan was golden brown, artificially so, Morris thought (but perhaps it was only envy), and her way of moving was coquettish. Age around twenty-four, much older than Massimina. And showing it. Pore problems around the lower part of the nose. She sat down on Morris's towel and began to say how much she adored the heat. She switched from English to an awfully broken Italian for the sake of Massimina. *'Vengo in Italia ogni anno.'* It sounded like 'ano', but Massimina didn't laugh.

Morris tried to relax. What could they say to each other that could be damaging? Tourists didn't read the local news, even if their Italian was good enough, and that didn't seem to be the case with poor Sandra. In fact it might be better to have Massimina tied up in a painstaking conversation with an Englishwoman, rather than wandering free amongst all those Italians. Consider it a stroke of luck.

'How long have you been in Italy then?' he asked.

'Myself? Not too long,' the toothy woman said. 'We drove down from Venice this morning in fact,' and she began to talk about how much she adored the sunshine and citadels of *La Serenissima*, the sparkling water . . . *'Per me è stato meraviglioso!'*

Morris saw an opportunity. 'I'm just going to go and get today's papers,' he interrupted. 'I'll leave you two to chat.' He picked up the copy of *Panorama*, holding it carefully so that the cuttings wouldn't fall out, and hoped this exit would be sufficiently abrupt to discourage the girl.

'Bring us some ice-creams, will you, Morri.' Massimina seemed proof against any offence. 'What flavour do you want, Sandra?'

'Zabaglione,' Miss Hadley called after him, half pronouncing the 'g'.

Morris laboured across the burning sand. The beach wheeled around him alive with cries, radios, balls being hurled, twitching oily bodies to step across. He watched two boys in sandy swimming trunks slithering about with a football, a girl on her stomach with tiny blond hairs on the soft skin of her arms. Tomorrow he must buy some sunglasses and just relax, soaking it all up, watching it all. Why couldn't he ever relax?

He reached the steps to the road and slipped on his sandals. The weather was too hot. Far too hot to think straight. He would just dash to the nearest big newsagent, pick up an *Arena* (if they had one) and a *Corriere della Sera*, check out the *Arena*, throw it away and take the *Corriere* back to the beach with some ice-creams. He couldn't leave Massimina for long. Then drag her away from the other woman as soon as possible and off to lunch. With any luck he might persuade her to buy some fish today, seeing they were by the sea.

Morris threaded his way across the busy seafront drive and scurried towards the centre in a gritty heat. He would have liked to take it easy and drink a long slow beer on his own, but there was no time for that. He had to try three newsagents before he came across a solitary copy of the Verona *Arena*.

Out in the street again he was just preparing to open it and turn to the local section when his eye caught a small headline at the bottom of the front page.

MISSING GIRL'S CLOTHES FOUND.

He was puzzled.

The red tracksuit of Massimina Trevisan, missing from her Quinzano home since last Friday afternoon, was found yesterday morning in a public waste bin at Vicenza railway station. Franco Galeardo, who has cleaned the bins in the station for more than ten years, said: 'I saw the thing was still in perfect condition and decided to hold on to it. I showed it to my wife, thinking we could wash it and use it for my daughter and then she told me she'd heard on local radio the police were after a girl in a red tracksuit, so I phoned them directly.'

After some hours police technicians were able to declare that hairs on the tracksuit corresponded with those found in Massimina's room.

Inside: AGONY OF FAMILY THAT WAITS.

Morris crossed the street, walked directly into a bar and ordered a double Scotch on ice. He straddled a stool. She'd thrown the thing away! In a public bin of all places. Without even telling him. (Thank God she hadn't left it in the hotel!) And if there were some of *his* hairs on that tracksuit too? A single blond hair. Had he leaned his head against her at any moment that first day? Or could they tell just from dandruff? He must have sprinkled a couple of flakes over her. We all had scraps of each other all over us. It was inevitable.

He downed his drink in one and turned to the inside pages, scanning the columns quickly.

. . . no blood, but police fear worst . . .

And the letter? There was nothing about his letter. The post had let him down there obviously. Three days and it hadn't arrived. The next one would have to go Express. Unless they were keeping it from the press for some reason.

Morris caught a glimpse of himself in the mirror between

bottles of alcohol. His face was flushed with the heat and the drink, not to mention the worry, his hair ratty and unkempt after his dip in the sea. Just his luck. Of all the bins she had to leave it in, it had to be the one emptied by a cheap scrounger on the lookout for second-hand clothes. (And for his daughter of all people! If Morris ever had children, he'd give them the best, for Christ's sake. Why bring them into the world otherwise? Why had Dad brought *him* into the world?)

He stood up and left the bar in a blinding temper.

'You're just jealous. He wasn't interested in me at all. He . . .'

'I'm not having dinner with them.'

'But for days you've been asking me to go out to a restaurant and now the first day I agree, you refuse to go. Oh come on Morri!'

'*Not with them!* If we go out, let's go alone.' His life had definitely become a farce. A real kidnap with the blindfolds, tent in the middle of the room and revolver always in your hand would at least give you the pleasure of knowing who was the boss. And it occurred to Morris that had his father ever taken part in a kidnap, that was most certainly the way he would have done it and he would quite definitely call Morris a pansy for having gone about it in this way.

She rubbed lotion into his burnt back (her fault) in the cheap room full of flies and he knew she would be smiling merrily under that silly chic perm with the big curl dropping over her plucked eyebrow. Because she honestly thought he *was* jealous. There was no limit to female vanity. Now that she'd had her hair done and bought some clothes she thought she was Venus, dragging him round the shops all afternoon like that for perfumes and make-up. ('Mamma never let me buy the make-up I wanted. I had to share it with my sisters.') And only two days before she'd been happy at the prospect of spending the whole month of June, not to mention July and probably August, sweating like a little pig in that red tracksuit.

'What on earth did you do with the tracksuit?' he demanded.

'I threw it away.'

'But why, for God's sake?' Anger helped him to feign the necessary surprise. He twisted his head round sharply on the pillow to catch her grinning. Strangle the girl immediately, he suddenly thought. Now. That would settle it. Dump the body safely and then he could just cruise through it, pick up the ransom and go back to his flat in Verona with no more of this awful fuss.

'Why though? You're always droning on about saving money and then you go and chuck out something perfectly good.'

*Strangle the girl.* It was strange, but his whole body suddenly filled with heat at this terrible thought. (And when he had been beginning to like her. When he had even had slight inklings of what love might be – that time she pressed her thigh against him with a wriggle and giggle walking along the sea front.) *Strangle her.* Nothing easier. And who would care in the end? (Hadn't life definitely been easier when Mother was dead, for all his ostentatious mourning, for all if he'd ever loved anyone it was her? The conflict had gone out of everything, the sense of guilt, of Mother-wouldn't-like-that. He'd felt freer. Perhaps all lovers in the end would be happier if their loved ones died.) Kill her. She was a nobody. Failed all her exams at school. (When had Morris ever failed an exam and look where it had got him?) Plus she deserved it. That letter she'd written to her mother ('. . . perhaps he does lie sometimes . . .'), plus going and dumping the tracksuit like this! Morris felt his mind suddenly slipping into a nausea of fury that was also the nausea of his sunburn and the unbreathably stale air in this darkened, fly-filled cheapest of cheap cheap rooms. He could easily do it, he was much stronger than her. Just . . .

'You said I didn't look nice in it. I only want to wear things that please you from now on Morri. I . . .'

What was he going to do with her at the end anyway? Imagine they gave him the money, what . . .

'So I did it for you, you see.'

She rubbed in the lotion, knelt on the bed beside his tortured back. She rubbed softly over the tops of his shoulders where it was worst. 'You have a gorgeous back,' she whispered, bending to his ear.

He shivered and was hot together, flexing his damp fingers where they lay above his head. Her voice became husky. 'I'd so much like to make love to you Morri, if only we were . . .' He didn't move. He seemed to be getting hotter and hotter.

'I'm not going to dinner with those two others. He was staring at you all the time.'

'Whatever you say, boss,' she laughed and her slim fingers slithering in oil down his back slipped inside the top of his bermuda shorts. His body tensed to a cord of steel.

'Morri . . .'

Any moment now, if she just . . . The heat in his body was intolerable. If she . . .

There was a knock at the door. Morris twisted over and sat up straight and sharp as if caught in the act. She likewise, shooting off the bed, so that her wrist caught him in the jaw. *'Avanti!' Who in God's name was it? Police? He brought his hand up to his face. One of her rings must have caught him and his mouth was bleeding. 'Avanti, prego.'* And Sandra came into the room with boyfriend Giacomo.

Having thrown away the *Arena*, Morris had returned to the beach with three cardboard cartons of zabaglione to find another development he hadn't expected. (And he'd considered himself so prepared, so sharp.) Sandra's boyfriend. Sandra's *Italian* boyfriend. Morris had imagined that when she spoke of 'we', she had been referring to herself and her English boyfriend, or girlfriend, or at the very worst a whole group of English people, none of which would have been the least bit dangerous. Such people were unlikely to know that Massimina Trevisan was supposed to have been kidnapped. But an Italian boyfriend was different. And especially one who seemed to have more eyes for Massimina than for his own companion. (Morris didn't actually think Massimina was quite so attractive as to deserve all this attention, though her breasts were certainly impressive – and that was precisely the department poor Sandra was weak in.)

Giacomo was obviously considerably older than Sandra, and smaller. He walked with a serious limp, wearing long trousers to hide whatever problem it was he had with his legs, and his dapper, inevitable Italian moustache was grizzled and grey. He snapped his fingers every few moments and rubbed his hands together and his conversation, which dominated everybody else's, was a constant stream of jokes, witty remarks and innuendos darting around the borderline of the acceptable.

Finally it came out he was a photographer, an art photographer in fact, which explained why Miss Green-Belt Plummy-Voice Hadley had taken up with such a dwarf, Morris thought, though the greater part of his mind was still wondering whether, having found the tracksuit, the police would have the sense to go and check the hotels and pensioni in Vicenza or whether, considering it a kidnap, they wouldn't bother. If only his letter had arrived. And if only the letter itself had been a bit more serious; if only he hadn't hung back, hedging bets, giving himself the let-out it might just be a practical joke. Because if they thought that, they might still follow up the 'runaway' hypothesis, which meant checking hotels. Damn and damn.

'From Napoli,' Giacomo was saying, eating the ice-cream Morris had bought for himself. 'But this will be the first time I've been back to the old breeding ground for a good ten years or so. I live in Verona now.'

Verona? Morris turned in one split second to stone, then waded into the conversation like a bull in a china shop. Before Massimina could swallow her zabaglione and start asking whether they had acquaintances in common, he said desperately:

'And how long have you been travelling then?'

Giacomo was a shade unsure for a moment, given the patently false, forced-interest tone of Morris's voice, whether the question indicated mere social incompetence or downright rudeness. But Sandra's Italian wasn't up to nuances and tones of voice.

'A week now,' she said. 'Four days in Venice, a couple in Ravenna . . .'

Morris breathed again. They'd left before the story broke. Get out now and it was plainest sailing. Sandra was saying how much she'd adored the mosaics in Ravenna, 'really breathtaking,' she suddenly finished in English, turning to Morris. For it was becoming embarrassing the glances Giacomo was throwing at Massimina's breasts and the part where her lime-green costume tapered up from crotch to hip. *Porco!* His face had a grin of typical Latin lasciviousness, the little crumpled man who can never prove himself often enough. The exact opposite of himself, Morris thought. He could perfectly well do without women in the end. A slave to no animal urges.

'I'm sorry,' Morris said, bringing up a hand to cover his forehead, 'but I'm afraid I feel rather ill. It must be the sun.' And to Massimina. 'Mimi, I know it's a bore but I'm going to have to go and lie down in the cool inside. Coming?'

'Meet us for dinner,' Giacomo said brightly.

'Okay,' Morris agreed, 'seven o'clock at the bottom of the pier.' Just to be rid of them. And he propelled Massimina back through the city to their pensione.


'How the hell did he find the place?' Morris whispered fiercely once they were in the back of the car. Faced with the fait accompli of the two of them actually arriving in their room in the pensione there had been nothing for it but to accept the invitation to dinner in a country restaurant. Morris felt as one who must run some awful gauntlet before he can breathe again. The whole evening, holding his breath.

'I'd told Sandra where we were staying. While you were off buying the ice-creams.'

'And what in God's name do you mean telling everybody where we're staying?'

'Why not?' she said brightly.

Why not indeed.

It had taken Massimina more than half an hour to apply her new make-up, purchased that afternoon. Against his better, that is his aesthetic judgement, Morris had advised her to buy brilliant colours, sharp reds and blues, thinking it would look common and take her even further away from her normal self. And instead, she applied them so carefully and well as to highlight her natural prettiness quite perfectly, so that her face had taken on the classic lines of that flattering picture they'd published the first day in the newspaper and would no doubt reprint every time they mentioned the case. Morris felt exasperated (he'd changed her, yes, but in the wrong direction). Then he could have sworn pastel shades were the thing for her camellia skin with its curious milkiness and breadcrumb freckles, and here she was looking an angel with these neon reds and blues attracting all the wrong kind of attention to herself. Giacomo's attention. A Veronese.

'I suppose it hasn't occurred to you how easily it could get back to your mother where we're staying.' She was wearing too much perfume too. It seemed to fill the car. 'Has it?'

'No,' she laughed, hugging herself into his arm. 'But there's no need to get neurotic, Morri. And then who cares if it does get back to her? We'll tell her it's too late and I'm pregnant and we'll have to marry.'

'We're eloping,' she said out loud then to the two in the front of the car. 'My mamma didn't like Morrees but we decided to run away anyway.'

Morris's fingers clenched tight into the skin of his thighs till the blood sang with anger.

'Shut up!' he hissed.

Giacomo's car spun quickly along the narrow country roads up into the Apennines with the sun throwing sharp shadows amongst the peaks. He wanted to take them to a restaurant on the steep terraced slopes under San Marino where he had been before and eaten well.

'We're running away too, aren't we, Giacomo?' Sandra said, ruffling the coal-grey curly hair at the back of his neck.

'*Proprio così*,' Giacomo said. 'Turtledoves all,' and despite the curving road he turned to the back of the car and winked.

Which meant he'd ditched his poor wife, the bastard, Morris thought. Like Dad with Mother. How long after her death before that Eileen woman was giggling downstairs on the couch, trying to wriggle Dad's hand out of her pants.

And Cartuccio too, most probably. Wife dead indeed! How the hell was Morris supposed to check up on that? Unless he'd killed her. Most probably that. Morris watched over one precipice after another as the car wound tightly up into the hills. If only you could tilt the wheel a bit and somehow manage to get out before . . . but the car was a two door and he was in the back. (Was he going mad? What had he done in the end: run off with her, written a letter, lied to the police. It was their fault for making it all so easy. Otherwise he would never have started.)

San Marino floated into view. Picture-book battlements and pink sunset castles rose hewn and cobbled a thousand steep feet above, like some corny illustration in *Lord of the Rings,* or a backdrop for a TV costume show. Relax, relax, play it as it comes. The tyres scrunched across the gravel surface of the restaurant car park and they bundled out to eat under a panoply of vines, the distant twilight view of San Marino half blocked by the silhouette of an illegally parked Dutch camper.

'There's a certain kind of tourist one just has to hate,' Sandra said in her plummy English to Morris, indicating the camper. She worked at the BBC as a production assistant apparently. Her father was a political analyst for Radio Four. (Surprise, surprise.)

'I know what you mean.' He was desperately trying to keep half an ear on Massimina's conversation in Italian with Giacomo, ready to intervene at the slightest hint of address exchanging. But perhaps because of his own delicate situation, Giacomo seemed to be steering thankfully clear of any attempt to find common acquaintances. He hadn't even had occasion to ask her surname yet, so far as Morris could tell. And why should he ask her? Did he know Stan's surname? Marion's?

'They come all the way down from Holland,' she went on, 'and then just spend the whole time on the beach eating pizza and blocking the views with their damnable caravans.'

Giacomo had put a friendly hand on Massimina's naked shoulder for a moment. No, it was really incredible the liberties people took. Morris would never have done that with somebody else's girlfriend. Sandra, for example. Sometimes he seemed to be the only one around with any morals, with any sense of who was whose. The older man whispered something in the girl's ear, but that would scarcely be a request for her surname, would it, Morris thought.

'And then if they do go to a museum they just browse around for ten minutes and think they've seen the whole thing – Italy. What they never do is actually try to soak in the real art of the way these people live and how that relates to the glorious past. The mosaics at Ravenna, for example . . .'

Morris poured himself another glass of wine. He was drinking too much. He must be careful. The thing to remember was that he was better than these people, genuinely better, smarter and quicker. In every way. Mentally, morally. So there was no need to be nervous.

'For you?' He offered the bottle.

At least it was exciting.

'Yes, please,' Sandra nodded and drained her glass. 'No savoir faire at all. All beer, beach and TV and no consideration for others. I often think the most important thing about artistic people is their sensibility towards others. I mean, they're more likely to be considerate because . . .'

Bullshit! Look how considerate gammy Giacomo was being. What the hell did she know about art anyway with that silly gauche mauve dress cut to a theoretical cleavage and geometric earrings like parts of some intellectual puzzle the well-to-do buy in Harrods for their children's Christmas stockings. Give a girl a plummy voice, a hockey stick before she's ten and a horse at puberty and a few years later you can bank on it she'll think she has carte blanche to talk about art till the cows come home.

'Mind you,' she was going on, 'half the people at the BBC are the same really. Like Daddy always says, culture's no more than screen-deep with that lot. Despite all their airs.' She hitched up the strap of her dress a little and, leaning nearer to Morris, smiled knowingly from all her Princess Anne-sharp teeth. This 'screen-deep' and 'airs' thing was obviously *the* family bon mot.

'I mean, in the end I'd rather a real pleb than half these twits and pansies who go on about theatre and culture on the television all day without really knowing anything about anything. There's no virility about them or contact with life, whereas there's something natural and earthy about a pleb, straightforward. He parks his camper in front of a view of San Marino and says, "What the bloody hell!"'

So now she had come round 360 degrees. And without him even contradicting. Dad would have fucked you black and blue, Morris thought. And sent you packing afterwards (as he had with Eileen – and the others).

But then so many women seemed quite happy that way.

Sandra leaned back, laughing. She must have drunk nearly a whole carafe all by herself and was obviously under the impression she was shining.

'Giacomo's a real artist, though. You should see the book he's done called *Middle Ages at Twilight*. It's really something else. Isn't it Giacomo?' And she took advantage of the opportunity to butt in on his conversation with Massimina and grab his arm.

'I'll pick up a copy,' Morris promised. And piss all over it. At which he suddenly realized he needed to go to the lavatory quite desperately, but couldn't of course, for fear of what turns the conversation might take in his absence. He was going to have to hold on the whole damn evening, which would ruin his first good meal for a week.

Eleven o'clock. A surprisingly dull morning with a spot of rain, but bright for Morris. He threaded his way from the pensione at the back of town through to the main street and headed towards the newsagent's. He definitely liked, he thought, the way they covered every empty wall with a great haphazard sea of posters in Italy. Every possible colour and message; dance lessons, ladies' underwear, the Radical Party. On the oldest buildings too. To show they weren't overly respectful of the past, that they lived now, in the present; at tonight's meeting of Democrazia Proletaria, for example. *Forza compagni!* Good for them.

And the girls walking arm in arm. That was another thing Morris liked to see. Not afraid of expressing an innocent affection for each other, not in danger of being considered lesbians the moment they linked arms or kissed each other's cheeks. Even some of the boys could grab each other affectionately without attracting the shameful inferences that such a gesture would inevitably provoke on the streets of suburban London.

Morris hurried through the fresh morning whirl, albeit under a grey sky, and felt at one with the world. He had dreamt of Dad last night; he had dreamt they were sitting together on the sofa watching TV. Nothing else, just him and Dad watching the box and laughing together, as if they'd never hated each other. The odd thing was that on the TV screen, he'd suddenly realized, they were showing himself and Massimina, her rubbing cream into his shoulders as he lay on the bed, and Dad was laughing – 'Christ, what a pair she's got, up hers any day,' and for some reason Morris was laughing with him.

Yes, the morning had got off to an exceptionally good start. Massimina had lain in quietly till ten nursing a terrible headache which had given Morris a clear couple of hours to finalize his letter, snip snap all the words from the mags he'd bought (a huge pile) and tape the whole thing together. At half ten he left the poor girl in the pensione, hashing up a picnic brunch with yesterday's bread rolls, and went down to the street. Apart from the hangover, she seemed in a state of semi-shock over the amount of money they'd spent the previous evening.

'Forty thousand lire, Morri! It's mad!'

'I told you we shouldn't have gone out with them. He was just trying to get you drunk, and for fairly obvious reasons.'

But the evening couldn't really have gone better as far as Morris was concerned. No addresses exchanged, no common acquaintances unearthed, no surnames mentioned even, and most of all, after Morris's coldness and fine show of jealousy towards the end, no mention whatsoever of a further meeting. Given that the two would be picking up the boat from Brindisi to Greece in a few days' time there thus seemed little likelihood they'd ever be in a position to cause trouble for Morris. All well then, and he hadn't killed anybody. (What a stupid idea that was, Morris was far too smart to be a killer.) He smiled his smile feeling the corner of his lip lift. He was going to come out of this clean with all the money and live happily ever after without so much as a smudge on his conscience. On the contrary, he was going to feel very proud of himself. But Morris remembered that strange tightening of the muscles he'd felt the evening before, the overwhelming sensation of physical heat, a moment's blinding determination. It was curious.

He popped into the same newsagent as yesterday, picked up one of only two copies of the *Arena* and there it was. The letter had arrived. A small headline in the margin of the front page led him to an article inside. The police were now definitely considering the matter a kidnap – excellent – though given the curious nature of the letter they still hadn't absolutely ruled out the possibility of some kind of macabre practical joke. Fair enough. It was oddball stuff. But the mole must have been convincing. (Unless even her family had never noticed it? Most people were blind after all.) The search was concentrating on the area around Vicenza, the paper said, where the red tracksuit had been found and Inspector Marangoni was quoted as saying that he expected there would be concrete developments within the next forty-eight hours.

Oh no he didn't, Morris thought, and positively skipped out onto the street. Oh no! He didn't expect anything of the kind. That was just the crap they fed the press with. No mention of himself either, which could only be positive. The only minus was a reprint of Massimina's photograph, admittedly in smaller dimensions this time, but now looking remarkably like the blow-waved, eyebrow-plucked made-up girl who'd sat beside him last night. (What had the photographer done, for God's sake? How much had they paid him?) A friend or even relation might never recognize the creature as she was now, but half the world would – if they were in the habit of scrutinizing photographs in out of town newspapers. Still, Morris was feeling sufficiently secure this dull humid morning to actually welcome a ghost of a challenge (where was the excitement otherwise?) and his face creased into its smile of sly triumph. He stopped a moment to share the smile with himself in the reflection of a window full of children's clothes. Tall, blond, quite handsome – a little indistinctive was the only problem. It wasn't a striking face. Rather boring. Thank God he hadn't kidnapped Sandra though: could you imagine having to put up with that kind of conversation day in day out? Count your blessings, Morris Duckworth.

He bought stamps and an express sticker and then enquired his way to the local S.I.P., the phone centre. Safely installed in a booth, he dialled the number Inspector Marangoni had given him. Perfectly safe, he felt. Ready for a long chat, ready to give his best opinion; he would even offer to go back to Verona if the police thought it could be of any help.

'*Pronto, Questura di Verona.*'

'*Pronto, vorrei parlare con l'Ispettore Marangoni.*'

The inspector was busy; if Morris would like to leave a message perhaps?

Morris wouldn't. He didn't want to communicate through some lackey and be misunderstood.

'This is a long distance call about the Trevisan kidnap. Tell the Inspector it is Morris Duckworth speaking and that I have some new information for him.' That should stir things up.

'*Pronto,*' Inspector Marangoni was on the line in a matter of seconds. 'Ah, Signor Duckworth, *come va?*'

'*Non c'è male.* I'm in Bari.'

'Marvellous, how's the weather?'

'Hot,' Morris said, which was scarcely taking a risk. 'Look, I saw the news about Massimina this morning. I don't know, I feel really shocked. It really is a kidnap then, you're sure? Did the letter ask for money, I mean . . .'

'I can't give you any of the actual details I'm afraid. Confidential. The man was obviously determined not to use his own handwriting though. Used bits of newspapers, lettroset.'

'Oh – is that unusual?' Morris asked.

'So, so. Maybe he has some special reason for hiding his handwriting. Someone close to the family. Or he could be left-handed, you can usually tell that immediately even from printed caps. Hence the lettroset where he couldn't find bits of newspaper.'

'Oh?' Morris felt a shade unnerved. The Inspector's voice was heavy and slow, professional, and Morris remembered the businesslike manner of the man in the garden at Quinzano, the impression of experience. How long would it take him to come up with the real reason behind that messy collage?

'Yes, in which case leaving the tracksuit in a bin in Vicenza – you heard about that, didn't you? Yes, they left it at the rail station – that might just be some kind of deliberate red herring, trying to take us away from the immediate family circle. But my assistant here tells me you have some new information.'

'Well, I'm not sure if it's really useful, but it's something I remembered yesterday and then when I saw about the kidnap . . .' Damn! How on earth could he have seen about the kidnap in Bari? No *Arena* there. Rimini was one thing, just a couple of hundred kilometres south of Verona and crawling with tourists from the northern towns, but Bari? Morris trembled, switching the phone from one sweaty hand to another. It was awfully close in the booth. Nobody would ever want an *Arena* in Bari, surely.

'Yes? *Pronto?*'

'Well, Massimina mentioned to me that there was some strange character always bothering her on the bus when she came home from school. He used to try and sit or stand next to her and stare at her.'

'She didn't give you any description?'

'No. Oh, only that he was very hairy, and that his eyes were odd. I got the impression he must have been around forty, but I don't know if she actually told me that. I just told her to stick near the bus driver or the other people and not to worry too much. I mean, the world is full of people like that and they're generally harmless. But now . . .'

'No other description? She didn't say where he got on, where he got off, what time of day it was?'

Morris left himself an authentic pause for thought. He was feeling confident again. The inspector was swallowing it.

'Well, she went to school at the Stimate and got the bus straight home when the school closes at one. So it would have been around that time. But where he got on and off I don't know. I can't imagine he got off at Quinzano itself because if so she'd have known him. Everybody knows everybody there.'

'Quite.' Inspector Trevisan was obviously writing as he spoke, which gave Morris a breather. 'Quite. We'll have some men check out the bus route around that time for a few days.'

'But if he's the one who kidnapped her he won't *be* on the

bus any more.' Morris managed to get some exasperation and fear into his voice. 'If only I'd asked for more information, taken it more seriously.'

'We can interview the passengers who regularly travel that line and maybe get something from them.'

'I think I should come directly back to Verona,' Morris said with determination.

'Why's that, Signor Duckworth?'

'I don't know. I'm so worried about it all and I'm not enjoying my holiday at all. Then maybe if I was in Verona I could help in some way. I could . . .'

'Look, Signor Duckworth, I really don't see any way you can help us here any more than you already have. Remember, you didn't see Massimina for a full month before the kidnap. As for her family, I'm fairly certain that they don't want to see you around. They appear to feel somewhat embarrassed in your regard, and hence hostile.' The inspector chuckled in quite a fatherly way. 'That's life. Now, you're with friends down there, right?'

'Right.'

'So you've got something to take your mind off it all.'

'But . . .' It was quite touching actually, this concern for his state of mind.

'The decision's yours, obviously, but I'd advise you to stay. There's no need to feel in any way guilty about not rushing back, seeing as there's nothing for you to do here.'

'And if I go with them to Turkey?'

'I've got no objections to you going at all. If you want information, just phone this number as often as you like and my assistant will tell you where we're up to. You remember Tolaini. He was with me when we met in Quinzano.'

'I'll think about it,' Morris said miserably, and after a few more moments the conversation ended.

He stayed in the booth and on impulse decided to call his father. He dialled out the code for England, then the Acton number, listening to all the click and echo of exchange connections until at last there was the English ringing tone. Its familiarity gave him something of a jolt, so near, so usual, he could have been at Victoria station announcing his return home to a life with the Milk Marketing Board. Perhaps he'd tell Father he'd earned a shit-load of money speculating on the stock exchange or something and that he was going to buy himself a house on the hills outside Florence and would Dad like to come over for a week or two in September to get a bit of a suntan? That should shake him up.

But there was no answer. After a moment or two, Morris realized it was just a regular Thursday morning back there in London and Dad would be sweating away over a hot die-drawing machine in Park Royal. Shame. Each to his own though. *Unicuique faber est* . . . etc. He went out into the foyer, paid, asked for the Verona directory and scribbled down Bobo's address.

No, but he should have been a detective himself, Morris thought, stepping out into the street. *He'd* never have missed a detail like how could somebody have got hold of the news of that kidnap in Bari. Maybe it still wasn't too late even. He could go back and sign up and be a detective before he was thirty-five. Quite feasible. Surely the police of all people wouldn't reject him. The only bind being those two years you had to spend on the beat, and then the image of course which scarcely conformed to Morris's idea of what a cultured . . . Unless the case had got a mention on the national radio news, or television? That's why the inspector hadn't been surprised. They had mentioned the kidnap on the national network with Massimina's face covering the whole screen!

Morris stopped in his stride, perturbed a moment in the busy street packed with disappointed beachgoers. But they couldn't surely. It would never have made it to the national news. A small town kidnap like that. This wasn't England where they had to dig and scrape for drama. Here they had the government dying and resurrecting itself every day and the mafia shifting more arms than the whole of the Warsaw Pact put together. So what did they want with Massimina's story? Morris regained his stride and hurried back towards the pensione. Mental laziness on Marangoni's part, that was all it was. He had a feeling though that they should get out of

Rimini as soon as possible. It wasn't a good idea being seen too much in the same place. People began to recognize you, to place you.

'*Ehi! Eh là!*'

Morris had reached the end of the main drag and was cutting through the more ancient side streets when he heard the sound of steps, half running, half hobbling behind him.

'Morris!'

Before he could even turn, a hand clasped his naked arm. And it was Giacomo. Gammy Jackie. Morris found he was trembling. The slightest thing.

'I was going to go over to the pensione, but then when I saw you . . .' Giacomo was out of breath and held on to Morris a moment for balance. Morris's mind hunted back and forth at the speed of light for some reason why Giacomo might want to talk to him. To apologize perhaps? For what a pig he'd been last night.

'What is it?'

'Well, you know you said Massimina had run away.'

'*She* said.'

'Right, well. What's her surname?'

Morris barely hesitated. He looked Giacomo straight in the dark eyes, his own cold and blue, as if confronting destiny. 'Trevisan,' he said. 'Massimina Trevisan.'

'From Quinzano? On the hill above Verona?'

'Right.'

And Giacomo started to laugh. 'But they think she's been kidnapped, man! Didn't you phone them or something to tell them she's okay?'

'What?'

'They think she's been kidnapped,' Giacomo insisted. 'Abducted, carried off. Look, I picked up an *Arena* this morning, by a miracle, the last one in the newsagent's, and there's an article about Massimina being kidnapped.'

'No!' Morris pushed a hand through blond hair, covering his face a moment. If only he'd bought both copies!

'But she telephoned. And then we've written. I posted the letter myself. There must be some mistake.'

'I don't know.' Giacomo was excited. He obviously thought it was all wildly amusing. 'Come back to the hotel and have a look at the paper. Maybe she was just too scared to telephone, you know what girls are, and then the post being what it is the letters mightn't have arrived yet. When did you post them?'

Morris was already falling in step with Giacomo in the direction of his hotel. His face was slippery with sweat and his limbs felt like wax. Think, think, think! He ran his front teeth back and forth along his lower lip.

'Right away. Saturday morning. We . . .'

Giacomo was roaring with laughter. 'It seems they've got half the police force in the Veneto scouring around Vicenza because they found a tracksuit there they thought was hers.'

'Oh no.' Morris was planless, in an abyss.

'You'd better phone the police or the family or something as soon as possible. You can phone from the hotel.' Giacomo turned a moment, laughing, eyes bright, and he clapped Morris on the back. 'Hey, no need to worry too much. You've gone pale as hell, man. It's her fault if she said she'd telephoned and then didn't. Anyway, you can sort it out in a second in a call to the police.'

'Yes, of course.' Thank God there'd been no mention of himself in that particular article.

Giacomo and Sandra were staying in the Albergo degli Ulivi, a name which appeared to be entirely unjustified by the broad flat street planted here and there with maritime pines and lined with the same modern ten-storey apartment blocks and hotels that filled every side street within five minutes' walk of the sea.

'Very apt,' Morris said with a grin and was faintly pleased with himself. He was still alive. He could still notice things, make dry remarks. And then when Giacomo leaned over the hotel desk and asked for his key, he registered the obvious at once. Sandra must be out! He turned abruptly away from the receptionist. Mustn't catch her eye.

'Where's Sandra?' he asked innocently as they stood in the elevator. Sweating blood.

'Out. She thinks she needs a new bathing costume for some reason, you know women. Doesn't like the straps on the present one. As if new straps could give her a pair of tits.'

And then Giacomo began to talk rather unpleasantly about women. He wasn't really serious about Sandra at all, he said. It was just a fling. And frankly, that was all women were good for. Otherwise they interfered with your work, with their marriages and homes and babies, and then wanted to make you feel guilty the moment you stopped paying a hundred per cent attention a hundred per cent of the time, or they'd dash off to flirt with other men in the hope it would bother you. His wife was a bitch, pure and simple, that was all there was to it. You could never live in peace and quiet with women. And so he was separating and would live on his own and work alone and save up his sex life for the odd fling like this with a lusty ticket like Sandra. She may not have much tit, poor girl, but once you got her between the sheets, God she was a goer. Oh yes! A real squeeze.

It was precisely the kind of conversation Morris had always avoided in male company. 'Does she know?' he asked politely. 'I mean, about you not being serious.'

'Sandra? No, she thinks she's going to come and live in Verona and play the artist's mistress game.' He laughed. (And the man was ugly as sin, Morris thought. Small, gammy, hairy as hell with a chewed southern toffee of a face. A real runt.)

*What in Christ's name was he supposed to do?*

'But I don't have any trouble telling them. You know? You have to be cruel to be kind sometimes, that's my motto. What about you and Massimina? Nice girl. Quite a pair.' And with barely a pause for Morris to reply, he said, 'Not interested in sharing and all that, are you?' His face lit up in a boyish, self-excusing little grin. 'I mean, we could all go on holiday together in a foursome, share and share alike. Sandra's quite into that kind of thing and she likes you. She thinks you're sweet. She was saying what a change you are from the snoots she's used to. We could even take some photos if you like. No holes barred. Share the profits. Have a hell of a holiday, I can promise you.'

Morris was quite shocked and had to swallow hard. It was the kind of horrible thing you read about in the worst magazines. (There'd been something like it in Cartuccio's *Penthouse* come to think of it – three people contorted together while somebody else took a photo. Awful.)

'What d'you think?' Giacomo had started talking again. 'It's a pretty big turn-on doing it with more than one,' he laughed, 'sucking and fucking, oral and anal, you . . .'

'We're very much in love, actually,' Morris got out, positively croaking. He felt nauseous. 'Really, we . . .' The lift stopped suddenly, shifting his stomach. He made a great effort to hold himself straight, to remain in perfect control of body and voice. 'We mean to get married just as soon as it's her eighteenth birthday. In six weeks' time.'

*Don't touch anything in the apartment. Nothing. Nothing!*

'Oh well then, congratulations, if that's the situation.' For some reason Giacomo made an absurd little bow, then changed the subject abruptly: 'I hope the police don't give you any bother over this kidnap business. There's the paper, look. I'll just go and mix a couple of drinks. Martini okay for you?' He went through a door into what was presumably the bathroom. Morris looked quickly round the room. What, where, how?

But there must be some other way, some . . .

'Pretty amazing, eh? Would you believe it?' Giacomo called over the sound of tinkling glasses. 'We'll have to phone directory enquiries to get hold of the Verona *Questura*. Phone the local police and they won't even know what you're talking about. All they ever do here is arrest nudists on the beach.'

The paper was on the bed, open at the accusing page. Morris picked it up and deliberately rustled. Table lamp, no. Chair, no. Radio, no. The room was so sparsely furnished. A copy of *Il Fotografo* with a dirty nude on the front. *And he only had a few seconds!* Dear God, there must be something. A paperweight? Paperweight was the classic. Wasn't one.

(Something to do what? What was he going to do? Morris!)

'With vodka or without?'

'With.' His voice was a croak. He should be making comments on the newspaper. He should be shouting, 'Oh no, but this is amazing, and some cranky bastard's gone and sent them a ransom letter.' The plant pot, the plant pot, it was the only thing. What a farce!

There was a tropical plant in the corner in a ten-inch deep earthenware pot. He lifted it carefully. It was certainly heavy enough. But could he wield it properly? No, he hadn't meant to do this at all. Morris Duckworth, always first in class, Mother's boy, a pansy his father used to . . .

He was behind the bathroom door now. Giacomo was putting glasses on a tray. Absurd. Television farce. Bad taste. He lifted the thing over his head, gritted his teeth and tried to tense his trembling arms. But instead of yesterday's heat, he was shivering. Muscles and tendons refused to tighten. His buttocks felt soft and wobbly.

The top leaves of the plant rustled and broke against the ceiling. And then as Giacomo's curly head appeared, he brought down the pot hard, with absolutely everything he had. Everything. The pot went into fragments and Giacomo fell to the floor in a mess of broken glasses and scattered earth. He hadn't even cried at all, but he twitched now and rolled to one side, then let out a long, low groan. Not dead. Morris cast about desperately for something else to hit him with. You couldn't kick with sandals. It was like having a live trout in the kitchen and the rolling pin nowhere in sight. Till finally in a flash of genius (because he *was* a genius) he turned and dashed to the bed. The pillow. Of course. The pillow!

He rolled Giacomo over, gasping and whimpering, and covered his face with the lemon coloured pillow. Then pressed down for all he was worth. The body offered only the feeblest resistance, twitching and at one moment lifting a weak hand. Morris looked at his watch, counted two whole minutes and then eased the pressure. Barely a trickle of blood from the head. He took a wrist and felt for some pulse. Nothing. Ten seconds, twenty, nothing. He stood up. He wouldn't take the pillow away from his face though. He could do without seeing that. Feeling utterly weak and exhausted he stumbled over to the bed and lay down flat on his back, eyes closed, fighting back a sudden nausea.

Five minutes later, less, and he was on his feet again. He'd have to get out before Sandra came. Or no? Or wait for her? It was quite mad. Thank God they weren't nice people. Partner swapping! 'She's into that kind of thing . . .' Scum. 'She was saying what a change you were from the snoots she's used to.' Filth. Go, stay? His hands were trembling violently. And Massimina? God only knew what Massimina mightn't be getting up to. Go then. But first he'd have to make this mess more plausible.

He went over to Giacomo and felt the front pockets of his jeans. Material didn't leave prints, did it? Nothing there. He slipped a hand under. The wallet was in the back pocket and tight. He held down the pillow over the face and tried to heave the body over. It seemed impossibly heavy. He had to take the hand away from the pillow and use all his strength to move the dead weight. The pillow came away, but the face was pointing down now. He snatched out the wallet and put it in his own pocket. Then to the desk drawer by the window. He pulled it out and spilled cosmetics, perfume and small change over the floor. Nothing of value. But cameras and camera equipment in the cupboard beneath. A glance out of the window into the street showed a clearing sky with thin sunshine that came and went. A plastic bag, that was what he needed. He looked all round. Nothing. Then into the bathroom. They had hung up a plastic bag on the handle of the little cupboard there to put tissues in and the like. Used rubbers. Pigs. Morris emptied the lot onto the floor. Water. He needed water, water, water. He was drinking directly from the tap when he realized he might have left fingerprints on the desk. Damn. He should find a cloth and rub the thing hard. A cloth. Sheet from the bed. He picked up the plastic bag, went back into the main room and loaded in the cameras, then the wallet too. Just wipe out the fingerprints and . . .

But now there came a knock on the door. 'Giacomo?'

Why the hell hadn't he heard footsteps? Oh Christ.

'Giacomo, it's me.'

'*Vengo.*' There was no time to think, nor prepare himself mentally. He walked quickly to the door, taking a long telephoto barrel out of the plastic bag; he pressed the release button on the doorhandle and opened. She was wearing a T-shirt over no bra and a short white pleated skirt; there was a packet in her hand. The new bikini, no doubt.

'Morris!' She couldn't see Giacomo on the floor because he was out of view to the right, but she could sense something was wrong.

'Morris, what are you . . .'

He backed away. Got to get her inside the room with the door closed at least.

'Giacomo asked me in for a drink.'

She came forward into the room but then must have caught a glimpse of something on the floor. Scatterings of earth from the pot and broken glass. Suddenly she jerked back and tried to get out, pulling the door behind her. But Morris was quicker. A foot in the door, he grabbed her hand from the handle and with a strength he hadn't expected of himself, wrenched her into the room.

'For Christ's sake!' she shouted. Having dropped the telephoto, Morris put both hands on her breasts and pushed her hard to the floor. Her head cracked back on the tiles and she screamed. The telephoto was rolling away and stopped against Giacomo's gammy leg. Morris made a dive for it.

'No!' Sandra screamed, and for some reason, instead of defending herself, she pulled down the hem of the white skirt which had ridden up over her knickers and held it tight down above her knees. Her narrow aristocratic toothy face was white with pure amazement. As if he would want to rape her! The vanity!

Morris hit her on the top of her blond head. Hard.

'No!' she screamed again and the hands came up.

He hit a second time, on the temples now, and a third, and a fourth and a fifth and again and again. He put all his weight into it, it was exhausting; until suddenly the blood began to stream, dark almost black. He moved to the pillow, but then realized there was no point. Her face was perfectly still, the eyes rolled to one side and fixed, mouth contorted, lips and teeth broken. Morris took a deep breath, went to the door still half open, for God's sake, anybody could have gone past – picked up the plastic bag, slipped in the telephoto lens and left, closing the door behind him.

The elevator hadn't moved since Sandra came up. Morris got in, rode down, breezed through reception without being noticed as far as he could tell, and was out in the street before he realized he hadn't brought down that copy of the *Arena*. Dear Christ! He stopped outside the glass door of the hotel and slumped against the stuccoed wall beside. Open at the very page. The kidnap spread out right there in front of the first policeman who came. He would have to go back up.

Why on earth had he done it? Why? It had been the moment to bow out, take the first flight home to Britain.

Unless perhaps he had done it because he wanted to stay with Massimina. No.

He looked at his watch and counted an interminable ten minutes just to be absolutely sure there had been no alarm. Nobody had paid any attention to the screams. Perhaps they hadn't been as loud as he thought. Then he started quickly back in. The receptionist was giggling on the telephone and didn't even glance. But the elevator wasn't there. Morris saw the stairs to his right and made himself, forced himself, to walk up the three floors slowly and normally, without getting out of breath. He would just go straight into the room, pick up the *Arena* from the bottom of the bed, slip it into his plastic bag, wipe the desk handles while he was at it (and the tap, of course, the tap!) and then out again.

But the door was locked. For a moment Morris panicked. He dropped the plastic bag, grabbed the handle and heaved at it. How on earth could he have been so stupid as to forget that the doors were self-locking? Why hadn't he taken the key for God's sake? He was nothing more than a stupid amateur, when all was said and done, a boy in a mess, and if they got him now it really was the end. He should have confessed everything to Giacomo and got out of it as best he could, taken the girl home and had done. Or he could have agreed to the holiday foursome and offered Giacomo half the ransom in return for his silence. He would have gone for that, the rat, the pig, you could see from his face he would have stopped at nothing to get inside a girl's pants. At least Morris wasn't like that. At least he had some sense of decency.

While these thoughts rushed wildly through his head, Morris was rattling and tugging at the doorhandle, until he heard the lift whine to a stop round the corner to his right. He picked up the plastic bag, made a dash for the stairs to his left and just got round the wall out of sight before a couple came into the corridor behind him. They stopped outside the door next to Giacomo's, laughing and joking in German. Morris peeped a glance round the wall to see when they would disappear and he could have another go at the door (he could pick the lock maybe). The couple, in their mid-forties, were embracing tightly against the wall.

It was at this moment, waiting for them to open their door and disappear, that Morris noticed a series of dark red smears along the creamy polished marble compound that was the floor of the corridor. He stared, not quite understanding for a few seconds, then lifted a leg to look at the underside of his sandal. The sole under the toes was sticky with blood. Standing on one leg as he was he swayed and almost blacked out. He grabbed the metal bannister for support, breathing deeply to recover. His vision seemed to narrow under a great weight of darkness all around and then slowly to open out again, despite a fierce pain flowering now in the dead centre of his skull. How was it those two hadn't seen the stains? He must have left them in the lobby too. Trembling, he slipped off the offending sandal, then the other, put them in the plastic bag with the wallet, the camera equipment, the bloody telephoto lens – there was a cluster of blondish hairs stuck to it he noticed – and then breathing hard, God you needed so much air in your lungs, he hurried barefoot down the stairs. Nobody passed him on the way down, but the lobby was busy now. It was lunchtime and people were filing through to a restaurant behind swing glass⁻

doors at the back of the lobby. Morris padded around a small group by the reception desk and out into the street.

Brilliant sunshine had replaced the clouds and the fresh black tar of the pavement was already burning. Morris went and stood under the meagre shade of a pine tree and quickly examined his clothes. His white cotton trousers had a speck of blood just below the knee and there was a small stain on his right cuff. *Make a plan*. He must make a plan and sort all this out. He looked at his watch. Twelve fifteen. He'd left Massimina alone for more than an hour and a half. God knows what she would be thinking. He started to walk down the street towards the canal, realized he'd taken the wrong direction and doubled back. His feet were quite scalded by the pavement now, so that he had to half walk, half run, always trying not to attract undue attention. A dog on a lead barked and strained after him.

'He doesn't like bare feet,' the owner laughed. Morris tried to smile back. Couldn't. He must have looked daggers at the chap.

The canal was glittering in the sunlight now, smelling strongly of diesel, dead fish and the sea. Morris walked quickly along the wharf where the painted fishing boats were tied end to end with here and there a pump rattling or a man spreading nets or painting a guard rail. What tranquillity! He walked a good two hundred yards, almost to the last of the boats where the path seemed completely deserted, and stopped. He reached inside the bag, careful to keep away from the telephoto lens and the bloody sandal and lifted out Giacomo's wallet. May as well profit by the crime now it was done. But there was only twenty thousand lire. There were documents, a driving licence, tickets for the Brindisi-Igoumenitsa ferry, a photograph, polaroid, of a middle-aged, pleasantish woman holding two young children and another of a naked, dark girl cross-legged on a double bed, hands behind her head to make her nipples point at the camera. This was neither Sandra nor the other woman and Morris was pleased to have this further confirmation of Giacomo's immorality. (Consider he'd done it for the wife's sake – those whom God hath joined together . . .) Finally, in a small pocket that closed with a stud, wrapped in thin tissue paper, there was a tiny St Christopher on a thin silver chain, wound round an old, worn wedding ring.

Morris took the twenty thousand for what it was worth, the two tickets just in case, and the St Christopher for no reason at all. Then he slipped the documents and ring back in the wallet and the wallet back in the bag and knotted the plastic handles tight. Looking around, he walked a few paces and quickly dropped the bag into the canal between two boats, where, under the weight of the cameras, it sank like a stone.

'For me?' Massimina was delighted. 'Morrees!'

'That's why I'm so late.' Morris felt weak, absolutely exhausted. He couldn't remember ever having felt so tired. And the police were bound to put two and two together with that newspaper right beside the corpses open on the very page of the kidnap. He sank onto the bed.

'Oh, and then one of my damn sandals broke, I caught it on a kerbstone, so I spent half an hour looking for some new ones and then of course when I found what I wanted I discovered I'd spent all the money on the St Christopher.'

'*Quanto sei caro!*' she laughed.

It was interesting, Morris thought, fishing for lucidity, how many different ways he could have spent that hour and a half and ended up coming home with no shoes on his feet and a silver St Christopher in his pockets. Murder might have been just a nightmare.

'To protect us on our travels,' she said solemnly, linking the thing round her neck. He hadn't thought of that angle. It was all terribly appropriate. She came over with a thank you kiss, but suddenly now he remembered the blood on his cuff and trouser leg and pushing her aside he sprang to his feet.

'I seem to be sweating like a pig these days. My clothes are stinking.'

The room was the typical pensione, suffocatingly small, a double bed, wardrobe and tiny table, bare wooden floor and a washbasin with a mirror in one corner. Morris turned on the tap, slipped off his trousers and unbuttoned the shirt; he plunged them into the water and without even turning round quickly rubbed the stain on the trouser leg against that on the cuff of the blue shirt. The marks dissolved and bled away to nothing almost immediately. So much for the 'Out damned spot' side. Nothing easier than washing away a bit of blood.

Then when he turned round to grab a towel he found Massimina was standing behind him, quite naked. She had let drop the pearl grey skirt which was crumpled now about her feet and peeled off the red T-shirt. Apparently she'd had no underwear on. Her pubic hair was a great bristling bush under the perfect curve of her belly. Morris froze. He was too tired to face another crisis so soon after the last. Very slowly he dried his hands, staring, tensing.

The room wasn't bright. The window was blocked by the buildings on the other side of the ancient street. Massimina stood, quite beautiful and more shapely than he had imagined, in the filtered half light. She cocked her head to one side with half a smile.

'It isn't wrong, Morri. You know it isn't. I know I love you. And you have such generous thoughts for me, bringing me presents like this, I feel so secure now . . .'

He felt he was swaying and shut his eyes a moment.

'Morri?' She lifted her slim brown arms, palms outward and upward in a gesture of offering. She thought it was oh so hellishly romantic of course. She was copying the crap she read in books. But his eyes were filling with tears. Affection was welling up inside him, overwhelming his old disgust, the visions of Dad and Eileen on the couch, the grunts.

'Come to me, Morri. *Vieni, vieni.*' She stepped out of the skirt round her feet. Her body swayed. Her belly eased against him.

'*Cara,*' he muttered, his arms around her, '*cara Massimina.*'

The dying afternoon had a liquid, dreamy feel to it in which even the room's dozens of flies moved lazily and silently.

'By the way,' Massimina was saying brightly. She had sat up now and squashed the grand straw hat gaily over her perm. 'While you were out this morning I phoned home . . .'

'You what?'

'I phoned home four or five times. The landlady said I could use her private phone and pay afterwards. But there was nobody there.'

Morris closed his eyes under a great wave of relief. Grandmother's funeral, it must have been. But he could cheerfully have strangled her.

## 13

They were on the train at eight fifteen. Morris wanted to take the rapido but Massimina wouldn't hear of paying the surcharge and so they were caught in a compartment full of the 'plebs' as dear Sandra would have called them. Massimina sat opposite and away to the right of Morris and gave him sweet little smiles every time he turned in that direction which was irritating. He was longing to read the report in the newspapers and yet couldn't buy himself a paper in the station because then of course she might have seen it. He tried to imagine the words they would use and he thought it was odd but you couldn't think of a murder – or a kidnap if it came to that – outside the words the press would use to describe it, not even if you'd done it yourself. It was like a football match, or a debate in parliament, or a new theatre performance, you had to read what the critics said before you really knew it had happened.

He was feeling a little more himself this morning and strangely (madly?) carefree. What if he had left the *Arena* in there? Looking back on it now in the clear light of another day he saw it would take a genius to make the leap required to pin the murder on Massimina's kidnapper. And then another giant hop, skip and jump to nail Morris as that kidnapper. Living in Verona it was perfectly logical that Giacomo should have bought an *Arena* and who cared what page it was open at? The other thing was that he didn't feel profoundly changed in any way. He had checked very carefully through his mind for some kind of trauma or horror or general mental handicap resulting from the event, and instead nothing. Absolutely all clear. No, all that bothered him was he couldn't be alone to read the papers and maybe dictate a jubilant letter to Dad, get his thoughts down. He hadn't intended to kill after all. There had been nothing premeditated about it – quite the opposite. He'd been forced to it by that stupid lascivious idiot who hadn't deserved any better in the end anyway and Morris was damned if he was going to eat his heart out about it. (Murder should be judged on the value of the victim, his claim to live, not on the merely academic aspect of whether the death was murder or not and if so who did it.)

Added to which, the experience with Massimina had been very promising. He could do their funny business as well as the best of them it seemed. He felt rather protective towards her. Happier in her company. It was almost as if one experience had cancelled out the other. He had slept all night with her, her warm smell and heavy breasts not unlike Mother's those times. Really, he felt quite tempted to tell her everything. Maybe she would play along perfectly happily.

'*Panino*, Morri?' They had stopped at Fano and Massimina wanted him to pick up a sandwich from the man pushing his trolley up the platform. She refused to pay a small surcharge to travel in relative style on the rapido and then wanted him to waste money hanging out of the window to buy dry sandwiches from some gippo on the platform.

'No,' Morris was firm.

Wait for her to go to the lavatory and then he'd ask to borrow the paper off the lady beside him and flick through what was important as quickly as possible. Massimina had to go to the lavatory quite often, he'd noticed, which was rather convenient. Ply her with drinks should be his policy.

'*Cara*, the sandwiches these people sell are terrible, but I'll get you a can of coke if you want. You can't go wrong with a can.'

'No thanks,' she said and sat back and smiled sweetly.

Morris had to wait until beyond Senigallia before nature finally called.

HORROR IN RIMINI HOTEL MYSTERY MURDER, the headline ran, though they'd relegated the thing to page four oddly. Morris felt the adrenalin stir in his veins.

136

'Terrible,' the lady who had been so kind as to lend the paper remarked. She was a frail decaying creature wrapped in a shawl despite the stale heat of the compartment. Morris smiled sadly, raising half a blond eyebrow.

Police have admitted they are completely baffled by the double slaughter of a man and woman in Albergo degli Ulivi, Rimini, yesterday. The corpses were discovered late in the evening after a receptionist realized that despite having gone up to their room some hours before, Signor Giacomo Pellegrini and Miss Sandra Delaforce, his English companion, repeatedly failed to respond to the telephone. A master key was used to enter the room where the two bodies were found horribly beaten to death by repeated blows to the skull. Police experts later revealed that a number of weapons had been used, including a heavy plant pot and an unidentified metal implement.

Funny they didn't mention the pillow. But then Morris had never really trusted the papers for detail.

ADULTERY CLUE – there was a subheading.

Although police were uncertain both as to the number of the assailants and the motive for the massacre, they were following possible suggestions that the murder may have been committed for passionate revenge. (How Italian of them.) Giacomo Pellegrini was a married man with two children only recently separated from his wife. 'Someone might have had cause to take revenge,' police sources said, 'though the clumsy, violent way in which the killings took place would appear to rule out a premeditated murder.'

Police found bloodstained shoe-prints both in the lift and on the stairs which would seem to indicate either that there were two killers, or that a single killer had left the room and returned again. If the motive for the attack was theft, the attacker may have realized that he hadn't taken Miss Delaforce's handbag which was found to contain 600,000 lire. Police believe that Signor Pellegrini's wallet was taken, plus some camera equipment.

'Morri.'

Barely two minutes and she was back already. She couldn't have . . .

'It's Ancona. We've got to get off.' They were rolling into a station and he hadn't even noticed. 'It was occupied,' she whispered as they heaved down the two suitcases.

'*Veramente orrendo*,' Morris commented, handing back the paper to the old woman (he felt more than ever the actor today) and when she asked if he would be so kind, he got her bag down and gave her a hand onto the platform. The thing about old people was they were so formal, so polite. You felt perfectly safe with them.

The original idea had been quite simply to cross the peninsula from east to west, putting as much distance as possible between himself and Rimini before he posted the ransom letter. Seeing as neither of them had ever seen Rome before, Morris had suggested, this elopement of theirs was an opportunity absolutely not to be missed; heaven only knew when they would find time to visit Rome after they were married, with setting up home and everything. So they had taken the earliest train from Rimini and were to change at Ancona with a half-hour wait before the espresso to Rome came in. Massimina dashed off directly to the ladies' while Morris lugged their two suitcases to a bench and sat down to think. He disliked travel of this kind, the dust and dirt of railway compartments, the grime you discovered on the backs of your arms that had got there you knew not how, under your fingernails, behind the elbow; and then the long waits for unaccountably delayed trains, the pushing and shoving. If one had to travel, it should be in style, Morris thought, with a little leg room, the possibility of buying a cool drink any time you wanted. After the purgatory of this awful business, when he could start really living, he must try doing some travelling that way.

Funny, it was somehow impossible to remember how life had felt before all this began.

Morris the murderer.

The four shaded platforms of Ancona's station milled with holidaymakers straining to catch the delays announced over the p.a., while the sun lay bright and white like four hot pokers on the gleaming lines between. A freight train clattered by and the inevitable workmen way up the line leaned on their spades to watch it pass. Morris tried to look at his situation logically. He tried to analyse each step he must make, one by one. But his mind rebelled. It was perilous but he seemed to be losing the desire to really think the thing out, to take it from now, the eye of the storm, right through every possible permutation to the moment when he, Morris Duckworth no less, would be perfectly free to live a life of ease with his ugly name, in an apartment in Rome perhaps, or Naples, or Verona again. (Why should he move if he came out of it right?)

Morris was perfectly happy reviewing the details of the life afterwards – he wanted to write a book, that was definite, and perhaps if he invested the money carefully he might even patronize one or two other intelligent young men from poor backgrounds who thought like himself – it wasn't impossible. (The Duckworth Scholarship, a year in Italy for budding young writers – that would be an amusing way to meet new people.) Morris enjoyed these thoughts like a cool soothing cream – but his restless mind refused to settle on the next few days and weeks ahead during which his future ease must be earned. (The careers of how many would-be Duckworth scholars hung on his every move.)

He bent down, unzipped a bag and drew out the dictaphone.

'Dear Dad, it might be worthwhile to compare our two respective futures. Yours stretches away on metalled rails, in an eternity of work, telly, beer and darts. Death will be an accident for you, a sudden hiccup, a derailment, not a destination. My future, on the contrary, is in the making every moment, as is my character; life for me is a maze where every choice is critical and hence formative (this was very good!). The contrast reflects our different positions vis à vis freedom and courage. I may come to grief but . . .'

'*Documenti, per favore.*' Morris's head jerked up like a jack-in-the-box. A tall carabiniere was standing over the only other occupant of the bench, a hippy looking girl. The policeman was heavily built with a pantomime Calabrian moustache, a white shirt soaked in sweat. Three or four other uniformed officers were moving up the platform behind, demanding documents at random (and just when he had really been in form).

Morris turned instinctively to his left, but saw that the platform simply petered away into a maze of rails after another fifty metres or so. Anyway, it would be crazy to get up and go at a moment like this. He slipped the dictaphone back in the bag, opened a side pocket and rummaged for his passport. If somebody had seen him in the hotel lobby and given a description? Or when he was dropping the bag in the river perhaps, if somebody had seen him then? Or even simply eating with Giacomo and Sandra the night before (they had found the restaurant receipt in his pocket, gone over there to interview the waiters, it was obvious). If they had got an identikit of him already and were doing the most sensible thing, combing all trains and train connections out of the city? Why on earth had he travelled by train? It was asking for it. And if they recognized him now? What to do? He would give himself up immediately. There was no point in struggling like an idiot and having himself shot at. Morris could already feel the hard metal of the handcuffs closing on his wrists, could hear himself speaking in court: 'They were no better than me, Your Honour. Signor Pellegrini made a number of lewd proposals to my *fidanzata* which . . .' But his *fidanzata* was Massimina for God's sake!

The policeman was turning over and over the small plastic card the girl had given him. He looked her up and down and asked her to show him the underside of her arms. She did so and he grunted, not finding what he was after.

'*Mio passaporto,*' Morris said with his frankest blond smile ınd strongest English accent. The carabiniere's southern face relaxed into an expression of generous servility and at the sight of the very respectable, short-haired, clear-eyed and patently undrugged Morris, he pushed the blue passport away.

'*Niente bisogno, grazie.*'

Morris made a cool show of examining his watch for a moment, fiddled in the pocket of his shorts for money, stood up and hurried directly to the ladies' room which was back towards the main station. He must stop her as she came out of the loo, stop her coming up the platform and being . . .

But he was too late. Massimina met him half way.

'Morri, they're looking for drug addicts! They . . .'

'Did they ask you for documents? Do you have any with you?'

'I showed my ID card. They're looking at everybody's arms to see if . . .'

Morris put a hand on her shoulder and gave her a resounding kiss on one soft cheek. He felt quite as if she'd done something extraordinarily clever of her own accord: showed her identity card to a carabiniere and not even been recognized! The police in Ancona clearly were not on the lookout for a kidnap victim from Verona. Not wandering free down the platform. It was obvious really, but Morris couldn't help feeling how marvellous it was. A little miracle.

'The train's in on platform four. Go and save us a couple of seats while I just dash and make a phone call.' It was so useful having an accomplice. If ever he was arrested he'd swear she'd been in on it all the way and bring her down with him. There were ways of proving one had made love these days. That should stick it up her signora mamma's arse with her oh so nice educated daughter stuff.

'But . . .'

'I've just thought of a friend's house we might be able to stay at. I want to phone before we get to Rome. Save us some money maybe.'

Morris found the station S.I.P. by the ticket office. He closed himself in a booth, fished for his address book and dialled directly. It was all instinct now. The thing was to do everything on the upstroke. As it came. That was living.

'*Signora Trevisan?*'

'*Si, chi parla?*'

'*Sono io, Signora,* Morris.'

'*Ah, dove sei?*' She seemed neither irritated nor pleased, but more resigned.

'In An – Bari,' Morris remembered. 'Look, I just wanted to know if you've had any more news about Massimina, I mean from her . . .' He let his voice trail off, as if overawed.

'No,' Signora Trevisan said. She was having to try hard to stop herself from crying, Morris thought, and he felt inclined to be kind to her. God knows if she hadn't been rude to him in the first place he would never have been anything other than kind and polite to her and most probably none of this would ever have happened. He could have married Massimina and had done. Brought a bit of style into the family. New blood. Good gene mix.

'Is there any hope it might not be a kidnap then, I mean . . .'

'The police say this is quite usual.' She was curt now.

'If I came back to Verona, is there anything I could do? Because I really would like . . .'

Signora Trevisan didn't think so really. The police were following up every line they could and her brother and Bobo had both come to live with them for the duration, for moral support and advice.

'I see.'

'But if you want some news you can always phone,' she added, rather grudgingly Morris felt.

'*Grazie infinite,*' he said warmly and after asking after the rest of the family hung up with a smile.

Then phoned Gregorio. If the worst came to the worst and one had to run, where better than a golden beach in Sardinia?

The phone rang for some minutes and was finally answered by another boy who was not Gregorio. After a moment or two Gregorio came on the line, giggly and clearly drunk. Morris was annoyed (the famous *figli di papà,* drunk at noon on their sun-drenched veranda) and explained his situation quickly and tersely, not at all begging. He was in Bari but had decided not to go to Turkey for reasons too complicated to go into. Would it be possible for him to stay in Sardinia for a while as offered? He'd be there in a week's time.

'But I won't be here,' Gregorio said.

His father had to have a gallstone operation, July 1st, and Mother had insisted he be back in Verona to visit and so on and keep her company, because she was always nervous in the house on her own and especially after that break-in when they took the bronze. It was understandable really.

But damn annoying, Morris thought.

'Oh, okay.'

'Well . . .'

'No, look, the only problem is I've gone and sublet my flat. Stupid of me I suppose, but now . . .'

Morris glanced at his watch. Three minutes before the train left.

'Well, you could always stay with us in Verona. My mother would be delighted. Take her mind off things having a guest you know. She laps up new people.'

'Thanks, okay, I'll think about it.' Morris let his voice fall with just a trace of disappointment. 'It's just that I have a rather close friend with me.'

Gregorio laughed a tiddly laugh and shouted something to his friend in the room. Morris, instinctively, had used the word *amico*, rather than *amica*. And he was right. After some background laughter, Gregorio said, 'Roberto here suggests I leave the keys to the house with him and he'll let you have them when you get here.'

'Well . . . only if you're sure it's okay, I mean I don't want to . . .'

But Gregorio was sure. It was absolutely fine, and he gave Morris Roberto's address and phone number.

'Friend from Verona?' Morris asked in passing.

'Roberto? No, he lives here. They have a hotel.'

Good. Morris signed off. He should have asked about the

exams of course, but time was ticking away. The next occasion would do just as well.

On the train he fought his way down the corridors looking for Massimina. It was packed with soldiers for some reason, all laughing and smoking out of the big open windows. There was nothing Morris hated more than soldiers, most especially slovenly ones, and he elbowed his way quite viciously along the corridor. Then having found the girl he plomped himself down in the seat opposite, breathless, all smiles.

'Why so late? I . . .'

Only now he noticed she had used the moments in the ladies' room to do herself up again. Soft pink lipstick and a dreamy eyeshadow. Too attractive by half with all these soldiers about. But it did give one a certain status. He'd have to find her a different bra though. Something more subdued and natural.

'My friend wasn't in, so I called Paola.'

'Who?'

'Paola, your Paola, your sister.'

'Oh,' Massimina relaxed. 'I was getting worried. When the train started I nearly got off it. I mean, how was I to know you'd made it, really?'

Morris smiled never-mindishly and glanced round the compartment. Businessmen, students, a couple of peasanty women and a soldier. No one they were likely to get into dangerous conversations with.

'So what did she say?'

'Well, it seems your mother's gone off with Grandmother to the mountains, Selva di Valgardena. The doctors suggested it for convalescence, and Antonella and Bobo have gone too.'

'Oh? So Paola's alone in the house then?' Massimina was dubious.

'No, she's sleeping at a friend's place she said and just checking up on things at the house every now and then. That's why nobody answered yesterday. Lucky I caught her really.'

'That will be Giuseppina,' Massimina said. 'Her friend.'

'That's right.' Morris noticed she looked rather down. 'Homesick? Miss them?'

The train plunged into the first of the long tunnels through the Apennines. In the sudden complete darkness and roaring echo of the walls, Massimina leaned across the compartment, slipped a hand between his knees and slithered it down to his thighs.

'Not with you,' she said, and almost had to shout. 'Not after last night.'

'She gave me an address where you can write to Mamma direct,' Morris said. 'Why don't we write her a nice long letter, see if we can't bring her round.'

They wrote the letter at the station in Terni where the train decided to stop for twenty minutes or so. They wrote it on sheets of lemon yellow notepaper with blue forget-me-nots climbing the left hand margin, which Massimina had bought in Rimini. Massimina said what she wanted to say, but even though he had only been in Italy a couple of years it was Morris who chose the elegant consolatory phrases. What it all amounted to was that they were very happy and would marry on her eighteenth birthday, for which they would like to have Mamma's consent. All doubts dissolved, they said. Morris signed his name too and wrote a note in his own hand saying how much he regretted that all this unpleasantness had come between them and wished the situation could return to normal as soon as possible. The curious thing was the sincerity and facility he felt: he could really see it all and really did his best to persuade his future mother-in-law. As if nothing had been decided at all . . .

The train pulled out of Terni towards two thirty and for the rest of the journey Morris hypnotized himself into a state of calm, gazing out of the window at brilliant yellow June corn broken by row after row of vines. If you didn't move your eyes to focus on any particular spot the effect of the shining green of the vine leaves against the golden carpet of grain became quite soporific and by the time the train pulled into Rome, shortly after four, his mind was completely empty, drained; and perfectly operational.

145

No sooner were they at the end of the platform than he sent her off to queue in the café, to pick up a couple of cappuccinos and a sandwich and find a table, while he went off to buy the stamps and post the letter. Taking the suitcases with him he found a tobacconist's just beyond the left luggage office, bought enough stamps to send an espresso, put them on the ransom letter now addressed in lettroset to Bobo and mailed the thing directly. The other letter he tore into the tiniest shreds before leaving it in a waste bin.

# 14

This was the evening of Friday, June 17th, a week almost to the hour since Massimina had left her home in the village of Quinzano, frazione di Verona, and six days before, according to the instructions in the ransom letter, the Trevisans would be required to place a mere 800 million lire in a holdall in the first class compartment of the 7:52 Milan-Palermo espresso. After which, as far as Morris was concerned, two possibilities offered themselves: on the boat, south and east to Greece, or on the ferry to Sardinia and a more relaxing time at Gregorio's house – returning to Verona at the beginning of autumn with all tracks well covered. Who knows, he might even accept a couple of hours' teaching a week for a while so as not to surprise anybody too much.

The night of the 17th was a halfway house then, with everything going swimmingly, so far as Morris could see. It was the morning after, Saturday, June 18th, that he was to wake up with a splitting headache and a fever burning its way well up into the hundreds, his body slippery and stale with sweat, his eyes dry and red, his ears singing like an untuned radio and his bowels ringing out alarms. Morris was ill.

It had been an evening of celebration. Morris had insisted that a first night in Rome was an occasion to live it up a little, so they found a slightly better pensione than usual in the side streets behind Piazza Quirinale. (Who cared if it meant leaving his passport this time? Nobody seemed to be checking where he was and he'd phone the police Monday to say he was in Rome, he'd changed his plans.) They were checked in and had the bags in their room before six o'clock and then set out at once to stroll and wine and dine.

They walked to Piazza Venezia in a balmy evening air,

took a look at the decidedly ugly monument to Victor
Emanuel II, then followed Via dei Fori Imperiali with the
sun throwing long shadows in front of them on the warm tar
and colouring the huge curved walls of the Colosseum ahead.
He should have kept Giacomo's cameras perhaps, Morris
thought; he'd always wanted to take good photographs; it
was something he imagined he would be rather expert at.

(It was the unreality of those murders that amazed him.
You realized the world was probably full of murderers, war-
criminals, child molesters, who couldn't believe they'd really
done it. The truth was, everybody was capable of doing it,
only incapable of accepting they were capable. Every kitchen
knife was a murder weapon and everybody had killed a
thousand times over in their heads. It was just a question of
bringing the two together, the desire, the opportunity. 'Dad,
it amazes me that with a strong character like yours you never
killed anyone.' Unless he had? Skinny Binny had disappeared rather abruptly from his life, hadn't she? That was
food for thought, dictaphone fodder.)

Morris bought a guidebook and after the Colosseum they
doubled back to wander around what was open of the forum
itself and the Palatine until the paths were all closed at nine.
Massimina chattered her continual amazement, which was
tiresome, but not so much so that it could upset Morris's
genuine enjoyment of the ancient city. He had always wanted
to come and here it was, infinitely more impressive than the
poor weatherbeaten English ruins that cowered in the city
centres amongst the fluorescent lights of Co-ops and the
stained concrete of the sixties building spree. No, here there
was more of a oneness, a cohesion, something that drew
together the raging traffic and the ruins sprouting with olives
and orange trees, the long burning streets with their splendid
names like banners from the past, Via San Teodoro, Via
Botteghe Oscure.

Massimina chattered on and he didn't hear. He was
learning perhaps what every husband no doubt learns after
the first days of living together, that there is a time to listen
and a time to close one's ears against all that is frivolous about

148

femininity, all he could do without. But even while ignoring her, he realized he was enjoying her company, the promise of her physical proximity. The truth was perhaps that forced cohabitation was doing him a power of good (he was open to anything in the end). And then on the purely practical side, nobody questioned you when you were with somebody else, nobody tried to approach you or bother you like they would if you were alone (although in a way in fact he felt more blissfully alone than ever – and never worried about it precisely because there was someone there). Plus she had the impression that he was an authority on everything, which in comparison with herself quite naturally he was, and she asked his opinion on everything they saw, whether it was Michelangelo or a shirt to buy, which Morris found rather enjoyable. Recognition at last. It would be amusing, he thought, to take the girl back to England and present her to his father, have her parade about with her most arrogant of arrogant bras and tell Daddy-O in her broken English what a genius Morris was.

They sat in a restaurant spread out across the flagstones of Piazza Navona and ate tortellini with ham and cream, then veal with a side salad and finally ice-cream. The waiter was fast and dapper, the square full of young people, girls on bicycles, groups of young boys watching hungrily or dreamily, being watched in turn. The air had something definitely Latin and foreign about it, the smells, the temperature, a hint of anarchy, and Morris felt blissfully calm and secure. Who would ever find you out in such a city?

'Perhaps we should live here,' he said, and almost added, 'when your old mum pays up.'

'Mmm,' Massimina said. 'Let's.'

And most probably she was thinking how much more scope there would be to show herself off here. And why not? Morris conceded generously. The glory of the whole thing was precisely the show. He wasn't going to be possessive about the girl for God's sake, though she must learn not to sit quite so carelessly when she had short skirts on.

As they came back through Corso del Rinascimento some

teenagers were dancing round a Vespa blaring music from a cassette player. Their bodies moved gracefully in the last of an inky twilight and staring streetlamps. Massimina had drunk too much wine and wanted to join in, but Morris drew a line here.

'A disco then, Morri. Let's find a disco. You know I've never been to a real disco, Mamma never let me, she . . .'

Morris said he didn't like dancing. Despite nightfall the air was still very warm and this was one of the things that always made him feel delightfully far from home. He wanted to relax now, soak it up.

'But how can you not like dancing? It's just moving your body. It's just fun. Go on, there must be millions of discos round here and . . .'

Morris was adamant.

'I bet it's because you've never tried,' she said archly. 'You spent all those years at university reading books and things and you never even tried.'

And when Morris was silent, 'Go on, I'll show you. It's fun.'

As they went past the Pantheon and into Via Seminario, she said, 'Morri?' Her voice was softer than before. 'Morri, you haven't been out with many other girls, have you?'

It was precisely the kind of conversation to get right on his nerves and ruin a good day. He said nothing. Ignore it.

'I mean, when you, we . . .' She tried to hug tight to him, but he hurried. 'When we, when we did it the other day, together, I got the feeling it was the first time for you too and . . .'

'And what?' he snapped. God damn.

'I felt so happy, Morri. I mean, don't be angry, I'm so happy if you've never been with anybody before, it makes it so pure and right and . . .'

'Well it wasn't the first time,' he said sharply. And she began to cry. They sat in a bar then in Piazza Quirinale and Morris drank two carafes of Frascati almost entirely on his own.

'You're very cruel sometimes, Morrees,' she said when

they were undressing at last in the pensione. The room was freshly whitewashed with a huge old double bed, a few items of recently polished furniture, a crucifix over the bed, Madonna opposite, and the pleasure of a clean window complete with modern and operable blinds. A step up.

'You're not easy to be with sometimes,' she said.

'Sacrifice yourself then,' he said. His first damn day in Rome and she had to ruin it like this. 'Or go home to Mamma if you like.'

'Maybe I will,' she said.

What a farce.

'Maybe I will,' she repeated.

Over somebody's very dead body.

And now he woke up sick as a dog. At first he thought it must be just the excess of wine the previous night. He climbed out of bed, shivering violently and hurried down the passageway to the communal lavatory. Diarrhoea. Very nice. What a moment for it too. Oh God, he looked in the mirror to find his face positively grey and glistening with sweat. His forearms were prickling with goosepimples. He washed his face and hurried back to bed, head swaying from side to side, unable to think, unable to balance himself. He mustn't vomit was all. Not here in the passageway so as to draw attention to himself.

Back in the room he half raised the blinds and seeing it was light outside, tried to get dressed. He must stay on his feet or how was he to keep an eye on Massimina all day? But he couldn't. Bending down for a fresh shirt from his suitcase he almost passed out and had to stumble back to bed.

Massimina went out to buy milk and brioches for breakfast. Morris managed a few sips of milk but couldn't hold down the food at all. He laid his head back and groaned.

'I told you you shouldn't drink so much.'

Bang. A shot in the head from point-blank range. Blow her to bits. He was dying most probably, hunched up in an embryo, shivering, and she had to talk about drink.

Or was it a punishment from God?

Or venereal disease somehow? What if . . .

She fluffed up his pillow. 'I'll go and have a word with the padrona. If I explain the situation I'm sure she'll let me have a change of sheets. You're sopping with sweat.'

'No,' Morris began, 'really, I . . .'

'You do what you're told when you're ill,' she said stoutly, with what was obviously her mother's voice. His own mother's too, come to think of it, her odd days of revenge with Dad when he was felled by his filthy colds. 'For your own good,' the archetypal woman was still lecturing him ('My own good'll be the death of me' – Dad, mid 1960s). She left the room. He felt too weak to follow. Too weak altogether, the muscles in his shoulder were twitching. Somebody could make a fortune, he thought, insuring criminals against illness during action. Advertize in the specialized press.

He must have dozed because when he looked at his watch again it was nearly eleven. She'd been gone an hour and still wasn't back. Morris heaved himself onto his elbows, alarmed. She had discovered something, spoken to somebody, read a newspaper, gone to the police. He would have to get up, get out. But he couldn't get up. He reached under the bed instead and fished for a while till he found his case and dragged it out, smothered in dustballs. (You wanted to live well, artistically, generously, to move gracefully among beautiful things thinking clear and accurate thoughts, and what happened? You ended up dying of some filthy Latin disease in a cheap hotel where nobody had swept under the beds for months – and he had thought the place above average!) He scrabbled through layers of clothes in the case until he came across the dictaphone, then lay back in the damp sheets.

'Dear Dad, I'm in Rome, where I appear to be suffering from some kind of serious illness.' Morris shivered. Just the effort of speaking and clicking the thing on and off was exhausting. His blond hair was sodden with sweat. 'What I ask myself about the major events of my life is . . .' Well, what was it? There was something. He had certainly meant to say something. It should be on the tip of his tongue.

There was something deep down he had really always thought about all this – himself, Dad, Mum, women, his life, his end. Something that explained it all in a nutshell, that the world ought to know. And why shouldn't he have profound and recordable thoughts? He had been to Cambridge with the best of them (the finals were a mere formality). And if he was going to die here, because this was serious, he could feel it – and he would rather die than simply be arrested anyway (would he? really?) – if he was going to die and they found out all about it then he would like these tapes to be published as a kind of justification, because they'd be falling over each other to condemn him of course, nothing better than someone they could trample all over and condemn without seeing anything of themselves there, as if they were condemning some kind of monster from outer space or something. Look at the fun they'd had with the terrorists. As if none of them would have given genital Giacomo the good hiding he deserved.

Morris played back the last sentence, '. . . ask myself about the major events of my life is . . .' The batteries were running down, damn it. His voice sounded heavy and comically drawn out. (Fate's last little joke? To leave him batteryless on his deathbed.) So now he tried to finish very fast. Partly because he felt tired too. God knows, he didn't have time to start a university thesis or anything. '. . . is how much of this is destiny and how much I chose myself. (Would I have killed Giacomo, for example, a psychoanalyst might ask, if his sexual promiscuity hadn't reminded me of yours, Dad? Or did I do it just for my own convenience?) Destiny or choice, then, or as if maybe the two are somehow interlinked and destiny has simply offered, and will go on offering, the choices I was made to take, that it knew I would and will take in a certain way despite the freedom . . .'

There were quick footsteps and somebody fiddled a moment with a key in the lock. Morris just managed to drop the dictaphone in his bag and roll back across the bed before Massimina came in. She was weighed down with two shopping bags and carrying a sheaf of newspapers and magazines under her arm. Her lightly freckled face was bright and busy.

'Slip this under your tongue and read the papers while I go and get the fresh sheets. The padrona, she's called Signora Ligozzi by the way, said they wouldn't be ready till eleven.'

Morris found a thermometer in his mouth and a copy of *La Mattina* in his hand.

RIMINI MURDERS, NEW FACTS, NEW MYSTERY. The article seemed to leap at him from the bottom right-hand corner. He even felt the pain of it striking his naked eyes. How could she not have seen it? He felt at once extremely grateful to her for being so thoughtful; she saw he liked reading papers, so she got him them (when had anybody bothered so much with him before?), and at the same time it was as if he was sinking into a nightmare, trapped in a space that was hotter and darker and more bloody and suffocating with every moment that passed. If he couldn't watch her then the only logical thing to do was . . . Morris was sick, his vision was blurring. His fingers trembled with the pages as she went out of the room and he sucked the thermometer, hard. He had never meant to kill anyone.

> Police have now definitely established that only one assailant was involved in the horrific murders that left two lovers lying in a pool of blood in their hotel room in Rimini, Thursday evening.

Pool of blood was a gross exaggeration, and lovers they most certainly were not. Adulterers was the word they should have used. He and Massimina were far more lovers than they were.

> So it is clear now that the murderer tried to return to the slaughter soon after the crime and from various fingerprints found on the door, police are convinced he was not able to enter, having closed and thus locked the door on his first exit. The question Inspector Rodari and his team must now answer then, is . . .'

At the sound of voices approaching down the corridor, Morris folded open the newspaper to page two and almost bit the head off the thermometer.

His temperature was 41. Multiply by 9/5 and add 32. No, he couldn't do it. High anyway, if the distance from the normal line was anything to go by. Higher than he'd ever had since mumps. The padrona, Signora Ligozzi, a big-boned, no-nonsense woman with a studied under-the-weather-but-bearing-up look about her and a pile of starched sheets in her arms, considered her young guests dubiously.

'Better see a doctor.'

'Right,' Massimina agreed and asked Morris if he had his health card with him.

Morris lay back watching from glassy eyes how flies whirled around the centre of the room. He managed a weak smile for Signora Ligozzi, which surprisingly drew a very warm motherly smile back. Obviously Massimina had told her something, softened her up in some way. ('We're running away together. We're getting married next month.') So that now the woman was going to be indulgent. No, he hadn't got his health card, he said, and didn't want to see a doctor. He had a thing about doctors. It was just a touch of diarrhoea, or something like that, a bug, something in the food he'd eaten yesterday maybe, and if Massimina got him something for it from the chemist that would be fine, it would go away in a day or so.

Massimina wanted to insist, but Signora Ligozzi changed her tune now and said she knew what he meant about not wanting to see a doctor; the problems they'd given her over the tiniest little polyps she'd had, being pushed from one doctor to another for examinations and signatures for authorizations for further examinations and long waits in surgeries and hospitals exposed to all the diseases everybody else had and then after wasting the best part of a month rushing around worrying herself near to death, the last doctor, the big consultant specialist, decided the whole thing was nothing at all, prescribed her a cream she could have bought at the chemist in the first place and that was the end of it.

Morris tried to enthuse to this conversation, but found his voice was breaking. When was the last time he'd been ill? A century ago. It *must* be a punishment. He tried to remember how stupid that idea had seemed when he had read the same thing about Raskolnikov – no, he must hold onto reason. But then he began to cough. Signora Ligozzi came over and put a hand on his forehead (as if there was any need for that crap now they had the evidence of the thermometer).

'You need clean sheets and a good sleep, *caro mio*,' she announced, and a moment later Morris was being bundled away to the bathroom in his drenched pyjamas with a blanket round his shoulders so he could sit on the loo while they made up the bed. They enjoyed playing mother of course. They enjoyed the reversal of normal roles, the strong man weak, the second fiddle happily taking the place of the first (and for Signora Ligozzi there was a few days' steady rent). Well, let them. Morris's only chance he thought now was to play ill enough to keep the girl by his bedside twenty-four hours a day like a guardian angel at death's door. He scooped up the newspapers and padded off to the bathroom.

She had bought *La Mattina* and *La Stampa*, neither of which would have anything about the Verona kidnap, Morris could be certain. Plus a few mags. *Panorama*, political, *Europeo*, likewise, and *Gente* which was just gossip, pictures of abundant girls with famous footballers and the like (got that for herself presumably). All safe as houses. He sat on the toilet, reread the Rimini article, tore it out and flushed it away. Tomorrow there would be nothing at all most probably. They'd made all the discoveries they were going to make and without new developments a murder wasn't worth anything after three days. And rightly so. Even he was beginning to get a bit bored by it. What was done was done. Morris leafed quickly through *Gente*, waiting to be called back to bed, and was about to put the thing down and relax (his bowels felt so weak, so shivery shivery), when a tiny item in the curiosities column caught his eye.

KIDNAP VICTIM SENDS GET WELL CARD.
Hopes were raised on Wednesday morning for the fate
of kidnap victim Massimina Trevisan when her family
received a get well card addressed to the girl's
grandmother who was seriously ill at the moment when
Massimina disappeared. Posted in Rimini and bearing
the message, 'Hope you're better now, I'll be back
soon,' the card was believed to indicate that the
kidnappers had established a human relationship with
the girl and were unlikely to carry out their threat to kill
her. It is the first known kidnap of a purely criminal
nature in which such a letter has been sent. Sadly,
Massimina's grandmother was not able to see the card
as she died less than a week after the girl's
disappearance.

What crappy writing, Morris thought as he stumbled down
the passageway back to his own bedroom. (He seemed to be
in a dream. He didn't believe it, couldn't take it seriously.) If
the kidnappers really had let a girl send a get well card he was
sure as a journalist he could have made a better story of it
than that. KIDNAP VICTIM'S MESSAGE JUST TOO LATE FOR
CROAKING GRANDMA. Something like that. But Morris had
applied for work with every halfway decent and indecent
newspaper in the British Isles with negative results.

What it did mean of course was that Massimina was less
likely than ever to suspect anything. She had mailed the
letter with her own hands.

Only a week to go now.

Morris shivered in the dim corridor, his hand on the door.
Stop. Wouldn't the police be surprised the kidnappers didn't
know Granny was dead? The criminals would be bound to be
reading the *Arena* every day, no? So the police would reason.
And if they knew, how could it be considered humane and
kind to let the girl send the card? Unless they were playing a
game with him perhaps. Perhaps the card had said something else. The card had given it away ('Morris sends his
love'), and now they were just waiting for him to phone with
all their tracking and tapping equipment at the ready so they

could nail his location once and for all and swoop. And then the Rimini post-mark – they must already have linked it up with Giacomo, with that copy of the *Arena* open on the bed beside the corpses. How could they miss it?

Morris breathed deeply, leaning against the wall. His forehead was bursting with sweat and his stomach was in knots. He closed his eyes. Was it possible he had been hallucinating? Still was? He should read the article again. But he had already flushed it down the loo. For a moment, with strangely perfect lucidity, he imagined a juggler who, in the middle of his most famous act, sees one more ball in the air than he thought he had thrown. Oh for another hand to catch it with!

## 15

Rome hummed outside Morris's bedroom window. The great metropolis he'd barely glimpsed, cradle of the culture and heritage he aspired to and yearned to be able to afford – it was all just a stone's throw away. Traffic throbbed in a distant street while somebody beat a tennis ball against the wall below his window. Caesar had been murdered not half a mile from here. St Paul had defended himself at the emperor's court. Michelangelo had worked just down the street. And instead of enjoying it all, soaking it up, Morris had to shiver there under a mountain of covers. He had to keep Massimina busy, he had to reflect on the fact that Signora Ligozzi still held his passport, he had to scrutinize each morning's paper with red and burning eyes to be quite sure there wasn't anything he couldn't let Massimina see. And even after checking every column inch of the thing, still when she casually picked it up and began to leaf through page after page, licking the tips of her fingers under the now painted nails ('I want to look nice for you, Morri, even when you're ill.') – still he could barely keep himself from biting his own nails in anxiety. All the old aplomb was gone.

The second morning Signora Ligozzi brought up an ancient valve radio and plugged it in beside the bed; for something to listen to, she said, seeing as he was stuck there for a while. And so now Morris had to keep his eye on that too and was scared of falling asleep lest Massimina should hear something on the news. He tried to keep it almost solidly on classical music and opera and the only spoken broadcasts he would listen to were the Radical Party's election phone-in and Radio Moscow's afternoon readings from the Black Book of Capitalist Imperialism. He really wouldn't mind working for Radio Moscow, and if the worst came to the worst . . .

'Your mother votes Christian Democrat?' he asked Massimina.

'Papà was going to be a Christian Democrat MP when he died.'

'Oh really. And you?'

She didn't know, she said. She wasn't interested in politics.

'You'd vote Christian Democrat,' he said. She was sitting by the window watching out and even that he envied her. Why was it always Morris who had to get the worst of a bad deal? All he could see, supine and shivering where he was, were the wooden feet of Christ crucified (rather clumsily) above him.

'You'd vote Christian Democrat because without them, all your money and property would dissolve away in a few years. I mean, if they started to tax people properly in this country, if they made people pay all the taxes they're supposed to, that is . . .'

'Mamma pays all her taxes.'

'I bet she doesn't.' He'd have burst out laughing if he hadn't been afraid of throwing up.

Massimina didn't want to argue. 'So what would you vote?'

'Me? Communist. For honesty and equity in the forma-tion of the New Man,' he added, which was something he had picked up from Radio Tirhana. 'Except after we're married I'll probably vote Christian Democrat like you. I'll have a vested interest.'

'No, Morri. If you believe it's right to vote Communist, then vote Communist. I don't care. Understand? I don't care about any of this money. As long as we can be happy together I don't care what happens.'

'But who is it always keeping the purse strings tight, cara?'

'Oh Morrees, why do you have to say these things? I don't know anything about politics and money. I only know that we have less than five hundred thousand now and . . .'

And he had made her cry. She didn't seem to appreciate, Morris thought, that seeing as he was English he'd never be able to vote in Italy anyway.

Pensione Quirinale was three battered though still genteel floors run by the widowed Signora Ligozzi and a mentally retarded daughter. The son was working as a cook in London, a large Italian restaurant in Clapham of all places; so that once Morris had begun to improve, the signora came up on a number of occasions to talk to him about England and when would be the best time to make a long delayed visit because Franco had a *fidanzata* now and she didn't want them to go and marry before she'd had a chance to meet the girl.

To Clapham, never, was Morris's opinion, but he plumped on September for some reason and extolled the virtues of Clapham Common in early autumn (the sun trailing its colours over yellowing horse chestnuts, the blacks straddled over their bicycles, turbaned Indians head down, hurrying to wherever turbaned Indians hurry to; and hunched behind this dubious oasis of green and dogshit there would be the remains of that great waste of industry that was the glorious past, plus those awful, awful houses that decayed away no sooner than some optimist had sacrificed his life savings to renovate them). But you couldn't say these things. You had to be kind. And if the lady nursed harmless illusions it was scarcely Morris's business to carve them up. He wasn't cruel.

'Clapham's a nice area,' he said.

Yes, she knew, she said. Franco had told her and sent postcards.

Postcards? Of Clapham? Morris said nothing.

Over the next few days Morris was to discover that Signora Ligozzi was particularly proud of the fact that her son was making a success of things in *England*, as if the Anglo-Saxon culture were somehow a step up in the world and Morris had made a pitiful mistake moving south to the land of mis-government and disorder. The bug he had caught she took as a confirmation of this opinion and she asked him constantly when he was going back and what sort of job he intended to take up when he got there. (Would he be anywhere near Clapham? Could he take a tin of *amaretti* to Franco?) He and Massimina should get married as soon as Morris was better and then go back directly, she advised. Morris sighed with relief when she left the room and Massimina giggled. Not that she wouldn't be very happy to go to England if Morris wanted . . .

On the second afternoon of his illness with his temperature down to 101 (his faculty for mental arithmetic had returned too), Signora Ligozzi moved them into a larger room on the other side of the building away from the fierce sunshine that beat on the windows of the south side. Morris collapsed on the huge double bed under a sad, gilt-framed photograph of a young man in uniform and looked out at a blank blue sky. This had been where she and her husband had slept, Signora Ligozzi smiled and hurried off to her cleaning. The room cost five thousand a night more than the other one.

All in all there were nine other rooms in the pensione, mostly taken up by foreigners, thank heaven, which reduced the likelihood of Massimina's striking up dangerous conversations. The only real problem was that Signora Ligozzi insisted on asking any American or English-speaking visitors if they would be so kind as to go up and talk to Morris and keep him company every now and then. On the third morning there was a graduate student from Yale who bored him for hours with endless questions about the Cambridge English department, comparisons with Yale, and, worst of all, detailed accounts of his thesis on a Structuralist Interpretation of Phantoms in Narrative.

Massimina left the room with an enjoy-yourselves-together smile almost as soon as the conversation began (who could blame her?) so that Morris didn't know where on earth she'd got to for a solid two-and-a-half hours, which left his nerves raw amidst the fog of what seemed an interminable headache. The police would be in there handcuffing him, he thought, before Ronnie Gutenberg had finished with his phonemes and phantasms. Thank God he'd left university anyway, rather prison than that. At least he didn't go around boring people to death. Then when Gutenberg had triumphantly resolved the function of Hamlet's father, the only remark Morris could make was that surely a real ghost was more interesting than one that turned out to be just a narrative sign slipped in by the author. (If Giacomo or Sandra came back to loom all bloody and beaten over his bedside? See if he could write that off as a complex introduction of the objective third person into dramatic narrative!) But Gutenberg was argumentative and said that sounded like a typical piece of Cambridge anti-contemporaryism (even the word conservative was out of fashion apparently). Morris grinned a weak devil's-advocate-found-out grin and said he needed some sleep.

Later it turned out Massimina had gone to a church in Via Umiltà to pray for him and afterwards she had asked the priest what documents they would need to get married. Romeo and Juliet stuff.

'You'll have to go to a *questura* for a *permesso di soggiorno* and a certificate of good conduct.'

'As soon as I'm better,' Morris promised. Good conduct! *Four more days.*

June is the beginning of the watermelon season and Massimina fed Morris great juicy red slices cooled in Signora Ligozzi's fridge and served with Signora Ligozzi's spoons. She changed Morris's sheets, rubbed cream into his skin and anti-dandruff lotion into his scalp and each long evening she read to him from *I Promessi Sposi*. This having himself read to, and from this book in particular, Morris regarded as a confirmation that genius was still shining in his feverish brain.

First, he had always wanted to read *I Promessi Sposi* – it was considered a sine qua non of understanding Italian culture, was it not? Second, it kept Massimina happily by his side and thus out of harm's way, partly because it touched just the romantic chord the dear girl was after and partly because it gave her the impression of being allowed to enter into that area of Morris's character she admired most, his intellect and cultured educational background. Third, and this was rather a surprise, he discovered that Massimina read quite well; her usual giggly and sometimes jarring voice evened out into the long periods of Manzoni's great character descriptions and she read with a remarkable dramatic sense and intelligence which made her failure at school quite interesting from an educational point of view. Something else one might look into later with time and money on one's hands. So all in all it was a wonderful way to pass the evening, if only he hadn't felt so shivery and ill, and then nervous too every time they heard the phone ring down in the hallway, or when more than usually decisive footsteps climbed the stairs.

Morris's illness had temporarily cut out any further sexual activities. But at the same time, because of the heat, Massimina moved around the room for most of the day very scantily dressed in just the green cotton skirt they'd bought in Vicenza and then one of his own loose white shirts, often completely open at the front (extraordinary how quickly she'd lost any sense of modesty with him), so that from his bed, from day to day more comfortable as the fever receded, he was able to follow the lines and movements of her body most carefully, the slight bounce of all her flesh as she walked barefoot across the boards, the way her breasts changed shape from standing to bending to sitting to lying, the pucker of her face as she concentrated on reading aloud, occasionally making as if to toss back the long hair she no longer had, a gesture that set her nipples a-quiver. (Yes, he would definitely buy a camera once he had the money. He might even paint, damn it. Who knew what precious stones the ILEA mightn't have left unturned.) When she sat cross-legged on the bed, creasing her brow over the melon she was feeding him, he was able to follow the soft soft contours of the skin that crept up from her knees to inside the skirt, whitening as it went. It was all novelty to him. And Morris thought really, as long as a woman was well-trained and stayed young, he wouldn't mind spending a lifetime with her at all.

On the fourth day in bed, sitting up and bright now, he persuaded her to cut away the hair under her armpits which had been bothering him (did you ever see a statue or painting with hair under its armpits?); and when she wouldn't actually razor them because she was afraid of cutting herself, Morris offered to do it himself with his own razor and she lathered under her arms and he did it without cutting her at all. (It would be the same with children, he thought, doing things for them, modelling them, the poor man's only chance to be an artist in the end. If only he could wangle his way out of all this.)

The fifth morning finally, a scorching Thursday, Morris had to slip the tip of the thermometer into his tea to get it over normal. A moment later, feeling right back to his usual self, he switched on the radio and for the first time braved the national news. Why not? What could there possibly be after nearly two weeks had passed since the kidnap, six days since Giacomo and Sandra?

Nine o'clock: the Russians had rejected an offer on nuclear missiles, the Italian political parties were making their final campaign statements before the elections on Sunday. The reader went through the headlines with a clatter of fake typewriters in the background to add a sense of urgency. The engineering union was coming out on strike over contracts, fifteen more mafia arrests in Palermo – Morris sipped his morning tea – 'and in a development in the Rimini murders case, police are now looking for a young blond man and his girlfriend known to have been staying in a pensione not far from the victims' hotel. The young man was seen in the victims' hotel shortly before the murder and is believed to have eaten . . .'

'*Morri! Come mai?* What on earth are you . . .'

He tumbled across the bed and snapped the thing off.

'I want to get up. I feel fine.'

'But you have a temperature of . . .'

Morris was on his feet, already rummaging for a shirt. Just today and tonight to get through, just today and tonight and then tomorrow morning around noon the train would be in

Stazione Termini: he'd pick up the money, train out to Civitavecchia, then the boat to Sardinia where . . . but he could decide on that when they got there. He wasn't obliged to think about that now. The thing was to get his passport off that woman downstairs and get out now before the newspapers were full of identikits.

Morris dressed and looked himself over in the mirror. He was quite conspicuously pale of course, his forehead more furrowed than he remembered it and the whole face a shade drawn, especially about the eyes. But he was okay. He would make it.

Massimina came and stood behind him: she rested her chin on his shoulder so that their two faces were reflected together, his thin and sharp and straight, hers wide and round with two full lips that pouted a smile, plus the little silver St Christopher of Giacomo's around her neck. Morris kissed her spontaneously. He put an arm round her and kissed her on her mouth, pulling her soft body into him.

What would he do without Massimina?

'Don't you think you should rest at least one more day, *caro*?'

'I thought we'd get a train down to the beach for the day and take it easy. Get some fresh air. Then I'll phone a friend of mine in Sardinia who's always inviting me out there and see if we can't spend a week or two by the sea. Before getting married,' he added.

'Morri.' She kissed his ear. 'But I thought you wanted to see Rome.'

'I don't think I can face it now. Trailing round a city. I feel too weak.'

And he did. Weak at the knees and in the bowels. Too weak to go down and settle everything with Signora Ligozzi, face to face. Who knew what she mightn't have heard on the radio, seen in the papers, what photofit pictures she mightn't have contemplated over her morning coffee? He sent Massimina, saying he would pack himself. He turned on the radio and worked quickly, folding his clothes into the suitcase. He was really looking forward to buying some new stylish clothes, something one could really cut a figure in, a change anyway from the endless round of two pairs of trousers and half a dozen T-shirts. And for her too. There would be bazaars and designers' shops in Sardinia no doubt. And if the money went back into her family in the end (if they got married and bought themselves a house) then where was the crime in it all? Nowhere.

While he was waiting for her to come back, Morris folded Massimina's things over the top of his own. T-shirts, two skirts, bras and pants. How on earth were you supposed to fold a bra? It was so curious being alongside someone who wore these different things. Who had a completely different inside from oneself. Could you imagine climbing into tiny pants like that, for example? The whole crotch part would feel totally different. Perhaps it would be fun one day to try out each other's clothes just to see how . . . Damn, the girl was taking forever. Morris suddenly zipped the case shut and looked quickly around the room. He had to hurry. He had to get out. Not sit here fiddling.

All set. He carried the cases downstairs, surprised to find how powerless and exhausted he felt. On the second landing he had to stop for a breather. He really was ill still, damn it. Which seemed a justification for everything.

'*Buon giorno, Signor Duckworth, buon giorno, come va?*'

Not so loud with the name, Morris thought. Two or three people were lounging in the tiny little lobby-cum-sitting room where Signora Ligozzi did business with her guests. The room smelt surprisingly of French cigarettes this morning. Morris smiled a wan, convalescent's smile and said *buon giorno*. Where was Massimina? Yes, perhaps he should stay just a day longer but he wanted to go to the sea and get some fresh air. He kissed the old woman on both cheeks and thanked her warmly for her kindness.

'Your young lady is just writing down her address for me so we can all keep in touch.'

'Good,' Morris gasped, turning abruptly to see Massimina standing at the makeshift reception desk, scribbling.

'It's under T,' she said, 'for Trevisan. I've put the phone number too.'

Signora Ligozzi barely looked at the thing and slipped the slim red address book high up on a shelf behind the desk. '*Grazie mille*. If I go to England I'll let you know so that I can bring you something back if you like.'

'*Bene, bene. Grazie infinite.*'

He had to get that book! Had to. It was one thing having his own name down in the register and quite another having hers there in the address book. Her surname. Because it would be her name in the paper after all at the end of the day, not his. (And why in God's name did they have to leave addresses like that when neither of them really had the slightest damn intention of ever seeing the other again? Rome was four hundred miles from Verona.)

Out in the street he said, 'Mimi, let's buy her some flowers. She's been so nice.'

Massimina thought it was a good idea. She wouldn't spend money on the rapido of course but she was willing to throw it away like this without a second thought so long as she could feel generous. They found a florist's on Via 24 Maggio. Morris didn't know anything about choosing flowers, he said, so he'd leave her to it while he popped a little further down the street for a paper.

It was a small newsagent's without an *Arena*, but the 'Cronaca' section on page four of *La Mattina* had a report on the Rimini case. Morris drew his breath. There was an identikit picture the spitting image of himself. He leaned against a traffic light and read, the paper trembling in his hands.

. . . Signor Alfredo Todeschini, owner of a pensione in Via Fama, admitted that he had let the couple have a room for three nights without seeing any documents or even putting a name on the register. The couple seemed very happy he said, as if they were running away from home and wanted to keep themselves to themselves. The blond man had a marked foreign accent, but Signor

Todeschini was unable to say where from. In the couple's room police have found a number of prints which correspond to those found on the door of the victims' room. The motive of the atrociously violent attack remains obscure, though police feel fairly certain that they must be dealing with some kind of maniac, or at least a mentally unstable criminal. All border points have been alerted under the assumption that the murderer may be a foreign tourist who will soon try to return home. Interpol has been asked to co-operate by providing information on similar unsolved crimes in other countries. Police said they would be considering bringing charges against Signor Todeschini and other hotel owners who failed to register guests.

Marked accent, my arse, he hadn't even managed to identify the country. 'Atrociously violent' was another newspaper cliché. What other kind of attack did they want? A rather gentle murder was committed today . . .

Morris gazed at the identikit. They had missed something about the eyes, and the bridge of the nose was too narrow. But all in all it was pretty good. He could grow a beard of course, but that was exactly what they would be expecting, a week's scrub of a beard would give him away immediately. (And if Signor Amintore Cartuccio of Gucci's saw the picture, if he read about the blond hair and the accent. What then?)

Massimina returned with a spray of roses, which seemed inappropriate to Morris, though he didn't venture an opinion. They sat for a while over cappuccinos at a small café in Via Mazzarino and Massimina said if he felt so ill perhaps they should just get the train back to Verona right away where he could be in his own flat and see the doctor and so on and . . .

But he hadn't even said anything, Morris protested. He hadn't said he felt ill. But he looked so pale, she said, and seemed so listless and down that . . .

He wasn't going back to Verona until after they were married, Morris said firmly, otherwise her mother would find some way of ruining it all. Massimina was solemn. After paying the bill at the pensione, she said, they only had two hundred thousand lire left which meant . . .

But they wouldn't have to spend anything once they got to Sardinia; Morris struggled to stay patient – why the hell did she have to bother him with this crap now?

So why didn't they go directly to Sardinia today?

Because Morris felt too weak to travel a long distance today.

(Just hold on one more day and the jackpot was his.)

He kept them sitting at the café until nearly eleven before going back to the pensione. Signora Ligozzi should have started cleaning the rooms upstairs by now. She had. Morris stayed in the lobby and sent Massimina up to look for her with the flowers. He glanced round quickly at the shadowy space where just one or two tourists lounged in ancient armchairs with their guidebooks and foreign papers open on their laps. He reached up above the desk, took down the address book, found 'T', released the spring mechanism that held the pages, removed the page, folded it in his pocket, snapped the spring home again and put the book back. But then he changed his mind. He took the book down again, found a spare page in the back, inserted it in the 'T' section and wrote, 'Massimina T . . .' Think of another name that began with 'T', an Italian name. But he couldn't, damn it. He didn't seem to know any other Italian names that began with 'T'. Tibaldo, Tramonto, Toloncino, but he was inventing. Who knew if they were really names or not? Oh God. Until something came back to him from the newspaper. Todeschini, the man with the pensione. Massimina Todeschini, and he scribbled a false address and phone number.

'Morri, Signora Ligozzi's out for a minute.' Massimina was at the bottom of the stairs with the retarded daughter who was twisting her mouth awfully to speak.

'Out?' (To phone the police?)

'Yes.'

But she had a phone here. She wouldn't have gone out.

'What are you doing?'

'I just wanted to check you'd put the Verona code with your phone number, you know how much bother it is looking for things like that.' And he slipped the book back. They left the roses on the desk with a message and set off for the station.

Massimina thought perhaps instead of going to the beach Morris should go to the *Questura* and sort out his documents for when they could get married; but Morris pointed out that the *Questura* in Rome would be much more of a crush than some quiet country place in Sardinia and anyway it always took a few days to get any document from the Italian bureaucracy and so if they weren't going to be here after tomorrow it wasn't worth it. And this was true.

'You're sure you want to get married, Morri?' She wasn't so much suspicious as simply after another of those lovey dovey moments again, like when they'd looked in the mirror together.

Yes, he told her and kissed her forehead. He really did.

If only it were that easy.

'You're a real nut for newspapers,' she said on the train out to the Lido as he scrutinized the *Arena* he'd managed to pick up in the huge station newsagent's. There was nothing about the ransom letter. Which was as it should be this time.

'I like to feel I'm part of things,' he said and he read her an article about town council proposals to put a plastic cover over Verona's huge Roman amphitheatre, an idea which made good old traditional Massimina quite indignant.

The beach at Lido di Roma is vast and on this particular day the sea was blue and the weather kind. Morris and Massimina hired a sunshade in the third row and Morris lay down and closed his eyes while Massimina read from *I Promessi Sposi*.

Morris listened only intermittently and it occurred to him that when he had a bit more time to relax and do as he pleased he might actually write a rather better book with the same title where the hero out of penury and desperation kidnaps a

171

girl but then falls in love with her and she with him and they decide he must give himself up and they will marry. But the police of course insist on putting the lad away for most of his life and the two can only see each other once a month across the grille of the prison visiting room and she dies of a broken heart while he wastes hopelessly away.

This was such a subtle little plot, he thought, and so amusing that he began to laugh out loud and when Massimina asked why, he told her the story (why not?) and she said yes, it was terrific, it would make a marvellous book or even film and she'd always thought just from the way he spoke and from the letters he wrote that Morris would make a marvellous writer. They laughed together under the sunshade. Only it would be better, maybe, she said, if during the actual kidnap, at the beginning, something goes wrong and he goes and kills somebody by accident. The girl falls in love with him and she makes a terrific effort to forgive him and to understand about him being poor and so on, but the crime destroys any hopes they have for the future.

Morris sat up, trembling. *She didn't know. She couldn't.*

'Good idea,' he said, clearing his throat to hide a broken voice. 'So what happens?'

'At the end?' She was sprawled in the deckchair in her green and white costume. She looked so much more adult recently. Morris noticed how the elastic sank ever so slightly into the flesh around the top of her legs.

'Well,' she puckered her lips to think, all her freckles smiling, 'the girl says for him, the kidnapper, to go and collect the ransom and run away and then she'll go to the police as if she'd just been released and say she was blindfolded all along and didn't know who the kidnapper was and then when everything's safe they can meet normally and marry. But he, the boy, is overcome with remorse. He says he isn't worthy of her, refuses that way out, confesses to the police and is condemned to death and executed.'

'They don't have the death penalty here,' Morris told her

quickly. Did they? No. He was sure they didn't. You would have heard about executions every now and then. And they hadn't executed the terrorists, had they?

'Pity,' she laughed. Oh God, she was really enjoying herself. 'But you can always set the story in some country where they do.'

'You cruel thing,' Morris said and lay down again. The sun on his closed eyelids burnt deep reds and blues.

'I'd love it if you became a writer, Morri. I'd be so proud.'

'It doesn't pay,' he said.

All afternoon he watched the vast sea of flesh shifting across the beach, padding off for their ice-creams, or for a swim, or to the loo. There were slender girls and bulky old women and young boys running everywhere kicking up sand and waddling their plump little bums. How could you say life wasn't expendable! If a hand reached down from the sky now and removed someone from the beach? The lad scratching his mosquito bite, for example. Who could possibly care? (Had anybody, bar himself, really and truly wept for his mother? Did anyone remember her? Did he really remember her himself, or was it just part of his own life, a feeling, an atmosphere he remembered?) And when you thought of Asia! BBC documentaries of streets in Calcutta, a solid wall of dark skin, unimaginably thick with bodies, shifting and squirming like maggots in a fisherman's bait box. Life, Morris thought, was like being in a burning cinema. You had to get well out of the crowd and the crush or you were dead.

'If we really want to save a bit of money,' he said towards six in the evening, 'why don't we sleep on the beach?'

And that was what they did. Ate in a restaurant, ham and mushroom pizza, then strolled through the town till late quite happily (truly) arm in arm and finally down to the beach at nearly midnight to stretch out their towels hidden between the deserted sunshades and try to sleep. Which saved registering at any more hotels, showing passports.

'I wonder what Mamma and Grandma are doing now?' Massimina whispered. She held his hand and squeezed it lightly from time to time. Heat lightning flickered out at sea. 'I was thinking today, maybe we should just go back now and have done with it. To Verona. I mean, I don't think they could do anything now. Not when they've seen how close we are and how happy together.'

'If you really want,' Morris said.

'I just don't want them to worry too much.'

He laughed indulgently. 'Why should they worry after all the letters and postcards we've sent? They can't have had so much post in years.'

'I know,' she said. 'I'm just being stupid, I suppose,' and she giggled nervously in the warm air.

'When we get to Sardinia,' Morris said, 'there'll be a phone and you can call them from there.'

## 16

Morris was rather pleased with himself for not having rushed to Stazione Termini too early and got himself caught there for hours trying to explain to Massimina why they didn't take the first of the frequent trains out to Civitavecchia and the boat. No, he had timed it perfectly. Their local from the Lido pulled in at a quarter to one, leaving them barely fifteen minutes to book tickets to Civitavecchia and check out the ferry times before the espresso would arrive from Milan. Then ten more minutes before their own train. Morris even felt an unexpected tinge of gratitude towards the Italian railway system which as yet showed no sign of letting him down. In her excitement at the prospect of a long boat trip Massimina had now forgotten all ideas of going home, and, ordering their tickets in the great throbbing entrance hall of the station, they felt quite like a regular holiday couple, her with her straw hat on and him with a bit more colour to his cheeks after yesterday.

To waste a couple of minutes he took her to buy a pair of sunglasses. (Why on earth hadn't he thought of that before?) His choice was the biggest and roundest and darkest pair there were and after something of a squabble over the price (she was right, it was absurdly high, but they were designer frames as the shop attendant patiently explained) the glasses were bought. Stepping out of the shop and back into the station, the p.a. announced the imminent arrival of the Milan-Palermo espresso on platform six. Right on the nail. Morris looked at his watch and told Massimina he just wanted to phone his friend in Sardinia to let him know when they were arriving more or less. In the meanwhile she should wait on platform fifteen where the train for Civitavecchia would leave.

Sensing her eyes following him, he went towards the station S.I.P. as she would expect. And had a stroke of genius. He did have four or five minutes before the espresso actually pulled in. The idea was right. He slipped into a booth and phoned the Verona police directly. Inspector Marangoni was out for lunch, but his assistant, Tolaini, was available.

'No developments then?' An apparently very discouraged Morris.

'No, Signor Duckworth. Nothing significant.'

'You didn't find that man on the bus?'

'Not a trace.'

'But I don't understand it. Surely if someone has kidnapped her they'd ask for a ransom or something, I mean . . .'

'Well,' the young detective was hesitant, but obviously happy to talk. He was there manning the phone through a lonely lunch break after all. 'Obviously we're expecting some kind of ransom demand any moment, but there's been nothing so far. My own personal suspicion is that somebody may have managed to get in touch with the family behind our backs and be arranging a deal without telling us.'

'Oh, I see. Is that normal?'

'So far as any of these things are, yes. It's a pretty desperate situation for the mother of course and the family of the victim have a natural tendency to think that the police aren't really doing enough and don't care and so on. From a psychological point of view it's a fairly well documented phenomenon.'

'I can imagine,' Morris said. He was positively itching to get at that train now. They didn't know a single damn thing. It would be rolling in any minute. Get on it and grab the cash. But he managed to go on talking to Tolaini with polite interest for a full two minutes more on his watch.

Platform six was in total confusion. All the better. On one side, to the right, the espresso was still hissing and clanking the last few yards down the oil-stained rails, while to the left a rapido to Venice was expected in at any moment. Soldiers, backpackers, old women, plus all the usual anonymous crowd buzzed about, jockeying for position, laughing and smoking, wishing they'd booked a seat no doubt, or hoping they'd be able to find the one they had booked. (How many hours in the corridor to Naples? The loos would be filthy.) Children whined and scampered and there was a group of toddlers all waving balloons in the care of a single ancient nun. Morris suddenly felt perfectly calm. It was a piece of cake.

The train was still. A slight final lurch and then every door was banging open and a great crowd of people tumbled out onto the platform into the equally eager crowd struggling to get in, each man and woman clutching his cumbersome bag and knocking it against the legs of all the others. Morris, without any baggage, pushed quickly through the mêlée glancing up at each compartment for the first-class stickers – and found the first one in the third carriage. He walked on to the fourth carriage, waited his turn in the confusion, climbed up and pushed his way down the corridor back to his goal. As soon as he was in the third carriage and the first-class section, the crowd eased off, the compartments were half empty: there were just one or two people standing around in the corridor smoking quietly. Which meant less cover of course. But then Morris wasn't expecting trouble.

An older man was standing outside the first compartment in a light silver-grey suit with thinning hair slicked back, watching the crowd outside. Plain-clothes policeman? They'd been taking him for a ride perhaps. And of course if they did know everything then naturally they'd give him that shit on the phone (and he shouldn't have posted the letter in Rome if he was going to collect here).

Except they couldn't know. They mustn't.

The compartment door was closed and all the blinds drawn. He couldn't see in. A trap? Morris bit his lower lip and tensed his body ready to spring into action. But the muscles still felt terribly weak. He had lost weight through the illness. He wasn't well. And then a scuffle was no good. If they knew about it, they'd be armed. If they knew about it, it was already too late.

To open the compartment door he had to squeeze round the man in the suit. (A suit in this weather? He had to be fake.)

'*Permesso.*' '*Prego, prego.*' Holding his breath, expecting the handcuffs at any moment, feeling them already on his wrist, Morris slid back the door. The compartment was in deep shade with only a pencil of light coming through from under the lowered blinds and just one middle-aged lady sat silent in a corner, head thrown back and mouth disturbingly open, breathing deeply. The air was stale with sleep.

His eyes went up to the luggage racks and two huge suitcases, hers and the man's outside presumably, matching Moroccan leather with bright buckles. They must be man and wife. And then above the woman's head a small brown holdall! Yes, as if he had dreamed it and there it was. As if he had willed it there.

Morris looked over his shoulder. The man by the window hadn't moved, appeared to be lighting a cigar. Morris took two steps to the far corner, lifted the holdall from the rack, stepped backwards, careful not to brush the woman's legs, and without waking her was already outside the compartment.

'*Permesso.*' He pulled the door to. The man in the grey suit glanced at him, curious, from over a cigar he was lighting.

'My wife went and left her bag there back in Milan,' Morris smiled a sweet smile with just a hint of 'you-know-what-women-are-like' about it. The man puffed, said nothing.

Morris hurried back up the corridor in the direction he had come and under his breath found himself muttering, 'Thank you God, thank you, thank you,' which was what he used to say after he read the exam results outside the headmaster's door. He laughed. Oh he had done it this time! He had really done it. If the money was in there, that is. But it must be, it . . .

Still in the corridor, feverish, Morris stopped a moment, balanced the holdall on one knee and pulled the zip. Clothes: T-shirts, blouses, skirts . . .? Yes, of course, he'd asked them to put the clothes on top. But underneath? A large man in overalls pushed out of a compartment, thrust himself past Morris and sent the precariously balanced bag tumbling to the floor. The neatly folded clothes spilled out.

'*Asino!*' Morris shouted involuntarily, desperately scrabbling after the thing. The corridor here in the second-class section was all a-bustle and people turned. Likewise the burly man in overalls. A wide aggressive face, low forehead, bulging eyes.

'*Dillo di nuovo e ti spacco la testa.* I'll smash your face in.' The man seemed ready to spit. '*Nessuno mi chiama asino!*'

At the first hint of trouble a half-silence fell on the scene. Morris, trying to bundle back the clothes, saw the stacks of fifty thousand lire notes tied in elastic bands in the bottom of the case, visible to all. Oh God, get the clothes in quick.

'*Mi scusi, mi scusi, colpa mia,*' Morris croaked. 'My fault. You know how it is in the rush.'

He was on his feet now. Incredibly, nobody had noticed. Traffic began to flow again down the corridor. Only a little boy was watching him agape. The burly man grunted and pushed along ahead, Morris following timidly. And at the first door he was out. Free! And the air seemed so fresh after the stale sweat and nerves of the train. Free. Rich! He should have brought a suitcase though, so he could have switched over the money now and got rid of this garbage, because Massimina was going to wonder where . . .

'Hey man, well would you fucking-well believe it! Morris buddy!'

He looked up. Was it a nightmare or what? He was hearing voices now. The platform was throbbing with movement, a great wave of passengers pushing down from the train towards the station end of the platform and then the undercurrent thrusting up along the doors, trying to find a compartment that wasn't crowded. On the other side a steadily clanging bell indicated that the Venice rapido must already be approaching. Right in front of him somebody was heaving a cart, trying to sell ice-creams and cold drinks – and, as the cart moved away to the right, from behind it there appeared the bearded, grinning face of Stan.

'Hey, one in a million, man, fancy meeting you here!'

And he had wanted this to be so organized, so cool, so professional. You were wrestling with the stars was the truth. He had been born to this.

'Hello,' Morris said. His smile must have been wax and ashes. 'Simonetta too. What a surprise!'

And now he saw that Stan, leaning heavily on the little girl's shoulder, had his left leg in plaster nearly up to the thigh.

'Pretty, eh? Drove the microbus into a wall coming off the autostrada. Marion did. Thing was a write-off. I've been in hospital here for more than a week and now Netty's taking me home.'

The mousy girl smiled brightly at Morris. More brightly than he remembered seeing from her before. She'd nailed her wounded soldier obviously. Got him to herself.

'What bad luck,' Morris said. You could say that again. His mind was whirling. Get out now and the thing still wasn't a disaster.

'What are you up to though, fancy meeting you here, I mean . . .'

'On my way to Sardinia,' Morris said. Tell the truth, why not? 'In fact I've . . .'

'Morrees! Morrees, Morreeeeees!!' The voice shrilled high above the crowd noise in the half-silence after the bell had ceased to clang. From across the space of two empty lines, where any moment now that rapido would come squealing in, Massimina was shouting and waving her arms.

'They've moved the platform, Morrees. It's leaving from number ten. Come quick or we'll never get a seat.'

'Okay,' he shouted. She'd think he was holding one of their bags. 'Got to rush.'

'Who's the chick?' Stan grinned. 'Hey man, I wish I was coming with you. This accident's fucked up the whole summer, not to mention the money side. Same girl you were with at the bus stop that night, no?'

What an eye the bastard had! Massimina was at least twenty metres away and completely changed. Or perhaps he only looked at breasts.

'That's right.'

'Whatever happened,' Simonetta asked, 'to the other girl, the one they said was kidnapped?'

Morris shrugged his shoulders: 'No idea. Still,' he added lamely, 'I wasn't actually going out with her any more when it happened.' It sounded awful.

'You men are all pigs,' Simonetta pouted from her little happy face. 'See if Stan would lose any time worrying if I disappeared.' But she had turned to look at Massimina who was shouting again, 'Morrees, come on, come on!'

'Pretty girl,' Stan said, and to annoy Simonetta. 'Too bad you can't introduce us.'

Morris was desperately trying to weigh up how dangerous the situation was. His body, which had been so gloriously cool and relaxed just a few moments before, was now coursing with heat so that he could feel the sweat trickling down his back between tense buttocks. Would they recognize Massimina's face when it appeared again in the papers? It looked like they'd be spending the whole summer holed up in Verona now and with his leg in plaster Stan wouldn't have much else to do but read the papers. If only there was only one of them! If Stan was alone he could help him onto the train, bundle him into a loo, get the door closed and throttle him there. Beat the life out of the stupid hippy hypocrite. (Worried about the money indeed!) The same with Simonetta; she seemed so small and frail you could have choked her with one hand. But with the two of them . . .

'Got to rush, sorry.'

'Send us a card,' Stan laughed. 'Hey and introduce me to that chick when you get back to VR!'

Morris was already moving away down the platform.

'*Arrivederci*!'

He turned to shout something reassuring to Massimina, but the Venice rapido was already rumbling in, drowning all sound in squeals and clanks, blocking the view. In the middle of the crowd, now getting frantic with the imminent departure of one train and the arrival of the other, Morris stopped at a litter bin where he'd caught sight of a plastic bag. He lifted the thing out. Full of orange peel. He emptied the peel back into the bin and hunched down, hiding the money under the clothes while he switched it from holdall to plastic bag. There was so much that the thing was full to bursting. Morris laid just one yellow sweater over it, which he could always swear blind was his own, tucked it down around the sides, tied a knot in the handles and checked that you couldn't see from outside what was inside. No. Good. He left the holdall on the platform with the other clothes, then hurried back to Massimina. He'd met a couple of friends, miracle of miracles, he told her, and helped them with their bags down the platform seeing as one of them had broken his leg. They were off to Venice any minute.

'Good job I saw you,' she said.

## 17

The boat plied a sea the blue of brochures. Not a ripple, not a cloud on the horizon. Certainly none of those awful northern buffets which made the Anglo-Saxons feel so gratuitously heroic. His father, for example, insisting they hold firm on the beach despite a near gale that lifted the sand and threw it in angry handfuls against the rented windbreak. You'd have thought they were the rearguard at Dunkirk for God's sake. The man's whole sense of self-respect hung on his being the last to surrender that beach – as if there was any chance, any chance at all, with all the other mad Brits there were there, every one quite as determined as himself; there was even a girl with her tits in the wind, a veritable pioneer in those days, with Mother watching Dad to check he didn't watch that way. And then when Morris had started whimpering because he was cold and still damp from the sea (yes, you had to *swim* for Christ's sake!), then it was the moment for Dad to explode with his 'pansy' and 'cry-baby' and 'next thing you'll be wanting me to wipe your precious bum for you' – and Mother would pour oxtail soup from one of a battery of thermos flasks, putting another towel round Morris's shoulders and telling Dad not to use foul language, Morris was far too young to hear . . . Morris appreciated now that it wasn't just his father had created the 'pansy/weakling' stigma that had hung over his infancy and youth: it was Mother too, her insisting on his delicacy, physical and moral, so that she would have a reason to protect him, but at the same time arousing (consciously? to keep them apart?) Dad's ridicule. Morris's erstwhile hang-ups (now thankfully overcome) were nothing more in the end than a by-product of their relationship, had nothing really to do with himself at all. He was fine.

Of the two of them, naturally, he vastly preferred his mother, except that dying on him like that she had exposed him to the full blast of Dad's ignorant spartan virility. True, there were no more trips to the beach, but there was always the house in Acton with the doors that didn't fit and the bathroom window that had to be nailed permanently open because there was no vent for the Ascot; there were always the heroic fishing trips Sunday morning on the Grand Canal (the *Grand* Canal! *Great* Britain. Great Great Britain). The sun would be rising in one vast haemorrhage over the wasteland Park Royal was (Park Royal! Sunbeam Road!) and 'shepherd's warning', Dad would announce with grim satisfaction so that half an hour later they would be sheltering beneath the umbrella, the one family umbrella, under a cold London drizzle with the worms swimming about at the bottom of their margarine tub, Morris hugging his shoulders, sucking a numb thumb through woollen gloves.

Oh yes, the Brits thrived on their hardships. (Look how embarrassed they seemed here in Italy to have found themselves in a place so beautiful, how they stooped and slouched about, spindly and Dickensian, squinting weak-eyed in the sunlight, trying to convince each other it must all be more than they could afford and they should really go home a few days earlier – 'We really ought to go home, you know, Doris,' – because whenever they started enjoying themselves they felt guilty). They thrived on their hardships, their difficult mortgages and windswept Sundays and if they read so avidly about the rich and soaked up facile TV celebrities night after rainy night ('I'll just take the old hound round the block, love,' – Dad buttoning up his plastic mac, no hat though, please God no hat for a piddling little drizzle like this – 'Be back in time for Parkinson.') – if they couldn't keep their eyes off *Titbits* and would have given a year of their wintry lives to know if Prince Charles had had it away with Di before their wedding TV appearance, then it wasn't because they had any ambition to be rich themselves, God forbid, but just so they could savour their poverty and sacrifice all the more – 'You get yourself a good honest job, my boy, and leave off all this university crap.' His Dad was the kind of person who, having voted Labour all his life, would switch to Thatcher just because she'd shown that the Brits could still raise the flag in a howling Antarctic gale and march across a freezing bog better than any other nation in the world. 'And 7000 miles from home, lad.' Dad glued to the wartime newsreel while Morris scribbled off his letters to the Milk Marketing Board.

'What are you thinking about, Morri?'

The boat plied its sea the blue of brochures. Morris had taken two deckchairs on the first-class sundeck and they were half sitting, half sprawling under a generous sun, roasting in a bottle of Noon Soon (Gloom Soon they'd probably call it back at Boots the Chem), holding their limp hands between the chairs. All around them were the elegant first-class travellers in their fashionable string bathing costumes and those dainty white leather sandals with golden buckles, that showed off painted toes. Painted toes had begun rather to interest Morris. He must get Mimi to paint her toes.

'Thinking? Nothing.'

'Nothing at all?'

*'Niente di niente di niente.'*

'You're happy, Morri?'

'Terribly,' he said and waited for the soft kiss below his ear. They would make love tonight. He was looking forward to that.

'You should go to a chiropodist, Mimi,' he said.

'What?'

'A chiropodist. You've been cutting your nails too low and they need some attention. Look how elegant that woman's feet are: over there, with the straw hat like yours.'

'But the chiropodist would cost so much, Morri, and . . .'

'We can manage,' Morris said confidently.

Because Morris Duckworth was a rich man. An extremely rich man. Morris Duckworth had 800 million lire stuffed in a plastic bag jammed inside his suitcase, presently located in the far corner of the boat's luggage compartment. He hadn't had time to count it yet but he was perfectly sure it was all there. Why shouldn't it be if they wanted their precious daughter back? Eight hundred million. It was a shame it was in lire of course with the inflation there was here and then the appalling exchange rates (good old Brits, belts tight now and keep the pound strong). Still, he could hardly go and try to change such a massive sum into sterling or dollars.

The thing to do would be to invest it somehow. Government bonds might be the thing, inflation-proof and available at any bank in Italy. Or perhaps he should simply buy a few houses and live in one off the rent from the others. The problem there though was the tenants. Would they pay up? Would they get out when you wanted to sell? Could you trust them to maintain the property decently? No, simple safe investment was the thing, live off the interest, get himself a nice apartment block in the fashionable centre of Verona, nice furniture, set himself up and then relax into doing what he really wanted to do with his life. A little writing. Articles perhaps. On art or politics. Italian politics were interesting. And then photography. *Women of Verona*, book of photographs with text. That might sell. 'Dear Publisher, I am a freelance photographer living (opulently) in Italy. I would like to present you with . . .' That all had a nice ring to it.

The only problem that he could see being Massimina. But Morris had decided not to worry himself with this, at least not for the duration of the crossing. He was taking a much needed mental break. Enjoying himself. And Massimina was almost the best part. You could see he got a good deal of respect from people, especially other men (men like his Dad) from having her around. Quite apart from the sort of light butterfly company she kept him.

Eight hundred million lire in the suitcase.

They sat outside on the rear deck for iced-lemon *granita*. A favourite that. Morris had two. Massimina stayed with one because she was tight of course. But then now the money was his, perhaps it was better that way. She was looking happy though. Happy to be going to Sardinia. Morris was well again and they were going to take a real holiday, without any more hotel bills either. (Why, she wanted to know, hadn't they come in the first place?) She smiled her round smile with the pearly bright teeth and that silver St Christopher winking sunlight in her cleavage. (The cover photograph for the book? Homage to Giacomo Pellegrini. Idiot. He'd been asking for it he had, wanting you to swap girlfriends before you'd barely met him – probably had VD too come to think of it, the kind of life he was leading, riddled with it. He should consider himself lucky, a quick end like that.)

The Sardinian coast appeared towards twilight, rocky and blue. The passengers were tired after a hot lazy day and the atmosphere at baggage collection was subdued and pleasant. They had all escaped from the city and the crowds now. They could relax and love their neighbours. It was just a question of getting one's bags and driving a few picturesque miles to hotel or villa and they'd made it. The few hippies and backpackers there were seemed out of place and unthreatening, apologizing even for bumping into you. All very nice.

Morris exchanged a few words with an elderly gentleman who turned out to be some kind of Venetian count and owned a spot of land in the Highlands too, for hunting. Marvellous people the Scottish, how they put up with their weather. Glorious centuries of it. Morris had always been a fan of the Scottish, he said, in fact his grandparents were from Scotland. Did the count know Renfrewshire? Pity. (Memories of 'O' level geography. Where the hell was Renfrewshire anyway? What a name! Still, at least it wasn't Great Renfrewshire or Renfrewshire Royal.)

'Meet my fiancée, Massimina, Count Verzi.' No risks with surnames.

The count's wife was about fifteen years younger than her husband, a very attractive and pleasant woman of forty-fivish. No, it was only their second time in Sardinia actually, a villa they had bought last year.

'But if you young people don't have a car, why don't we give you a lift? Are you going far?'

Morris told them.

The count said their villa was rather beyond that. No, no

trouble, he'd be delighted, so encouraging to meet young people you could talk to these days. (Massimina hadn't said a word.) And Morris's accent *was* impressive, my word, how long had he been in Italy? Only two years? Heavens, he had done well!

And so, forty air-conditioned kilometres later, Morris and Massimina were climbing out of a silver-grey Mercedes in the central square of the village of Palau.

'You're sure I can't take you right to some door or other?'

'No, really, we're just going to look for any old hotel for the night here and then meet up with friends tomorrow.'

'*Arrivederci* then. Do come and see us if you can.'

Morris said he would.

'But why do you have to make up stories?' Massimina protested as soon as they turned away towards a bar. She seemed angry for some reason. 'We're not going to a hotel.'

'I didn't want my friend to see us arrive in a Mercedes, did I? He'd think we were stinking rich or something and didn't need somewhere to stay.'

'Can I say something, Morrees? You won't be offended?' She had that determined pucker about her lips.

'What?' He was surprised. He'd been wondering how he should deal with this friend of Gregorio's who was obviously expecting a pair of homosexuals. Cold shoulder him completely was probably the best line. Just get the key to the place, get taken out there and then make it quite clear they never wanted to see the boy again. Play lovey dovey with Mimi, honeymoonish. Shouldn't be difficult.

'You really overdo it,' she said, 'the way you suck up to these people.'

'What?'

'You were sucking up to that man just because he was a count and had a nice car and it was so obvious really . . .'

Morris was suddenly boiling, furious, and at the same time uncomfortable.

'I was talking to Count Verzi and his wife because I found them very cultured and courteous,' he said coldly, 'which is more than I can say for some people.'

And suddenly he remembered that letter of hers: ' . . . but he does it because he feels inferior . . .' The bitch.

'But don't you see you were making a fool of yourself? I didn't know where to put my face, I mean . . .'

'And I suppose sitting there silent with your thumb in your mouth is the best way to behave in society?'

Morris ordered two coffees. It was almost eleven.

'Morri, don't be angry, I just thought . . .'

'Shut up. I have to go and phone this guy now who's going to take us out there. Okay? And I don't want to hear another word of this crap.'

If only she knew the kind of fire she was playing with she wouldn't come out with shit like that.

Roberto arrived at eleven thirty and was not at all what Morris had imagined. Tall, athletic, with a lively step, Gregorio's friend was a big lad with huge shoulders, thick reddish hair brushed stiffly back and a proud, slightly hooked nose. His eyes, as he hunted about for them on entering the café, were deep-set, quick and sharp. On appreciating that it was Massimina who was with Morris, he did for a moment seem just faintly surprised, but was neither put off nor ill at ease. He sat down at their table in the warm evening air, spread his arms wide and lazily across the table top, drummed a little beat with long fingers, sized Morris up at a glance that ended in a wink, and then shouted out loud to the barman:

'Enrico, three peach grappas, house special here,' and he turned and gave them a big smile. His lips, Morris noted, were slightly loose and extraordinarily wide, his smile was friendly, sensuous and mischievous all together.

'Massimina,' Massimina said.

Roberto took her slim little hand from the table and lifted it laughing to his lips. Winking again, this time at her, he said, *'Piacere, Signorina,'* and made a little mock bow.

Morris had meant to be cold-shoulderish to him, lovey dovey to her. He had meant to demand that they be taken out to Gregorio's place immediately. But after the flare-up with

Massimina he had no desire at all to be left alone with her or show her any affection whatsoever. And then he was immediately attracted to Roberto who was full of good humour and ready to make their acquaintance thoroughly and immediately. So he didn't object to the grappa, not at the first round nor the second, and he found after a while that he was having a good time, even going out of his way to shine for the boy, to show he could liven up a party as well as the next man. Massimina was giggling already, holding her nose to down the grappa. Morris had never seen her so lively, nor so willing to drink. Reaction to their little argument perhaps. Roberto, meanwhile, was poking fun at her, mimicking her little pouts, her sudden righteous frowns and she had realized but didn't mind it seemed. Morris joined in and found himself feeling at the same time contented and protective. Was this what mellowing out was?

Not that alarm bells didn't ring from time to time to spoil things. When the Trevisans realized that they weren't going to get the girl back. When they told the police. What then? Would they be able to trace the two people who had had reservations in that compartment? Would they find the holdall on the platform? They'd know then he'd picked it up in Rome. Or if the elderly man actually managed a description of him, which meant another photofit that would correspond perfectly with the Rimini one, not to mention with Inspector Marangoni's knowledge of Morris. (Were all incoming calls to the police station automatically traced? Because if so, they'd know he'd called from Rome, from the station, and it would all add up. What a fool he'd been to call, an idiot.) And just from the routine point of view, wasn't it crazy to expose Massimina to someone for such a long time like this, to let an imprint of her face sink into his memory? Yes, Morris heard the alarm bells ringing, but he chose to ignore them. He chose to ignore them because he was weary of worry and alarms. And what was the use of 800 million if you couldn't sit back and enjoy it. Have a joke, a laugh, for God's sake. The boy was fun.

Roberto had taken off his clogs now. He put his hands in

them and made them do a little dance on the table, after which he told Massimina the joke about the woman who showed her breasts to a gorilla, and so then Morris told the one about the woman who wouldn't say a word in the sperm donors' queue – one of Dad's worst – and Massimina spluttered her grappa all over the table and said she'd never have started going out with him at all if she'd known he could be so disgusting. But she was enjoying it.

It was two o'clock before they rolled in drunk to Gregorio's place after a hair-raising ride across the cliffs. And nearly four before Roberto went home.

In bed he said experimentally, 'I'm sorry, Mimi, snapping like that.'

And she kissed him and said no, it was her in the wrong.

(Oh, he was adaptable, Morris was!)

# 18

Morris liked to see the children well dressed. Their knee-length pants and brightly coloured shirts, carefully groomed hair, made a picture that contrasted strongly with his own childhood of dirty shorts and torn T-shirts. The fact was, they were rich of course, otherwise they wouldn't be holidaying in Sardinia, but all the same you had to hand it to these Italians, they had a flare for things like this.

'When I have children,' he remarked, 'I'd like them to be as well dressed as that.'

Massimina was solemn, cross-legged, her skirt spread between her knees, slicing tomatoes into a sandwich. She lifted the knife to scratch carefully under her chin.

'It may be sooner than you think.'

'What?'

She smiled and then blushed faintly through the tan of the last few days.

'Don't play innocent, Morri. Come on.'

'Come on what?' he smiled.

'Well, we didn't use anything, did we?'

Morris glanced up sharply to find that faint puckered serene smile spreading like melted butter all over her face. Why hadn't he thought? He'd been so surprised to find himself doing it at all, he'd never thought of the much publicized precautions. He picked up a round pebble and tossed it into the postcard Sardinian sea, careful to avoid the group of children near the water. They were sitting in a tiny stony cove at the bottom of the cliff beneath Gregorio's villa. Only two other families from another luxury holiday home shared the space, their well-behaved, well-dressed children playing a game of tag.

'You can't be late already,' he said coolly, realizing as he spoke that he didn't know the Italian word for period. 'It was only a week ago.'

'No, but I'm sure I will be.' And she smiled gravely. Oh so very gravely. She thought this was romance par excellence obviously. She thought this beat the pants and underpants off *I Promessi Sposi;* and you could see she was dying to be perfectly sure, just dying to dash out for her predictor test the moment her period was ten seconds overdue, so that then she could phone Signora Mamma with the fait accompli that would leave the two nunnish sisters howling with jealousy. And send Morris scurrying off to complete the matrimonial documentation tout de suite.

On the other hand, he really wouldn't mind. A child, a rich wife, the well-dressed afternoons in the square, at the theatre, the *passeggiata,* and with his own private income now so they could never hold him to ransom or accuse him of sucking the family dry.

Except there seemed no way to reproduce the girl without hanging himself.

*(Take the money and run, Morris. Get out!)*

They ate a picnic lunch – the one o'clock radio news was the thing to avoid – then climbed steeply back up the rocky path to Gregorio's villa and an hour's siesta on the big double bed in the parents' room. Roberto was coming over at three to take them along the coast to Porto Torres, where Morris hoped he would be able to find at least some sort of newspaper. He hadn't had any news for three days now.

He lay in the half-dark of lowered blinds, Massimina dozing naked beside him, and tried to force himself to face up to things seriously. The point was of course he shouldn't need any news at all. This hankering after news was just another way of marking time. News couldn't help him at all now. He had the money. And the longer he delayed his re-entry to Verona, the worse things would be. Plus, Massimina was extremely dangerous. Any moment she might hear something on the radio, see her own portrait photograph on TV, or simply pick up the phone and call home. Morris had told her that Gregorio had left a note saying they absolutely mustn't make any calls to the mainland as these were all registered and would give away to his parents that he had let friends use the place in his absence. But actually the note Gregorio had really left had said that he, Gregorio, would probably be back in Sardinia around July 1st, less than a week away. Morris felt caught in a trap that didn't seem somehow entirely of his own making.

He really hadn't foreseen this problem with Massimina at the beginning. He honestly hadn't. He hadn't planned for it.

He could try to persuade her to run off to South America of course. But she would want to know why, and with whose money. At a push he might get her to England, but she would be determined to see Mamma and sissies first. If only to gloat. Unless he could forge an extraordinarily negative letter from Mamma. Disinherited, never-want-to-see-you-darken-our-doorway-again stuff. But it was too far-fetched, and anyway, she would know her mother's handwriting to the last dot and comma.

Or he could run off to South America on his own. This was a serious possibility. Except that Morris didn't want to go to South America. Or any other far-flung, half-civilized place if it came to that. (Australia, for example, no desire whatsoever to see Australia.) It would defeat the whole object of the enterprise after all, which was to establish himself in some civilized cultural centre living a civilized cultural and tasteful life. And if he had to run off and hide in the jungles of Bolivia or swamps of Paraguay with a troupe of ex-Nazis and mafia fugitives, then it wouldn't have been worth doing the whole thing in the first place.

Plus he didn't actually want to leave her. Christ, he really didn't.

If only he had kept it to an elopement. He could have married her and got the money that way.

Morris lifted her slim arm off his chest, tucked it under her a little where her breasts were squashed against the sheet, and eased himself out of bed. The floor was tiled white and pleasantly cool. He slipped on his shorts and padded through the spacious rooms. Incredible they could be so kind as to let somebody like Morris stay. He must send a thank you letter. Everything was rich, sumptuous, down to the last detail; the television on a corner of raised floor, the white touch-button telephone, ornaments, paintings, a tapestry on one wall in deep reds and blues, a sense of stillness, of sound suffocated and nothing stirring. Why couldn't it stay this way for ever?

Morris picked up the paperweight on the desk in the second bedroom, Gregorio's room. He weighed it in his hand, a great glass globe, big as a cricket ball and quite solid apparently. In the centre a tiny bubble of twisted colour seemed to revolve as you moved the thing round. But his eyes were filling with tears. He turned abruptly to the window which looked back away from the sea over a rugged countryside of gorse and rocky outcrops. Caves? He must check up on that.

In Gregorio's wardrobe, behind piles of clothes (Morris had helped himself to an exceptionally well-cut pair of linen summer trousers), was the plastic bag with the money. He undid the knots – the thing was still smelling faintly of orange peel – slipped a rubber band off one of the wads and took a couple of fifty thousand notes to be getting on with. With inflation running at 16 per cent though, he thought, the stuff was losing 16/365 per cent of its value every day. Which was – he would have to buy a calculator – about a twenty-fifth of a per cent every day. Yes. One per cent of 800 million was 8 million and a twenty-fifth of that was about, let's see, three hundred, maybe three hundred and twenty thousand. So that not doing anything with the stuff he was losing about the same amount every day as he had been earning in two weeks last year. And if he delayed the return to Verona until just before Gregorio came, that meant a loss of two million and more – two months' salary for the average man. No, you had to invest and you had to do it quick. There was no point at all in having money rotting in the back of a wardrobe tied up in a plastic bag. A day in Milan, find a good stockbroker and unload a hundred million of it right away, that would be a start at least. This afternoon he would buy a calculator and some new batteries for the dictaphone and in the night he would talk it through and through on the tape until he came to some firm and final decision.

'Morri, where are you Morri?'

She was in the hall. You couldn't hear anybody when they moved barefoot on these tiles. Morris shoved the plastic bag back behind a pile of folded sweaters and stood up sharply, catching his head on an upper shelf.

'Morrees,' she was already at the door. 'You shouldn't really look through his things you know.'

She smiled and frowned together as if to say, I do love you, but this is a part of your character that will have to change, like the way you suck up to people sometimes. She stood in the doorway in a white T-shirt and panties, fingering the St Christopher round her neck. And then she said:

'Where on earth did that money come from?' Because the coloured bank notes were still held between the finger and thumb of his left hand.

The paperweight was only a couple of feet to his left, arm's length; and even if there were no caves out there, the countryside was one empty mile after another of gorse, gorse and more gorse. But Morris stayed calm. He loved her, didn't he? If ever he had loved anybody. He might still find a way out. Anyway, Roberto was due any minute.

'I was trying on a pair of Gregorio's trousers and I found it in his pocket.'

'Oh, but you shouldn't,' she said. 'I mean, trying on his things is a bit . . .'

'Gregorio is a very close friend of mine,' he said coldly. 'He'd be happy for me to use his clothes. And the money if I need it.' He was aware of almost wanting her to make him angry.

'I'm sorry,' she said, biting her lower lip. But he had hurt her now. 'Morrees, why do you have to talk to me in that tone of voice?' She stopped and stared at him and he stared back, struggling to keep his expression normal. He must blink to stop the eyes from going glassy. 'And this morning, when I said I might be pregnant, I didn't expect you to jump for joy or anything; I know it's a problem; but you might have been a bit more supportive. You haven't even talked about it. You act as if . . . Oh Morri, what's happening, one moment you're so friendly and loving and the next you seem so peculiar, so distant, I . . .' She burst into tears.

Morris hesitated, stepped towards her, but indecisively, lifted an arm to the warm flesh of her shoulder, her neck.

'Massimina,' he said, 'Mimi, honestly I . . .' Her neck and shoulders were beautifully angular and proud: you would photograph them from a forty-five degree angle and then slightly above (if she knelt a little now for example) to give a sense of the length, the firmness. 'Honestly, I didn't mean to . . .'

Perhaps it was like this for all lovers, the affection, the warmth, friendliness, sex, and then those unspeakable things hidden beneath, the attraction growing alongside the horror, the desire to . . .

'Mimi, I . . .'

And then somebody hit a horn outside and it was Roberto.

Roberto's father was a hotelier with three hotels all along the coast north of Palau. Roberto helped in the office sometimes in summer and very occasionally in the restaurant of the largest hotel, but otherwise he made no contribution at all and none was expected of him. His studies in medicine at the University of Rome, where he spent most of the year, were progressing steadily but slowly and he seemed in no particular hurry to finish. He had excellent contacts in the hospital in Sassari, he said, and was bound to get a job there when he did finish, so what on earth was the use of hurrying? He smoked a thin cigar and the car he drove was a white Golf convertible which bowled merrily along the balmy cliffside roads with steep hills of gorse to the left and a sudden rocky drop never far away to the right. Precisely the kind of car he would like to have, Morris thought. He had always admired the Golf convertible. Style with a usefully low profile.

Massimina was a shade sombre and said she was worried her perm was going to blow out altogether in the wind that swept over the windscreen, and after all the effort she'd made not to let her hair get wet when they went swimming. She sat next to Roberto and turned round occasionally with a pouting anxious frown, probably thinking how embarrassed she was going to be, asking after the pregnancy test in the pharmacist's, Morris thought. And he leaned forward and whispered that he would go and get it for her himself. She smiled and kissed him and was obviously relieved.

'Oh no!' Morris said then when they were twenty safe kilometres on their way. 'I forgot my passport. I can't sort out my documents at the *Questura* without my passport.'

'But Morrees, I told you . . .'

'Look, I can pick up the forms at least and then have them all ready for the next time.'

'What documents are those?' Roberto asked, and Morris appreciated his mistake at once: he should have whispered it.

'We're getting married,' Massimina came out promptly. Oh she really enjoyed saying that. Roberto was amused, he was delighted even, and now Morris saw he was going to ruin the whole afternoon by ribbing them about it at every possible opportunity.

'I wouldn't marry *him*,' he began at once.

'And why not?' She was immediately playing his game, having fun.

'Well, he looks a hell of a suspicious character to me.'

'No Morrees is . . .'

'And then English too. You know what the English are like. And too old.' Roberto glanced round to wink at Morris. 'You should try out a few younger men first, take a look around. Don't bury yourself with the first man you fall for.'

'No,' she was almost giggling, 'it's him that's burying himself with the first . . .'

'Shut up,' Morris said sharply.

Porto Torres turned out to be a bustling seaside town thronging with holiday-makers who drifted between the modern hotels that stretched in a ribbon along the seafront and the ancient stone warren of shops and restaurants that was the port's original centre. The place was rather too vulgarly colourful for Morris's taste with too many adverts for cheap camera film, too many balloons, jokey postcards, seaside toys and plastic flags.

He went directly into a newsagent and bought *Corriere della Sera* and *La Mattina* and then hurried to the tobacconist for stamps and postcards that Massimina had asked for. As long as she kept writing to Mamma's mythical address in the mountains he would let her post everything herself, he thought, but he must still keep a close watch and be flexible.

'Don't post it before letting me sign,' he told her and went off to the chemist now. Roberto came with him, looking for some kind of medically recommended footwear, and Morris, for no reason at all, decided to let him see what he was buying. Massimina had stayed behind to scribble messages to Mamma and Grandma sitting on the pedestal of a monument to the fallen of various wars.

'You're not getting married just because she's got one in the oven?' Roberto's eyes were dark and lively. He put an arm round Morris as they left the shop.

'I'm marrying her because she's rich,' Morris said.

'You're kidding.'

'Actually, to tell the truth, I'm not marrying her at all. It's her who's got that into her head. And she's created this whole pregnancy scare to hurry things along. I'm sure she isn't pregnant really.' How could she be? It was only a week and a half since they did it.

'No need to defend yourself,' Roberto said, still with the light of needling fun in his eyes. 'She's a nice girl. If you want to marry her, do. I wouldn't mind myself if I was that way inclined.'

But Morris had suddenly seen his way now, understood why he had let Roberto see what he was buying in the first place.

'Quite, I'm not saying I won't marry her. But there's no hurry. Hence the forgotten passport. In fact we're going to have a hell of a row about that tonight. You can see it a mile off. She's threatening to run off back to Mamma if I don't marry her immediately, and to show her who's boss, I may just let her go.'

'Well, if you need anybody to give her a lift to the ferry . . .' and Roberto gave Morris a not unpleasant little squeeze.

'Thanks, I'll bear it in mind,' Morris said coolly.

They sat on the beach. Miles and miles of white beach. The sun was scorchingly hot. And Morris suddenly felt fed up. It was too hot for him and too lazy. He wanted to be up and doing, getting on with things. And not things like making sure Massimina hadn't sent a letter or made a phone call; he wasn't going to spend his whole damn life babysitting the girl for God's sake. He wanted to be investing that money and having it working for him. He was just itching to start. Heaven knew, if he had the opportunities Roberto had he'd be acquiring a new hotel every week and building up a business empire as fast as he could, not sitting on his arse pretending he was studying medicine.

'No, I don't want another swim,' he told her. 'You go in with Roberto.' (They had bought a big red plastic ball to play with, of all things – and Morris had thought the boy was going to give them a cultural trip round the old centre or some ruins or something, the way he'd talked about it being a 'fascinating place'.) 'I'm just going to take a little walk through town while the shops are still open.'

He would take his risks now, Morris thought. If she found out, he would escape. If not, so be it. Leave it to fate.

In town Morris shredded her postcards into a bin. Because on second thoughts it might be wise to avoid an accumulation of cards from a certain Massimina and Morris to a fictitious address in Trentino-Alto-Adige. After the discovery of that red tracksuit you never knew what bad luck might come your way.

The newspapers had been reassuring though: *Corriere della Sera* had had a small report of a ransom being paid, but to no avail. It didn't mention how the money was paid (a compliment, Morris thought: they didn't want anybody else to get wise), but said that Inspector Marangoni now feared the worst for the young girl's life. Suspicions were growing that Massimina may have been dead all along, the mysterious get well card having been written the first day and then sent later to give the impression the girl was still alive. A last paragraph added that the card had provoked some puzzlement among handwriting experts who insisted there were no traces of its having been written under duress: this had led to some speculation that the girl herself might be involved in some kind of hoax against her parents. Police interviews with family and friends had excluded this possibility, however. *La Stampa* had nothing on the Rimini case. The thing had obviously petered out onto the back pages of the local papers.

Morris chose a calculator made by Texas Instruments. The shopkeeper assured him that the thing was suitable for somebody who had to deal with a lot of business administration, and showed him how to operate the mechanism for calculating compound interest. The batteries for the dictaphone, which he picked up at the same place, were exorbitantly expensive, Morris noticed. In fact, perhaps he should invest in the electronic components industry. The thing seemed to be booming.

Passing a S.I.P. in the centre, Morris considered the many possible telephone calls he could make. They would probably be expecting one even at the *Questura*. But he felt nervous about it now. They might automatically be tracing everything. And with the 800 million actually in the bag there was too much to lose to go playing fun and games.

Should he tell her? She might play along with him. She was a good kid in the end and he would miss her otherwise. She might think it was hilarious. Carefully edited of course.

Morris walked down the bustling main street of Porto Torres, itching to be back in action and at the same time caged in his dilemma. The sun beat down on his now tanned skin. From the harbour the steamer off to Genoa sounded its horn. (Why wasn't he on it?) In the mirror of a shop window displaying jugs and pottery, Morris noted he was more handsome than ever. Which gave him a lift.

Roberto had somehow managed to accumulate three friends (male) and they all went to dinner together. Morris again had an acute sense that he was letting things drift. The number of people who had seen and spoken to Massimina in his company was rising steadily and getting out of hand. He didn't feel hungry and ordered a simple grilled fish, no trimmings or extras. In a week it would be over. It must. One way or another.

The young men talked about the general election of the previous Sunday, which Morris had forgotten about, and he was disturbed to hear that the Christian Democrats had lost six per cent of the vote and the Communists had now pulled up just about even. A left wing government was therefore on the cards, a remote possibility, yes, but real enough to have caused a massive ten point slump in a single day on the stock market. Thank God he hadn't invested the cash last week. Still, the political turmoil should be keeping all the TV news programmes very busy.

Massimina fanned herself over a lobster – the evening was close and sticky – and when one of the other lads began to flirt with her (in the way queers will, Morris thought), Roberto laughed and said not to touch because they were about to get married.

'He's even bought her her first pregnancy test today,' he announced with a smile.

Massimina blushed to the colour of the forkful of lobster she was slipping into her mouth. Morris felt outraged by such a vulgar taking-of-advantage and would have liked to hit back and to show affection to the girl too, except that the idea of comforting her under the gaze of those laughing, dark Latin eyes unnerved him. The last thing he wanted to appear was a gooey fool. And so in the end he just sat there stiff and silent.

'Bravo, bravo!' they were all cheering. 'What are you going to call the brat?'

Massimina rather surprisingly recovered from her embarrassment and began to giggle through her blushes (so much for that strict Catholic education again). She took Morris's arm with both her hands, put her head against his shoulder and asked, what *were* they going to call him? She hadn't thought of that. If it was a him.

'Leonard,' Morris said automatically, giving his father's name, just to have a name out and have done with this stupid game, but everybody thought this was doubly hilarious – a new Leonardo – and Roberto remarked that Da Vinci had been homosexual, hadn't he? Always digging up dead men's bodies and everything and cutting them up to boot.

Morris saw red. Eyes flickering open and closed, he held his breath a moment, fighting back nausea – and recovered.

'Well, my son won't do any of those things,' he said coldly.

To which Massimina echoed an annoying, *'Vero Morrees,'* and kissed him on the cheek, provoking further 'bravos'.

## 19

Roberto drove them home early after a sudden thunderstorm had washed out the idea of drinking late on the beach. The rain was heavy and persistent and they travelled in near complete silence, sitting on their towels, having failed to get the top on the Golf before the rain started. They were back at eleven and Roberto came in a moment to use the lavatory. Massimina was in a bright mood and insisted on shouting to him to stay for drinks. (Gregorio's drinks; now who was taking liberties with other people's property?) Leaving Morris in the kitchen she walked through to the lounge where the bar was, casually switching on the television on the way. Where the first thing she saw apparently was her own face.

'Morrees! Morrees!'

The tone of her voice told him everything. He was in the lounge in a flash, soda bottle in his hand.

'No, Morrees, it's incredible.' She was standing in the middle of the room, one hand ploughed into her hair, the other clutching her skirt. 'Morrees, I don't understand. They think I've been kidnapped.'

'They what!'

'They've even paid a ransom. It's impossible.'

Morris was just in time to see the familiar portrait photograph fading away over the newscaster's head. For a moment then he was afraid they were going to have Signora Trevisan come on and make some desperate appeal or something that would send the girl flying to the phone before he could get Roberto out of there. But already the picture had shifted elsewhere – a fire in a chemical factory in Milan.

'How can they think that, Morrees, after all the letters

we've sent. And you even went to speak to them, I mean, it's impossible, I don't . . .'

'Nor me.'

Morris was trembling. But he made himself put down the bottle of soda. He could feel the sweat just pouring out of him.

'I don't believe it,' he whispered huskily. And it was the truth. That she had managed to snap on the TV at just that moment after nearly three weeks of rigid vigilance – it was perfectly incredible.

She was staring at him and he knew it wouldn't take long even for her slow mind. He hung his head, a gesture of humility.

'I never told them you were with me, Mimi,' and he hurried on. 'I have a confession to make – though I had no idea this was going to happen, I promise you; if I'd even remotely suspected such a . . .' He heard the lavatory flushing and the door opening. 'Let's get rid of Roberto and then talk it over. I'll tell you everything.'

Hold onto your nerve, Morris Duckworth! He strode quickly into the passage and met Roberto still closing the bathroom door behind him. His voice he made low and dramatic – low enough for Massimina not to hear, dramatic enough to impress Roberto.

'Robbi, you know that row I told you about this morning, the one Massimina and I were about to have? Well, it's started. You don't think you could . . .'

Roberto grinned. 'Sure, sure.' And he winked. 'Don't be too cruel now. And remember my offer, if she wants to . . .'

'Thanks,' Morris was terse. A man in no mood for joking.

'Attaboy!' And Roberto called, '*Ci vediamo!*' to Massimina in the lounge, but she didn't reply. Roberto grimaced, as if to say, 'that bad, eh?' and punched Morris lightly on the shoulder. 'They're not worth the trouble.'

*When the hell was he going to go!* Get him out. Morris had heard the tinkle of a receiver being lifted. And he almost pushed the lad to the door.

'See you tomorrow,' Roberto said.

'Right, ciao.' Without even waiting for the door to be closed he was rushing back to the lounge in time to grab the receiver from her hand with the ringing tone still sounding.

'But I want to speak to her now. I have to tell her. She must be worried to death, Morrees.' Massimina had begun to cry with anger, frustration and disbelief. Behind her back the television was still on, advertising brandy now. Morris guarded the phone and tried to take her in his arms.

'You have to let me explain first.'

She struggled and backed away. Her staring eyes were full of suspicion now and a hint of fear. But Morris wouldn't give up.

'Explain what?' she asked.

He searched for his softest tone of voice. 'Just sit down, sit down there and I'll tell you, okay? Just promise not to do anything until I've told you.'

The roar of the car outside told them Roberto had gone. They were alone in the villa with the next house a good half mile away on a road where the asphalt was only a memory.

Morris snapped off the television.

'The point is,' he said, 'I thought at the beginning that if I told them we'd run off together, they'd come after us directly out for our blood. Or rather my blood. So I simply didn't tell them. I thought they'd just take you away from me and split us up for good and always.'

'But . . .'

Morris sat down opposite in one of the great white leather armchairs. His nerve was coming back now – it was a part he could believe in and act well. And then he felt a sort of decision had been made. He would give the girl this one chance. It was up to her. Her decision.

'When I went to see them in Quinzano I said I didn't know where you were and then I destroyed the letters we wrote to them . . .'

'You what!'

'Of course, after the first couple of days I regretted it, I saw it was stupid, but I was in it up to the eyeballs by then and I couldn't change my story because then they'd all know I'd

206

been lying in the first place. You see, the awful thing was, when I was at your mother's the police arrived and I had to tell them the same story I'd told her, so that . . . I think this was why I was ill in Rome, really. I mean, I was getting so nervous and worried about it – you remember how tense I was – that I . . .' He let his voice tail off.

Massimina was bearing up better than he had hoped. The tears had dried up and she had just the usual worried frown on her face while the eyes watched him searchingly.

After he had been silent for some moments, she said 'God, you *are* an idiot.'

'Yes.' He was humble.

'But for heaven's sake, after the first days, when you began to worry, why didn't you tell me? We could have worked out some story. I could have gone home and said I'd run off on my own accord, but now . . .'

'I didn't want you to go home,' Morris said grimly, pushing out his jaw with an air of manly decision. 'I love you.' (It was true. And he was almost beginning to enjoy himself. She was coming round.) 'I wanted to hang on until you reached your eighteenth birthday and we could get married. That way would have settled it. How could I know they were going to think you were kidnapped – and even less that some tricky bastard was going to start writing ransom letters for heaven's sake! It sounds like a film. I thought they'd imagine you'd just run away.'

'But almost everybody who disappears in Italy is assumed kidnapped.'

'Well, I'm not Italian,' Morris said bitterly. 'I never dreamt it would come to this.' Should he tell her about the phone calls to the police, to her family? No, he'd have to get round that at a later date somehow. He'd think of something. 'I didn't know your family *had* enough money for anybody to want to kidnap you,' he went on sullenly. 'How much did they pay, anyway? I didn't hear when they were talking about that.'

'Eight hundred million,' she said in a low whisper.

'Not very much.'

'Not very much! Eight hundred million! My God . . .' and her voice trailed off, genuinely overawed by the enormity of the sum, and the futility perhaps, Morris thought, of all her little economies. Well, serve her right.

'I know,' he said. 'It's terrible. But what can I say? We can't get the money back now, can we?'

'I don't know, maybe the police . . . Oh God, I can't believe it,' and for a moment she lost her courage and wept again. 'When it comes home to you,' she sobbed. 'And I was having such a marvellous time. I thought I was really happy at last, honestly. Oh, it's like a nightmare.'

Morris crossed from the armchair to the couch to hold her and noticed for a second how they were reflected together in the bright black panes of the window. He should get the blinds down if it was going to come to anything.

'Oh Morrees!' She buried her head in his shoulders.

'*Cara*, look, the thing is we've got to decide what to do. If we go back and tell the truth, they'll probably go and put me in prison or something, I don't know, for perjury, and certainly they're never going to let us see each other again. Mimi' – his voice suddenly changed, softened, and not especially on purpose either – 'you're the first girl I've ever had. Honestly. The very first I've felt at home with. If I lose you I . . .'

She looked up, red-eyed. 'So what do we do?'

'You have to say you were kidnapped and they've just released you.'

'What?'

'Say you were kidnapped and make out they've just released you,' he repeated.

'But Morrees, you're crazy, we can't do . . .'

'Look, we go back to the mainland directly, tomorrow morning; and as soon as you're in Rome you go straight to a police station, or better still you go out to the outskirts of the city near the *autostrada* and you phone the police and tell them the kidnappers have just let you out of their car and dumped you there.'

She was silent for a minute. It really would be tremendous

208

if they could do it, Morris was thinking. 'You tell them you were kept blindfold the whole time in a cupboard or something and you never even heard them talk except when they brought you food and then you thought they had Neapolitan accents. You can do it. Then after a month or so, I come back to Verona just around your birthday and you'll be of age so we can marry without your mother's consent if necessary.'

'And what happens then if they find this man who asked for the money?' she asked.

'They won't,' Morris said with conviction.

'But . . .'

'It's the only way that I can see. Otherwise I'm in it up to my neck, and most probably you too and we'll never be together.'

'And the baby, Leonardo?'

He hadn't thought of that.

'It'll be born six or seven months after we're married at maximum and everybody will know it must have been conceived in this period now.'

'But you're not even sure you're pregnant yet, don't jump the gun for God's sake, it'd be pretty bad luck if you were and we've got enough problems on our hands for the moment.'

'I *am* sure.'

'How? You can't be.'

'A woman knows,' she said.

'Oh claptrap. You can't be sure until . . .'

'But I am sure.'

'Well then you'll have to say you were raped, for Christ's sake,' he snapped. He was losing his patience now. She was pushing him to the limit. 'You'll have to say that was what the delay was all about after the ransom was paid. They wouldn't let you go until they'd had sex with you. You resisted for a couple of days and then gave in. That way *cara* Mamma will even be happy I'm marrying you because she'll be thinking no one else ever would.'

'Oh I hate you,' Massimina spat back at him, thrusting him away, eyes wild.

But Morris didn't touch her. He still stayed cool as cool: all aplomb, Morris Duckworth. He was sorry he had offended her, he said, his eyes finding hers, his voice straining for sincerity, intensity: honestly, it was just the desperation of the situation, she must see that. What they should do now was to go to bed and sleep on it, not do anything rash after all the wine they'd drunk, then decide in the morning. And he turned to draw the blinds.

They lay in bed, Massimina trying to whimper herself to sleep, Morris caressing her lightly. The sheets were hot and sticky and crickets trilled incessantly from the garden behind the house. He really did want to believe it could work, in spite of all the obstacles that would have to be overcome. She was a hell of a girl and she had a lot of courage and the idea was so clever. Then from the purely financial point of view, he had been thinking, it was by no means certain that 800 million was really going to be enough. A handsome sum, yes, but maybe not enough for a lifetime. Not the kind of life lived to the full that he intended to have. There was no doubt he would be much better off being married to the rest of her money. Of which there was a great deal more than a piddling 800 million when all was said and done.

There were drawbacks though. It meant a whole lifetime lived in the fear that something might come out. It meant continual dependence on the girl. She might even try a little emotional blackmail every now and then. 'If you're not a nice Morris I'll tell.' Or she might blurt something out getting drunk at a party, because she was showing rather more of a propensity for getting drunk than he had at first imagined. But Morris felt he could handle all this. He had got so used to being near her. The only time in his life. And the thought of being without . . .

So he would risk it. They would be married and she would give him respectability and a family (the pregnancy test was all set up there in the lavatory with little bottles and chemicals that were supposed to form rings and things). They would have enough cash for a life of leisure with nurse and nanny and plenty of business and cultural interests. He watched her curved back.

'Mimi, are you asleep?' Nothing. 'Mimi?' Nothing.

He could let himself doze a little then. Not that he was likely actually to fall asleep in this oppressive thundery heat – and for that he was thankful. He felt it could be important to stay awake tonight. He settled down to listen to whirring crickets and the distant thunder that rumbled on the very edge of the auditory horizon.

The next thing Morris knew he was waking in the black dark. Forcing himself awake, groping his way out of sleep with tremendous urgency. The bed beside him was empty. His hand, moving to touch her, grabbed at the empty sheets. He had bounced out of bed before his mind had even fought its way out of the dark cave of sleep. His fingers felt for the light. Where was it, God damn! His ears picked up the sound of dialling though. Morris's trusty ears. He blundered through to the corridor and then the living room where she was standing in the almost complete dark, so that it was only the white of her skin that led him to her.

'Mamma, oh Mamma I'm safe, I . . .'

He had the phone out of her hands and slammed it down.

'You promised, you promised not to phone her till you were back on the mainland.'

'I didn't promise anything. I said I'd sleep on it.'

'But why this? Phone her now, they trace it and we're done. They may already have traced it. They find out we were here for the last week and we're done.'

'You always have your little plan, don't you,' she said coldly. She was stark naked, the big breasts lifting and trembling in the dark in front of her. She was panting with anger. 'I've been thinking about it. Everything that happens. This, that, the other. You always have your devious little plan to sort things out.'

'But Mimi . . .' God knew it was her life he was pleading for. He turned and switched on the light.

'Those phone calls you pretended to make, the letters you had me write and then never sent, the address in the mountains. God! How can I . . .'

'But *cara*, I did it for your . . .'

'What you don't seem to realize is that my mother is suffering at the other end of that telephone and has been for some time and all I have to do to help her is to lift it and dial.'

'But . . .'

'You think too much of yourself,' she said determinedly and picked up the receiver. 'You're selfish, egotistical and vain.'

'So you're giving me up,' Morris said self-piteously and leaned back against the door. He was surprised to find how much he really did feel hurt. She wasn't willing to go through with this for him. Although in another way her words were just what he had been waiting for.

She held the receiver, pouting. 'No, I'm not giving you up. I'm just saying, let's face the truth, tell the truth and get through it. They won't put you in prison. You haven't actually done anything. And then maybe they can set about finding the . . .'

'But Mimi,' he was almost whining now and hating himself for it. 'Mimi, they're bound to . . .'

'I'm not having everybody thinking my child's father is some kind of awful kidnapper who raped me.' Her fingers were on the dial.

Morris was exasperated beyond patience. His body was trembling and prickling with heat. 'But you don't even know you're damn well pregnant yet. Shit and fuck!' He paused, but she wouldn't even look at him now. 'Don't dial, Mimi. If you love me, don't dial, for God's sake.'

She scratched a breast and turned a finger in the dial. 'I don't love you. And I won't ever love you again if you go on shouting like that.'

She hadn't even looked at him. She didn't love him.

It was only three paces to Gregorio's room and there was the sitting room light to guide him now. He reached across the desk behind the door, found the paperweight, felt its heaviness in his hand and was already moving back through the passage while her fingers were still dialling.

'Mimi, *please* don't, we'll never be able to be together ever again, I'm telling you.'

She glanced up, must have seen the paperweight with its twisted pink bubble, but didn't connect.

'Oh shut up.'

Her fingers went back to the dial for the last number, and so he hit her. He hit her just above and behind the left ear, raising his arm high above his head to get the full strength. (There was even a moment's huge shadow of that arm thrown up against the wall, but she didn't see.) He gritted his teeth and the glass ball came down with tremendous fury. She slumped backwards, naked on the tiled floor, banging her head hard. Not even a scream, though it wouldn't have mattered. And then it was the work of a moment to have her over on her stomach and one of the Ferroni family's red silk cushions under her face. His fingers jammed in her hair and he pressed and pressed, knowing that really there was no need. The single blow had been more than enough.

Morris sat in the dark again. He turned out the light for safety and sat in the dark, watching the faint white of her body. He felt different this time. Sicker. Stranger. His face was wet with tears. Mimi! Why couldn't this cup at least have been spared him? Why couldn't she have been more sensible? It was her fault.

Perhaps he was going to go to pieces completely this time. He could feel it. He closed his eyes and great areas of dark gathered and pressed against throbbing burning brilliant lights inside his skull. Bright blues and reds were squeezed and crushed into darkness by the encroaching black. When he opened his eyes there was just that pale indefinite, lifeless shape, floating upwards from the shadows. It wasn't his fault life was so fragile, that you could solve all your problems with a single blow. And then he'd never planned to kill her, had he? He'd wanted it the other way (he should have recorded the conversation), and it was pure bad luck that . . . but he had to stand up and hurry to the bathroom to throw up in the sink.

For a moment, coming back across the corridor, he had the idea she might somehow still be alive and he ran the last few steps into the sitting room, ready to roll her over and breathe life into that pouting little mouth. But beside the body he stopped and turned away. Her nakedness frightened him. No, he had to get rid of her and do it fast. He had to get the body a hundred miles from here and perfectly hidden. If possible destroyed. How, he didn't know. But these were the kind of problems that would help him get himself back together again. If he just sat down and looked at her he was done.

It was five o'clock. Outside there would be the first grey light. Morris dressed quickly, went out of the front door, round the side of the house to the right and opened the door of a small garden shed, forlorn on the edge of an unkempt rockery. He had sniffed about inside here before and noticed some big plastic sacks full of fertilizer. Potassium something or other. There was one empty sack laid over a lawnmower and three full ones against the wall. He took a full one, dragged it into the pale light outside the shed, split open the top and emptied the stuff. A stream of blue crystals piled themselves into a heap. He took the empty sack, plus the one in the garden shed and went back into the house. The electric light was still needed here because he hadn't lifted the blinds and had no intention of doing so. At the door he wiped his feet carefully and then went back across the tiles through to the dining room and the corpse.

There would be no need to turn her over and see her face, nor even to touch her much with any luck. Just jerk out the cushion from under the head, then slip the first sack over her as far as it would go. And if she was alive? If she gasped, turned, looked? She wasn't alive. Morris bent down over the naked girl, drew a deep breath and then did it. It was clumsy, the arms wouldn't go in, then the breasts caught and for a moment he thought they were going to be too big, she was too wide for the sack, but no, they went in, a little pressure and they went. He worked the sack down, lifting her and pulling the thing until it was right at her waist. No further. Looking at her then, or what was visible, he felt a surge of affection, a desire to bend down and kiss the soft round bottom. But he held firm. He mustn't get into stuff like that.

Absolutely. He picked up the other sack and had worked it up as far as her knees when the telephone rang.

The bell hit Morris like a physical blow or a bullet. He felt dazed. The phone, at six o'clock on a Thursday morning? They had traced the call she'd made and phoned back perhaps. But you didn't phone back when you traced a call like that. You sent round ten cars full of police tout de suite. Still, it would be better not to answer, nerves too shaky. After ten rings or so the thing stopped.

He worked feverishly now. The ringing phone had impressed him with a sense of flight, a closing net, given him that hunted animal feeling he seemed to have lived with all his life and had learnt in a rather curious way to enjoy. He moved very quickly and efficiently, getting the second sack up to overlap with the first, then back into the bedroom to tidy.

He gathered all her clothes, everything, knickers, bras, swimming costume, slip, and then the dirty things she'd left in the bathroom, plus her handbag of course, where was her handbag? Here. Every single possession, he got them all together, took them back into the sitting room and stuffed them up inside the sacks. Which was when he remembered the St Christopher. Shouldn't he get it off her? If they ever found the body, for example, then identified the thing, what then? They must have appreciated that it had been stolen along with Giacomo's wallet, mustn't they? No, he was just getting paranoid. Forget it. He wasn't taking the sack off her body again anyway. Under any circumstances.

With all her clothes, belongings and shoes stuffed in now, he rolled the body over so it would be face upwards, lifted the feet end so that they pressed down on the face, held them there with his own foot while he undid his belt, and then slipped the belt round head and feet and tightened it, hard. Done. Coming adrift a bit at the middle but he could see to that later. The first thing was to have her out of the house and clean the place up. He took the two sack ends where they met at her bent waist and dragged the package down the corridor, down the two stone steps outside the front door, wincing as the head cracked on the second step, and then out behind the garden shed.

Oh what the hell was he going to do with that fertilizer, sitting there in a damn great shining blue pile? Nothing. Shovel it behind the shed and leave it there. Nobody would notice. Certainly not Gregorio anyway, and his parents wouldn't be coming again this year if the father had had an operation. Next year if anybody came across it, it would just be one of those little domestic mysteries of which life offered examples enough for heaven's sake – a big pile of dust behind the bathroom door, an ornament you've never seen before wrapped in tissue at the back of the visitor's bedroom wardrobe – these things were fairly normal. You didn't have to suspect murder just because there was a pile of fertilizer unaccountably dumped behind your garden shed. He shovelled the blue crystals round there, swept the path with a twig broom, then dragged the corpse behind the shed too. Just a temporary arrangement. The thing to concentrate on now was the house.

He went back over the bedroom, cleaning meticulously. Every sign of her must go. He had overlooked a nail varnish bottle, a box of Tampax, a tissue on the bedside table with toe-nail parings (after telling her to let the things grow!). And then there was the pregnancy test. How on earth could he have forgotten it? Morris stopped a moment to read through the instructions on the box, but it was too complicated, he didn't have time. And who cared anyway? He swept the thing into a plastic bag with the other odds and ends, carried them outside and pushed them inside the open mouths of the fertilizer sacks. He would have to tie those up later. Keep his eye open for a good piece of rope.

Towards eight thirty Morris was giving the sitting room floor a last careful wipe with warm water and alcohol, whistling now because he was almost through, singing sometimes – 'Through the night of doubt and sorrow, Onward goes the pilgrim band' – when his voice was suddenly drowned by the sound of a car racing up the drive. A squeal of brakes, scrunching wheels on gravel, a slamming door, running feet.

216

Still wearing Signora Ferroni's apron that he'd put on to clean, Morris blundered towards the door, the confession already forming on his lips. What was the point of denying it? If only they'd come an hour or two earlier to stop him. Morris felt close to tears and suddenly desperately lonely. Dear Mimi. If only they'd come earlier.

'Ciao, Morris! So you *are* here. Why didn't you answer the phone earlier? It did ring, didn't it?'

Gregorio ran up the steps. He was in shorts and his long athletic legs had a strong brown healthy look to them. Likewise his face under a mop of dark curls. Oh he was so terrifically glad to be back! And he'd just got his exam results, he said. He'd done it, passed, would you believe it? And he burst out laughing. Morris stared, backing away into the darkened house. Did he have to kill Gregorio too?

'*Buono*, in English. *Buono!* Mamma nearly fainted.'

'Congratulations,' Morris croaked.

A moment later he was helping the boy bring his bags in.

'I know it was early but you might have answered, you lazy bastard. I came on the night boat and was hoping you'd get me some breakfast ready.'

'You're back earlier than you said.' Morris was almost accusing.

'Yes, they let Papà out of hospital early and I . . . What on earth have you been doing in the sitting room; washing the floor at eight in . . .'

'I was about to go,' Morris said, looking for a voice with something natural about it, and putting down the suitcase he'd brought in, he moved quickly to lift the shutters so as to dispel that air of covertness. And the smell? Did the room smell, it suddenly occurred to him? Only of cleaning alcohol surely.

'Going?'

'Yes, that must be why I missed this call you say you made. It's all a bit complicated though. Come into the kitchen while I make you a coffee and I'll tell you about it.' His voice sounded about as natural as something from Wagner. But foreignness was on his side here. Gregorio would put it down to his English way with Italian. Put on a bit of an accent perhaps?

They sat on stools watching the coffee pot, Gregorio munching biscuits, and Morris explained how he had had a girlfriend with him and . . .

'Oh, a *girl*friend, I thought you were coming with a boy?'

'No, really? How come?'

'You said *amico* on the phone.'

'Did I?' Morris looked innocently at Gregorio and held his gaze until he caught the faintest blush behind the boy's tan. 'No, no, a girl. Anyway . . .'

'Not the one I saw you with in Piazza Bra that night? With the red tracksuit.'

'Who? Oh no, this was my real girlfriend.' He tried a little grin and thought he made it. 'Anyway, we had a hell of a row last night – about getting married inevitably enough, she thought she was pregnant – and then when I refused, she took it into her head she was going to leave immediately, on the first bus from the village, so I had to walk her down there, carry her bags.'

'But I phoned at six, you weren't surely . . .'

'The village is a good five kilometres and the first bus back to Olbia was 7:10.' Morris had no idea when the first bus was, but then nor would Gregorio. The only time Gregorio noticed buses was when he was overtaking them in one of Papà's cars. A warm feeling of justification began to throb back through Morris's veins. He too would have a car soon. (Oh damn, he must get the cash out of Gregorio's wardrobe!)

'Yes, I told her she should wait till nine or so and then call Roberto, but you know what girls are; I was a beast and she was going to get away as soon as she could. So of course "the beast" here ended up lugging her cases five kilometres down there and himself five kilometres back.'

He could see it all, was even beginning to feel hard done by. 'Anyway, when I got back I thought I'd just clean up and go myself, seeing as it's not too much fun being in a place all on your own.'

218

Actually, now he thought about it, there was nothing he would have liked more than a few days' rest here on his own.

Gregorio appeared to swallow it all and then while he was swallowing his coffee too Morris said he had to go to the toilet for a minute. He dashed into Gregorio's bedroom and quietly eased the plastic bag out from behind the pullovers. Excellent. He padded into his own room and packed the thing into his suitcase. Had he forgotten anything? Was there anything at all anywhere that could give him away? He had washed the paperweight and put it back. Traces of blood in the sink? He thought not. There'd hardly been any blood. The floor was clean. All her things were gone. Everything.

'You'll stay a few days though now I'm here?' Gregorio's voice behind him had him starting a moment.

'A day or two maybe, but I'm kind of eager to be back. Find myself some work before the money runs out.'

How long would it be before the corpse began to smell, before Gregorio for some reason wandered behind the garden shed?

'What are you doing today?' Morris asked point-blank.

'I thought a lazy day on the beach with Roberto would hit the spot. Then I need a haircut.'

These people didn't do anything but spend lazy days on the beach. And it was a scandal they'd passed him in English. His mother must have known the examiner or something. He followed Gregorio into the bathroom and watched him beginning to shave.

'I was wondering if you could maybe do me a favour then.' And he explained that when he had come over on the boat he had met a rich industrialist who was apparently a count or something and this man had hinted that Morris might be able to work for him in his office in Vicenza. He'd invited Morris to drop over and see him at his villa in La Caletta, and what he'd been intending to do was get the bus down there and from there to the ferry, but if he was going to come all the way back here to stay another couple of days, then . . .

'Sure, take the car,' Gregorio said, slicing through white foam on his neck. Morris noticed a pack of old-fashioned

Gillette blades on the glass shelf in the corner of the bathroom. People really were so vulnerable. It was ridiculous.

'We'll just go to Roberto's first, I'll get off there and you can go on.'

## 20

The only problem was that to go back and load Massimina into the car he would have to turn round and drive back in front of Roberto's hotel, going in the wrong direction for where he'd said he was going. There was no other road. Could it make them suspicious? It could. But Morris had learned by now that where there was no choice it was better not to worry about the danger of doing something. You just did it. He drove quietly past the white hotel, careful not to accelerate or do anything unusual, then once out of sight cruised moderately back to the villa. He'd seen an old skipping rope somewhere in one of the cupboards that he could use for tying her up.

Morris backed the car almost to the shed and went to the house for the rope. But the door was locked and he didn't have the key now. He'd given it to Gregorio. Damn. He'd have to buy a rope then. He could get a skipping rope when he passed through Palau. No problem in a seaside town.

A scuffling behind the shed as he approached froze him. Bird. It must be. It was. A sparrow was scrabbling around the sacks. He dragged the corpse away, imagining it would have stiffened now and be easier to move, bent up as it was. But no. The thing flopped and seemed determined to come out of the sacks. So much for rigor mortis. It was unmanageable. One didn't want to be undignified with the girl but there you were. He heaved the package any way he could as far as the back bumper and fiddled with the keys. He must have the key to the boot, damn it. Try them all again. Yes, there. The boot was half full of clutter. Old shoes, jeans, a few tools, accessories for skiing. A knife. Morris shoved them to the back and wrenched up the corpse. But shapeless as it was in the sacks and with all her clothes and odds and ends swimming about and occasionally falling out, it was difficult. He couldn't tell what he was grabbing. Then the belt slipped away from neck and feet allowing the whole body to open up. The top sack with her head was just inside now but the bottom slipped down, the sack slithering away to show her white backside.

Morris was suddenly boiling with anger, furious at this continued rebellion of the now inanimate girl. Anybody might drive by any minute. Somebody might be looking down from the hill behind. Damn and damn. He slapped her hard and the skin was cold as putty. 'Get in for Christ's sake!' He heaved up the legs, jammed them in somehow and slammed down the boot. A pair of blue panties lay on the ground by his feet. No. He picked them up, found the key again (he mustn't mustn't mustn't go and lock the keys in the boot or something stupid like that), shoved the panties inside a sack, which brought his hand in contact with her skin for just one unpleasant second, and had the boot down again. Morris stood up straight and made himself breathe deeply for two or three full minutes.

Ten o'clock. He turned off the coast road and drove southwest along Route 133. The rain of the evening before had left the country glistening and freshly scented. The car climbed steeply through hills of flowering gorse, occasional thickets, sheep, broken-down farms, modern holiday villas. Sardinia wasn't really all it was cracked up to be, Morris thought.

It was a long time since he'd done any driving and he had to go easy, especially in such a powerful car. His experience was limited to his father's old 1100. He turned on the radio and twiddled the dial a little, hoping for news or business reports, but it was all light music crap. There was nothing he hated more than light music. He settled down to enjoy what there was of a landscape, driving slowly and carefully. At Lake Coghinas he joined the main road and stopped a little later in Oschiri to get hold of every paper he could lay his hands on. With the car parked safely in sight across the road he sat in a small dirty café and went through the lot of them. But nothing. There wouldn't have been time for them to get ything in on her phone call of course. If they had managed to trace that he was done.

He was going to order a second coffee when it suddenly came to him that with the sun beating down on the car like it was, she would be smelling awfully in no time. And for some reason it was this idea of smell that bothered Morris most of all. As if once to experience the smell of a victim's corpse would taint him for life. He jumped up, paid and left. Seeing a petrol station open just a hundred metres away he thought for a moment he might buy a can of petrol and arrange a little cremation. But it would probably attract more attention than it was worth. Like digging holes.

A further ten kilometres and he left the main road at Ozieri, taking the car snaking up into the rugged hills around Biti. This was the heartland of Sardinia now – bandit country: sheep, shepherds, roughnecks and miles and miles of wild empty country. No tourists either, by the looks of it; no expensive villas, no people wandering across the country-side on exploratory walks every day. Morris watched the occasional untarred tracks that snaked off the road to either side, looking for one that was overgrown, disused.

He found it a few kilometres before Nuoro. The ground was wet, which was unfortunate. He would leave tracks. But then there was no search going on, was there? He put the car into second and took it very slowly up the rutted track into the hills, until, passing through a thicket, he had trees brushing their branches against both sides of the car. He stopped and walked a little way. Bushes, undergrowth, no sign of a path. It was as good as he was going to find.

Back at the car he heaved her out again, textbook stiff now. But he had forgotten the rope. He was going to have to drag her tugging at the edges of the plastic sacks again, tearing out his fingernails. And he did, any old how, through bushes and nettles, the hell with respect. He was making far too much damage too, but what could you do? Nature would repair herself in a couple of days. A bit of luck was all he needed – a bit of luck. 'With a little bit, with a little bit . . .' No, he must try to breathe only through his mouth in case it smelled – and look away when the lower sack continually slipped down round her nether parts. But better that than her face. He felt like a long-distance runner, exhausted, but nearing the end of the course. If he could just hold on a bit longer. After a few hundred metres he found a particularly wild bush, crept under the branches and pushed the body around the trunk, grunting and sweating with the effort, shivering and boiling together.

It was ten minutes' driving later that Morris realized that leaving all those clothes and things in the sack with her was pretty well the craziest thing he could have done. They would be bound to identify the body sooner or later, they were geniuses at that kind of thing these days. And then all those tags from Vicenza, Rimini, Rome and Porto Torres would trace out the itinerary of the kidnap down to the last detail and thus give the police just the lead they needed. He pulled into the side of the road and turned the car round. He felt rather proud of himself really to find he had the courage to go back there, and when he arrived proud again to see how quickly and efficiently he stripped the sacks off her and took all the clothes and shoes and odds and ends away. He didn't seem to mind the body at all, nor its faint smell. It did occur to him that he really ought to smash up her face with the car jack. But there were limits. And the St Christopher? Leave it. It was a gift he had given her and she could keep it. Nobody would connect it with Giacomo anyway. And it was a challenge, a snub to fate. Like Gregorio's bronze left on the coffee table in his flat.

Coming out of the track for the second time onto the country road, Morris almost ran over an elderly man walking with a stick.

'*Scusi, mi scusi Signore, buon giorno,*' Morris said from his open window at his breeziest and best. He looked the old peasant straight in the eyes. Tonight he would whoop it up with Gregorio and Roberto, get thoroughly drunk and then tomorrow or the next day back to Verona.

'*Buon dì,*' the man with the stick replied from a leathery old face.

Morris returned via Genoa, which meant a thirteen hour trip. He travelled at night with a private cabin and kept himself to himself. Before turning in he stood at the boat's rail and watched a warm Mediterranean moon shining full and bright over the boat's lazy wake. Not a wave was in sight. The sea was a pond. He looked backwards towards the last winking lights of Sardinia and added up the cards, for and against.

There was the box of tampons Gregorio had come across by the garden shed, a strange place to lose such a thing. Then the corpse might be discovered immediately and identified immediately with the Sardinian papers publishing photographs good enough for Roberto or Gregorio to recognize. Give it a month though and they'd both be back on the mainland. There was the heap of fertilizer too, plus the two hundred extra kilometres he'd put on Gregorio's Alfa Romeo that day. There was Stan who had seen the girl from a platform away in Rome and knew Morris was going to Sardinia. There was Signor Cartuccio who might have seen the identikit of the Rimini murders suspect, not to mention the possibility that the police could have traced his phone calls, might decide at any moment to check up on his supposed trip to Bari, who his friends were, where he had stayed. And against all these dangers Morris held but one card, which he must trust and pray would prove the ace of trumps – his unsuspectability, the leap of imagination that would be required on the part of a group of people who had shown themselves sadly lacking in that quality.

As soon as he was back in Verona he would get over and see Inspector Marangoni and have a frank talk about it all, especially about that last strange phone call, which according to yesterday's *Corriere* had been too brief to trace. He would ask the policeman if there was anything he could do, if there was any hope left at all. He would weep maybe and beat a fist on the man's desk. Yes, he could see himself doing it already.

Back in his first-class cabin with a bottle of spumante to celebrate, he drank quietly, going over his plans – the investments, photography, the book (he must buy a type-writer) – then rummaged in his suitcase for the dictaphone. Where had he put the new batteries? In the zip pocket. Good.

He installed the batteries, lay back and reflected. What was it he had said last? He wound back a little and switched on. '. . . the choices I was made to take, that destiny knew I would and will take in a certain way because . . .' His own voice stopped, to be followed immediately afterwards by a crackle and then a strange female voice.

'*Che cosa mai dici in tutti questi nastri, Morri? Non capisco un cavolo. Sei così misterioso sai.*'

The voice stopped. Morris, with his heart in his mouth, replayed it. It didn't seem her voice. The words were long and drawn out by those dying batteries he had just replaced. A moan it seemed; a moan from beyond the grave. '*Che cosa mai dici . . . Morri . . .* What do you say in these tapes, you're so mysterious.'

A moment later Morris was at the rail again, hurling the dictaphone far out on a moonlit sea. He wouldn't have been surprised really had a female arm reached out to take the thing. He was going crazy. Quite mad. And he stood at the rail for a long while, weeping quietly on his own.

## 21

It was late August, an ominous thundery day, and Morris, sweating in his new black suit, was following respectfully at the rear of the procession as they carried the coffin through the cemetery to the family vault. When a hand fell lightly on his shoulder.

'May we have a word with you, Signor Duckworth?'

Inspector Marangoni stood plump and sombre-faced beside his wiry, moustached assistant.

'If we can leave the family alone for the very last rites and drive down to the *Questura*, there are one or two things we'd like to talk to you about.'

So they had found him out at last. For which of the crimes? He mustn't confess until he knew what they knew.

The three men walked back down the white shingle paths of the cemetery. The policemen had left their car outside the gate. (Could he say she'd fallen, banged her head?)

'But I've been invited to the supper afterwards,' Morris managed to get out now, to test the water.

'Don't worry, this won't take a moment.'

The tone appeared to be cynical. Morris was obliged to climb into the car, the same kind of Alfa Romeo Gregorio had, he noticed. He felt surprisingly resigned. At least they weren't beating him up.

'The thing is' – it was the only remark anybody made during the short trip and Inspector Marangoni made it – 'there are one or two things that don't add up about this whole affair.'

They sat in a small blank empty room and Tolaini, the assistant, went out to get something. The tape recorder for the confession most probably.

In two months of burning sunshine Inspector Marangoni hadn't managed to get a tan. His balding head was pale under the room's fluorescent light as he leaned across the table.

'Did the Massimina you knew used to pluck her eyebrows?'

'No, I don't think so.' He mustn't fidget. He must sit perfectly still.

The assistant came in with a small metal box, set it down on the table and opened it.

'This,' Marangoni said, lifting out a lock of hennaed hair. 'Would you say it was hers?'

'No,' Morris said, 'Mimi's hair was just very dark, near black.'

'Did she wear necklaces?'

'Sometimes.'

'Anything you remember in particular?'

'No.' It wasn't the way he would have gone about the questioning, Morris thought. And he began to feel curious.

'This?' He lifted out the St Christopher.

Morris looked at it quite coolly. 'No. I don't think so.'

'Signor Duckworth, the young girl found in Sardinia, plucked her eyebrows, had this colour of hair, wore this charm. She . . .'

'Then it isn't her,' Morris said quickly. 'It must be somebody else, there's been . . .'

'It is her, Signor Duckworth. The dental test was conclusive.'

Morris waited. What did they want from him? What did they know?

'What's more, the corpse we found in Sardinia was pregnant . . .'

'No,' Morris cried.

Inspector Marangoni held up his hand. 'Only a week or so. Most probably she didn't even know. But pregnant she was.'

He sat still as stone.

'Let's throw in one or two of the other strange facts in this case. The red tracksuit in the station in Vicenza, the get well card from Rimini, the ransom picked up in Rome, a mysterious phone call to her mother which doctors tell us was probably made at least in the last days before her death, then the discovery of the corpse in Sardinia of all places. And one other thing. Shortly before becoming seriously ill, the girl's grandmother withdrew three million lire from the bank, apparently to buy a wedding present for the eldest daughter. That money has never been found.'

Three million, not two, Morris noted. Never trust anyone. Probably as well he hadn't risked . . .

'So what does that all add up to, in your opinion, Signor Duckworth?'

Morris looked the heavy man in the face. It added up to life imprisonment, obviously. But he shook his head.

'Doesn't it seem to you a rather strange kind of kidnap where the girl learns to pluck her eyebrows, henna her hair and gets pregnant, where the kidnappers are so lax in vigilance that they let the girl send get well cards and phone home?'

'Yes,' Morris said humbly. Though he hadn't been lax. It was just impossible trying to do everything on your own. And then, taking a plunge, he tried: 'If I didn't know her better I'd say she'd taken the money and then gone and run off with somebody else.'

Morris waited. Inspector Marangoni was watching him.

'What we want to know from you,' he said, 'is who that somebody was.' There was an agonizing pause before he continued. 'The point is that the family absolutely refuse to consider this possibility and they haven't been at all co-operative with lists of friends, etc. They even refuse to believe the medical evidence of the pregnancy. Now, if you can offer anything at all on her friends, habits, the places she visited and so on, or if you can very discreetly get something out of the family, we would be . . .'

And they took him back to the funeral party.

Morris had expected dust and ashes and a sorrowful, mournful silence of desperation and horror. And instead there was laughter and tittle-tattle in the Trevisan household, plentiful cocktails and spicy help-yourself titbits on silver trays. He was annoyed. The least you could expect was sobriety.

He went for a solemn handshake with Signora Trevisan and instead she hugged him, she pressed him against her bosom, she wept, but not sobbing, simply shedding tears as she spoke, and she said it was a terrible terrible thing that would haunt her all her life long, but at least it was over now, at least they knew the worst and the doctors had said from the way the blow was struck the girl couldn't have known anything about it. Probably done while she was sleeping. And she and the family had really done everything they could, and the police too, she thought. There was nothing on their consciences, nothing they need reproach themselves with, and they must remember that. There was no point in feeling guilty. Vengeance was the Lord's and the Lord would find the murderer out.

She was probably thinking, thank God it was dumb little Massimina, and not one of the other two, Morris thought.

'Oh, by the way, Morris, could I have a little word with you afterwards? I was wondering if you could do me a small favour.' And she smiled through her tears.

Morris nodded politely, without the slightest curiosity. He supposed he could afford the woman a favour if it was nothing too time-consuming. He had a lot of business to be getting on with and he wanted to make a brief trip to England for a couple of weeks to buy his father a flat and show him who knew how to be a success in the world.

He sat on a stiff, straight-backed chair, keeping as aloof as possible from the small group of friends and relations, and was surprised when Paola, the middle sister, came over to talk to him. She didn't mention Massimina at all. She talked about Antonella's imminent wedding with Bobo and how expensive it was all turning out to be and the cost of redecorating their flat in the centre and how difficult it would be to have fun after, after . . . this. Her eyes blinked, but were quite dry. Did she have a *fidanzato* herself, Morris asked, or was she going to be left alone when her sister moved out?

Paola blushed – rather softly and sweetly, Morris thought, rather as dear Mimi would have. No, she said, she didn't have a boyfriend, but her eyes didn't move and held his for a second, soft and brown. Her cheeks had the same shape as Massimina's, only not a freckle.

Morris poured himself more Verdicchio and helped himself to mushrooms.

'Actually, I'm going to England next week for a while,' she went on quickly, lowering the eyes now to show her long lashes. 'To get over it, I suppose. I'll be studying English. In fact, that was the favour Mamma was saying she wants to ask you. We heard that you were going back to London and she thought, maybe, you could travel with me.' She smiled. 'Poor Mamma's terribly worried about us being outside alone after all this.'

'Of course,' Morris said cordially. It would be infinitely better to visit his father with a girlfriend, he thought, and one couldn't mope over the dead for ever.

Tim Parks

# MIMI'S GHOST

*The brilliant sequel to* Cara Massimina

'Tarantino meets Peter Mayle'
*Independent on Sunday*

Morris can't get over Mimi. But then he should have thought of that before he murdered her and married her sister. Now Mimi's back, as a ghost, and she seems to be suggesting the way to redemption for Morris. He must help the poor immigrants of Verona; but if anybody should get in his charitable way then so much the worse for them...

'*Cara Massimina* was a triumph of the darkly-comic-thriller-and-something-more-besides genre. This is an even greater one'
*Daily Telegraph*

'Parks writes with a brutal, snapping wit, reinventing the crime novel as a capricious campy romp...A piece of conclusive reasoning that leaves the reader collapsing into squeamish giggles'
*Sunday Times*

VINTAGE

## BY TIM PARKS
## ALSO AVAILABLE IN VINTAGE

| | |
|---|---|
| ☐ HOME THOUGHTS | £6.99 |
| ☐ LOVING ROGER | £6.99 |
| ☐ FAMILY PLANNING | £6.99 |
| ☐ GOODNESS | £6.99 |
| ☐ SHEAR | £6.99 |
| ☐ MIMI'S GHOST | £6.99 |
| ☐ TONGUES OF FLAME | £6.99 |
| ☐ EUROPA | £6.99 |
| ☐ ITALIAN NEIGHBOURS | £7.99 |
| ☐ AN ITALIAN EDUCATION | £7.99 |
| ☐ ADULTERY & OTHER DIVERSIONS | £6.99 |

---

- All Vintage books are available through mail order or from your local bookshop.
- Please send cheque/eurocheque/postal order (sterling only), Access, Visa, Mastercard, Diners Card, Switch or Amex:

☐☐☐☐☐☐☐☐☐☐☐☐☐☐☐☐

Expiry Date:_____Signature:_____

Please allow 75 pence per book for post and packing U.K.
Overseas customers please allow £1.00 per copy for post and packing.

**ALL ORDERS TO:**

Vintage Books, Books by Post, TBS Limited, The Book Service, Colchester Road, Frating Green, Colchester, Essex CO7 7DW

NAME:_____

ADDRESS:_____

_____

_____

Please allow 28 days for delivery. Please tick box if you do not wish to receive any additional information ☐

Prices and availability subject to change without notice.